My Man's Best Friend III:

Severing Ties

My Man's Best Friend III:

Severing Ties

Tresser Henderson

www.urbanbooks.net

Urban Books, LLC
97 N18th Street
Wyandanch, NY 11798

My Man's Best Friend III: Severing Ties

ISBN 13: 978-1-60162-412-3
ISBN 10: 1-60162-412-3

First Trade Paperback Printing June 2014
Printed in the United States of America

10 9 8 7 6 5 4 3 2

Distributed by Kensington Publishing Corp.
Submit Wholesale Orders to:
Kensington Publishing Corp.
C/O Penguin Group (USA) Inc.
Attention: Order Processing
405 Murray Hill Parkway
East Rutherford, NJ 07073-2316
Phone: 1-800-526-0275
Fax: 1-800-227-9604

My Man's Best Friend III:

Severing Ties

by

Tresser Henderson

Acknowledgments

First and foremost I want to thank God for all the many blessings He has bestowed upon me. He is the head of my life and I give all glory and praise to Him.

I can't believe this is my third book. I remember the day when I never thought my dreams would come true but look how God works. And I have so many more dreams to accomplish and I know with God on my side, this is just the beginning. I can't wait to write more books. Not only am I a writer, I'm a reader as well. Of course it's hard for me to pick up a book when I write so I purposely don't read anything until I'm finished with my writing. But as soon as I finish, I pick up a book and enjoy the many stories other authors bring to pages.

I want to thank my husband Wil for being my partner in life. He gets tired of me sitting in bed with my laptop on my lap typing away until the wee hours of the morning. I appreciate his patience. You are a wonderful man and awesome father to our children. Honey, I love you.

To my children, you guys are so funny. And you have the worst timing sometimes. As soon as I get deep in a thought when I'm writing, here you come. I can look back and laugh about it now because I know the day is going to come when I'm going to miss that. I love you guys.

My parents Clarence and Rebecca Atkinson, thanks for always being here for me. Anything I need, you are always there to support me. Mama, when I'm feeling some kind of way, your motherly instinct calls me to see how I'm doing. Your timing is amazing and I always wonder how you know. But I know that's the connection we have. I am so blessed to have you and Daddy as my parents. I love you both dearly.

To Carl Weber, I want to thank you for this opportunity and taking a chance on me. I will continue to bring it.

Natalie Weber, thank you for putting up with all my e-mails. I feel like a pest sometimes but you always answer me and help me when I need it so I thank you.

Rochelle Cicero, thank you for reading everything I write and being such a great friend to me. You are my go-to reader and awesome friend. I love you.

I want to thank all my family members who have supported me and encouraged me. And last but not least, thank you to all the booksellers who carry my books, book clubs who have chosen my book, online Web sites and readers who support my work and took a chance on picking up my book and reading it. I appreciate your support because without you, I wouldn't be able to continue my journey of writing the words that encumber my mind.

Prologue

Ten Years Earlier

Chapter 1

Trinity

I stood outside the house as it went up in flames. With no shoes on my feet, lavender pajamas incased with the residue of smoke, and a blanket that a fireman wrapped around me, I stood and watched the flames try their best to reach heaven. The fire lit up the entire neighborhood as my neighbors were now standing outside and watching the firemen try their best to save the home I grew up in. But I knew it was too late. All the memories I had within those walls rose as if wiping away eighteen years of my life.

"Ma'am, are you okay?" the paramedic asked.

But, I had zoned out. I couldn't believe this was happening. I felt a soft hand try to lead me away but my feet were planted to the cold, wet ground.

"Ma'am, come on. Let us help you," the lady said, pulling me.

I slowly walked in the direction of the ambulance.

"Trinity! Trinity!"

I heard a voice call but I couldn't see who it was with the crowd of people and the police trying to keep order by keeping them back.

"But, she's my sister."

I knew then it was my brother. I looked in the direction of his voice and saw him arguing with an officer. The policeman looked back at me and then back at my brother.

He said something. I couldn't hear what he was saying. Then the officer let my brother through. Steven ran to my direction. By now I was sitting on the stretcher with the paramedic trying to put an oxygen mask over my face.

Steven kneeled before me asking, "Are you okay?"

Tears filled my eyes when he asked me that.

"What happened?"

I shook my head.

"Where are Mom and Dad?"

I stared into his eyes and then turned my attention back to the fire. Steven turned to look at the fire with me. He dropped his head in agony.

"No. No. I'm going to believe they got out like you. Our parents are not in that house," he said, pointing as the flames were starting to lose their battle with the water the firemen were spraying on them. "They are going to be okay," he struggled to say.

"We are going to transport her to the hospital to make sure she's okay. She may have inhaled too much smoke. We want to have her examined as a precaution," the paramedic said to Steven.

"Okay." He nodded. "But can I please find out if my parents made it out?" he asked. "Can you please wait for me to come back so I can ride with her, please?" my brother begged.

The paramedic nodded.

Steven went to one of the fireman and I could tell by the expression on his face he was shocked to hear someone else could be in the house. The solemn look let me know that there was no way they could have made it out. Not after the inferno that had captured our home.

I saw my brother's head drop again. This time he began to weep uncontrollably. The fireman placed a comforting hand on Steven's shoulder and was talking with him. The fireman then proceeded to walk Steven back over to me.

"Ride with your sister. As soon as I find out what happened, I will call you."

Steven nodded and the fireman patted his back. He looked at us both sympathetically knowing deep down that we had lost both our parents today.

Once we were at the hospital, I was examined and was cleared to go home a couple of hours later. Steven did get the call he did not want to hear: that our parents didn't make it out. They found their badly burned bodies still in the bed. Their deaths were ruled an accident due to smoke inhalation. Steven was devastated but I was numb.

He asked, "What happened? How did this happen? How did you get out? Where did the fire start? Why didn't you try to get them out?"

I just stared at my brother with as much sympathy as I could muster. This was hard when I felt the people who died in this fire deserved exactly what they got.

Present Day

Chapter 2

Derrick

Good guys do finish last. I'm a living witness to this fact. I obeyed my parents. I went to church. I believe in God. I tried to make the right decisions and was kind to others. I respected people and made women feel like the treasures I thought they were. I could go on and on. And look where that has gotten me. I've been stepped on, walked over, cheated on, and lied to. In a matter of months I went from this happy man who had it all together to defeated and not knowing what my true identity was.

They say a good start in life starts in the home. I thought the home I grew up in was the best home a child could grow up in. I had a mother and father who loved me unconditionally and who I thought were always truthful with me, especially with them being the pillars in our home church. Mama preached all the time about truth. I guess she never thought about practicing what she preached.

The lies she told me about who my true father was had destroyed me. The fact she didn't want to tell me had driven a larger wedge in our mother-son relationship. I hadn't seen or talked to her since I walked out on her and my dad. That was never me, since I had a habit of stopping by several times a week, checking up on my folks, making sure things with them were well. She tried to call to talk with me but I had nothing to say; not until she decided to tell me the information I needed to know in order to move forward.

Yes, I was a grown man now and shouldn't have let the things that had been exposed affect me like they had. But, when the world you thought you knew and the new one rear their ugly heads, clashing with your reality, how are you suppose to come to grips with that?

I was going to become the person the universe was pushing me to be and that was inconsiderate, angry, unsympathetic, and a playa. Yes, I said it. A playa. I was going to play people and the first person I decided who deserved this more than anyone was Zacariah. She wanted me back and she got me. All that scheming and conniving worked, or so she thought. I gave her a stipulation with me taking her back and that was me being able to keep Trinity as part of my life, too. That meant, if I wanted, I could sleep with both of them. I knew she didn't like it, but so what? Now she got to feel like she'd made me feel those years when were together. And so far, she didn't argue with me too much about it.

Other than Jaquon, Zacariah was second in line to go after what she wanted, despite the consequences. She cheated on me with I don't know how many men. Just so happens, one of those men was my best friend Jaquon. She shattered my life, also, by revealing to me and Kea that we were brother and sister. Later, we found out we really weren't due to the fact she had a family member who worked in the paternity facility tamper with the results to make it look like we were related. This was Zacariah's way of keeping Kea and me away from each other. And it worked because Kea decided to marry Jaquon.

Thinking about all of that, it makes me look crazy for taking her back into my life but I thought about some things; where I came from a home of love, even though later it was filled with lies, she came from a background filled with survival. Both her parents were alcoholics and didn't love her like they should have, so she never had a demonstration of what love truly was; the only love she knew was loving herself. I don't know if that was genuine, especially with her making herself disposable to men. No one who truly loves themselves allows themselves to be used. So, I knew a part of her couldn't love who she was.

Zacariah explained to me why she did what she did, cheating on me and everything. As bizarre as it sounded, I understood where she was coming from. She always had to be one step ahead to survive so having me was too good to be true for her. Even though I provided everything she could ever need and want, she still felt it necessary to use men by giving them the only thing she felt valuable and that was her sex. In return she would rob them for cash and stack her papers for rainy days. She couldn't see I was her rainy day. She was supposed to fall on me when she couldn't stand on her own.

But there I was; Zacariah was back in my home with her clothes, baggage, and all. She was happier than she'd ever been. I have to say with everything else that had been going on in my life, I was glad to have her back despite the things we'd been through. I knew I was settling. Hell, why not? The woman I wanted in my life decided to accept my ex–best friend's hand in marriage after turning down my engagement proposal. Talk about confused, hurt, and angry at her terrible decision. I was all of those things. Even after all Jaquon had done to her, he was who she chose. I guess she was a sucker for a broken heart. I still loved her but I couldn't stop moving on with my life to wait until she came to her senses to know I was the man she needed to be with.

Chapter 3

Kea

"I'm getting married," fell out my mouth when Terry came walking through the door looking like she had been beat over the head by a ton of work. To other people she may have looked like she had it together with her all-white pants suit with a red cami and matching shoes. Her makeup was done to perfection and hair was pulled up into a cute little 'do. But her face said it all. Her eyes screamed, "I had one rough day."

Now that she was back from Los Angeles assisting a trial, which she won, she came back home to more people wanting her to represent them. Yes, that meant more money but it also meant more work. Terry had been so busy lately that it was hard finding any time to hang out with her. We used to meet at least one day a week to do lunch or dinner before she went to Los Angeles. Since she'd been back we'd managed to start that back up before all this work began to bombard her. Little by little our once a week was lucky to see each other once a month. We'd talk on the phone but she didn't have time to do that because she brought her work home with her. I knew Terry was increasing her clientele to start her own law firm, which she was very well on her way to doing, but I felt like I lost my best friend. I know it sounds selfish of me but I wanted her to take time out for her friend.

So, finally, after begging her for over a week to come see me, she decided to make time and drop by my place after work. Even though she looked like she could fall asleep any minute, I was happy to see my friend. I guess I was too happy since I blurted I was getting married to her, which immediately piqued her interest.

"You're what?" she asked, staggering in my apartment like she couldn't wait to sit down. She tossed her briefcase and purse on my glass coffee table. I prayed it would withstand whatever she was carrying. It seemed like she slammed it down, which didn't help my table any. It sounded like she had bricks in it.

"I'm getting married," I repeated, watching her face go from tired to gleeful.

"Congratulations, Kea," she said, hugging me. "I can't believe this. When? Where? What? Girl, you need to sit down and tell me the details," she said, kicking off her five-inch red stiletto shoes.

"He proposed to me awhile ago but I haven't been able to get a hold of your behind to tell you."

"You have been talking to me on the phone. You could have told me during one of those conversations," Terry said.

"I wanted to tell you face to face. Besides every time we talk you know your mind is occupied with the work you are doing when you supposed to be talking to me."

"You have a point there," she said, slumping deeper into my sofa.

"You are here now and that's all that matters. I've been bursting to tell you," I said with excitement.

"I knew my boy Derrick was going to come through and treat you like the queen you are," Terry said, bringing her left foot to her right knee. She began to massage it for some relief.

My expression changed from one of merriment to one of despair. When Terry looked at me, her smile changed to a frown.

She asked, "You and Derrick are getting married right?"

"No, Terry, we're not."

"What do you mean no? Who . . . ?" she asked, pausing. I could see the answer resonate within her. Terry's frown looked like it was starting to turn into anger.

I was almost scared to say Jaquon's name knowing it would send Terry into an uproar.

"Spill it, Kea. Who are you marrying?" Terry asked, letting her aching foot fall to the floor and leaning herself back on my sofa. She crossed her arms and her legs like she was protecting herself from what she knew the answer was going to be. Her exhaustion caused her not to catch on as fast as she usually did but now her mind raced to furiousness as she blurted, "Please don't tell me, Kea."

"Terry, please be happy for me."

Again she said, "Please don't tell me, Kea."

"Well then I won't tell you," I said, laughing nervously.

"You are not marrying Jaquon," she shouted furiously.

I held my hand out and said, "Look at the beautiful ring he got me. Isn't it gorgeous?"

"That's a guilt ring just like the one Kobe gave his wife Vanessa after he committed adultery. The only difference in this case is this dog has been cheating before you two had a chance to say 'I do.'"

"Terry."

"What are you thinking? Why are you settling? What is it about this man that makes you lose all logic of common sense?"

"I'm thinking straight. All that matters is I love him."

"Since when?" Terry asked, bouncing her foot in the air. "Just a few weeks ago you were in love with Derrick. You were doing him, too, right? What happened to him?"

"We're friends."

"The test did prove you two are not related, right?" Terry asked.

"Yes, Terry," I said, frustrated that she was coming at me so hard.

"So, why haven't you dumped this loser and gotten back with Derrick?"

"I was with Jaquon first."

"So were half the women in this city. That man is a compulsive dog. He can't keep it in his pants. Did he drug you or something? Is he blackmailing you into this marriage?"

"No, Terry. I made this decision on my own."

"What does Derrick think of this?"

I was afraid to see him. Every time we got together, this desire always ignited between us causing me to do things I knew I couldn't do if I wanted to be faithful to Jaquon. Just the thought of how easily I could fall into bed with him made me doubt accepting this marriage proposal to Jaquon.

"Kea," Terry said, snapping her fingers at me. "Come back to earth."

"I've been listening," I said.

"So, tell me the last thing I asked?" she asked cockily.

"You wanted to know why I chose Jaquon and not Derrick."

"Wrong," she said loudly. "What I said was you haven't told Derrick about this joke of a proposal, have you?"

"First, Terry, it's not a joke."

"Like hell it ain't. I'm waiting for Krusty the Clown to jump out with Ashton Kutcher and say, 'Terry, you've been punk'd.'"

"Why do you have to exaggerate things?"

"Because this is some bull, Kea. Straight up cow shit from the pastures of fields of VA. I feel like a part of you thinks so too since you haven't told Derrick." Terry scooted to the edge of the sofa to get closer to me and then asked, "Do you want him to hear about your engagement in the street? After everything you two have gone through, you doing him like this."

"I'm going to tell him. I will call him up today."

"This should have happened immediately but I guess Jaquon is your priority now. Why, I have no clue, because I guarantee you, Kea, you are not his."

"He's changed, Terry."

"Oh, he's changed all right, into an even bigger woof woof," she joked but was serious as a heart attack. "You keep telling yourself that but I know he's a liar."

"How do you know?"

"Because men like Jaquon don't change. They get off on the high of chasing other women and them falling at his feet."

"He's been faithful since we've gotten back together."

"Maybe for now. Once that ring is on your finger he's going to think he owns you. Then he's going to go back on the hunt again, sticking that same ring that made you two husband and wife in his pocket or, even worse, up in some other woman."

"Must you always be so dramatic?" I said, sighing at the visual she had now given me.

"I'm being me and I'm trying to be your friend right now."

I nodded thinking I never should have told her. Trying to convince Terry that Jaquon was the one for me was like trying to convince Spike Lee he's really Caucasian. I knew I couldn't blame her for her opinion. She'd been the one here every single time Jaquon hurt me. Why would she support this matrimony now?

"Please tell me you are getting a prenup."

"For what?"

"Oh my goodness," she said, falling back and then sitting back up abruptly. "Really, Kea? To protect the money you just inherited. Come on, think," she said, taking her finger and tapping at my temple.

"It's not that much."

"The amount you inherited is a lot of money. Girl, with this economy right now, you are rich. People would give anything to have a quarter of that money and you sitting here acting like it's nothing. If it's nothing, then give it to me. I'll find a few things I could do with it. I'd rather spend it or put it away for you when that rainy day comes than have you let Jaquon get his grubby hands on it and spend it on himself or, worse, some other skank women."

"My money is my money."

"No. When you get married, your money is his money too in the eyes of the law. Why do you think people like Donald Trump get prenups? To keep what he's earned. Look at Paul McCartney. That woman came with nothing and left with millions all because she wanted to stick it to him and continue to live a lifestyle she couldn't afford before she met him."

"Jaquon won't do that to me."

"That man will have you broke within the year. You need him to sign a prenup."

"I want to go into this marriage able to trust him."

"Like you have for the past several years when you've cried on my shoulders about him dipping deep into the crevices of other women. Come on, Kea. Wake up and feel the fleas biting you. He's a dog and always will be one."

I had to laugh at my friend. If I wanted honesty, I would always get that from Terry.

"This isn't funny."

"Wake up and feel the fleas biting," I said, repeating her words to her.

"That's right. Just wait. I hate to say it but it's a matter of time before the true Jaquon surfaces again. You are going to be sitting here mad at yourself because you let a good man go."

"Can't you just be happy for me?"

"I would be happier if you dumped this loser."

"But it's not going to happen. I didn't call you over here to hear you dog Jaquon. I called you over here to ask you to be my maid of honor."

"I don't know," she said seriously. "I might object and then you would be mad at me."

"You wouldn't do that to me," I said.

Terry's expression, with mouth twisted up and left eyebrow raised, let me know she would.

"Please support me. Be there for me. Be my friend. Stand by my side and watch me marry the man I have chosen to be with. Can you please do that for me without objecting?"

Terry rolled her eyes and sighed her frustration.

"Please, Terry," I begged.

She still didn't answer.

"Kea, I'm sorry but I can't."

"Are you serious?" I asked, surprised at her reaction.

"Yes," she said strongly. "I can't stand up there in the house of the Lord smiling at this lie."

"But it's not a lie."

"You keep trying to convince yourself of that."

"I can't believe you. All I asked was for you to support me and you can't even do that," I said, raising my voice a little.

Terry held up her hand, saying, "Wait a minute, Kea. Don't sit here and act like I've never been here for you, because I have. So don't trip."

"You must be jealous. You don't have a man and—"

"Hold up," Terry said, sitting up on the edge of the sofa.

"No! You hold up. You either jealous or you want my man. So which is it?" I asked.

"I want your man," she said, frowning.

"All you talk about is him. I think you are curious and want to try him out for yourself."

Terry stood, saying, "I'm leaving before I say something I can't take back."

"Say it," I dared as I stood with her.

She pointed, saying, "If you knew . . ." Terry paused like she was trying not to say what she was about to say.

"Knew what? Say it."

"I'm done. I had a bad day and you made it worse by accusing me of being jealous of you and wanting your man. I have nothing to be jealous about."

"Then why get mad?" I said. "Only guilty people retreat."

"Don't stand here interrogating me like I'm Jaquon because I'm far from him. If you really want to know why I'm angry, it's the fact you don't know me better. How can you question our friendship? I've been here for you but can you say you have been here for me? This friendship has been a seventy-thirty friendship with seventy leaning my way, for being here for you more than you are there for me."

"See, that's your problem. You think because you this big-time lawyer now, you better than everybody. The one thing you don't have is a man."

Terry shook her head giggling a bit. She walked past me and picked up her briefcase and purse. She turned to me and said, "If you thought about your friend sometimes and genuinely asked me how I'm doing, and gave me time to answer before going into your issues, you would know I do have someone in my life I care for deeply. But hey, thanks for making the conversation all about you again."

I was stunned with the revelation and didn't have an opportunity to respond before Terry said, "Good luck with your wedding," and she walked out.

Chapter 4

Derrick

I was back in the coffee shop that started my and Kea's descent down a road filled with love and happiness only to end tragically, in my opinion. Kea called and asked if I could meet her here and I agreed. Zacariah was not happy at all about this. Of course I understood why. Kea and Zacariah damn near hated one another.

"Why does she want to meet with you?" she asked, walking back and forth with her hands on her hips in the bedroom we once shared. I thought she looked cute with her fleece pink pants and matching tank. Even though we weren't sleeping together, or in the same room for that matter, her body was still magnificent. I couldn't help but admire how she managed to keep it tight. And her ass, it was one of those you had to use your entire hand to lift as you entered from the back. In my opinion, you didn't have a behind if you couldn't lift and enter.

Trying to concentrate on how frantic she was getting about this meeting, I said, "Zacariah, calm down."

"Don't tell me to calm down," she snapped.

Frown lines crept across my forehead. She must've noticed because she said, "Look, Derrick. I'm sorry for snapping at you, baby."

She stopped pacing and walked over to me. She sat down beside me on the bed and took my hand into her freshly manicured fingers. I peered down at the bright lime green–colored fingernails as she began to speak again.

"I don't want to lose you again," she said.

"Zacariah, you do know nothing is going to happen, right?" I asked.

"Yes, I know," she said with uncertainty. "But, you have to understand why I feel like I do."

I could see she was trying to be different and trying to show me she was willing to do whatever it took to make us work this time around. Since Zacariah had been back, the old one, who was all about herself, was somewhat gone and the one who sat before me now was all about me. I didn't know whether to be happy or sad about this and I say this because, before, this was the one thing I required from her. But now, after everything that had happened between us, now it meant nothing to me.

I used my index finger to turn her to face toward me. I gazed into her brown eyes before placing a soft kiss on her glossed lips.

Breaking our connection, I said, "Kea and I are over. She chose who she wants to be with. I'm sitting next to the one I want to be with, okay?"

Zacariah smiled. I could feel her confidence about us returning.

"I want us to work, Derrick," she told me.

"And we will," I retorted.

"But—"

"No buts. I'm going to go meet with her and as soon as she leaves, I'm going to call you, okay?"

"Okay," she said, defeated.

"Now, give me another kiss."

Zacariah leaned in and kissed me deeply. She kissed me like she wanted more than a kiss. I knew this was her way of trying to make me change my mind about meeting with Kea. As sensual as this kiss was, my Johnson began to rise to the attention she wanted it to. She reached over with her free hand and gripped my manhood. I'm not going to lie, it felt good. But this wasn't going to work. I released our kiss, patting her on the leg as I got up to leave. She stuck out her bottom lip but I grinned at her as I adjusted my now-stiff extension.

I couldn't bring myself to get into bed with her yet. Making love was not an option because I didn't have any love for her. I was still sleeping with Trinity but I didn't love her either. She'd told me she was in love with me. I cared for her but that was as far as it went.

I said there are consequences to our actions and I did wonder if there would be any for me. Even though I'd decided to do me despite everyone else's feelings, I hoped nothing would happen that would be detrimental to me or my livelihood.

Chapter 5

Derrick

The sweet smell of the pastries brought back memories of me and Kea sitting here together relying on one another as we both dealt with individuals who cheated on us. That day we were just friends helping each other cope with our partners' deceitful ways. Now look at the irony. As much as we ran away from them, both Kea and I ended right back where we started, her with Jaquon and me back with Zacariah.

I looked at the young woman, who was very attractive, taking the order of an elderly woman who couldn't seem to make her mind up as to what she wanted. The young woman rolled her eyes a couple of times until she saw me staring at her. She then straightened up a little bit and smiled at me. I knew that smile and wanted no part of what she may have wanted to offer me. My choices in women these days were not good ones so a pretty face with a smile wasn't going to work on me today.

I really thought things were going to change for me and Kea once the results proved we were not brother and sister. Hearing those words made me the happiest man on earth. That was until Kea crushed my imaginings of being with her by not choosing me.

I started to get heated. My anger simmered as I stirred my black coffee with no sugar. I watched as the steam rose from it, thinking the heat exuding from my body might have been doing the same thing. I looked back up to see the young woman handing the elderly lady her purchased items, telling her, "Have a nice day." I guessed for my benefit. Just seconds ago she looked like she was ready to scream, "Will you please hurry up and order, old lady?"

I turned my attention to the window watching as people went on with life. The sun was out, cars were maneuvering up and down the street, and people were walking. Life went on and here I sat feeling like mine was at a standstill.

"Derrick," a voice called out to me, breaking my deep thinking. A sweet voice I wished would say my name every day. I looked up to see Kea standing there looking beautiful as ever. She was wearing a long, strapless sundress, which exposed caramel shoulders I wanted to plant soft kisses onto. Her hair was freshly done, too and big silver hoop earrings swung from her earlobes.

I stood when I saw her. My instinct automatically led me to go over to her. She didn't stop me as I draped my arms around her. She smelled so good. She felt even better. My embrace was unyielding and overbearing but I wanted her to feel my love and my grief. She tapped my sides as an indication that this was enough. But it wasn't. I didn't want to let her go. I wanted to hold her in my arms forever. But I knew I had to let her go and I eventually did release myself from her. I stepped back, pulling her seat out for her to sit down before sitting down myself.

"It's good to see you. I missed you," I said nervously. I didn't know why but I was. It felt like it had been ages since we had seen one another.

"You look good, too, Derrick."

"Thank you. You look amazing as always," I complimented her.

Then there was that silence. Again that damn silence. When did we get here? We used to be able to talk as soon as we saw each other and now it was like we couldn't find the words to say.

I stirred my coffee again, looking down at it instead of in her gorgeous face. The sun decided to illuminate the ring that was on her finger and I glanced at it. She saw me notice it and immediately removed her hand from the table, putting it in her lap.

"So, you are marrying Jaquon," I blurted, now looking her in her eyes. I had to see for myself this was something she really wanted to do.

"Did the ring give it away?" she asked timidly.

"That, and the fact Trinity told me."

She nodded, looking like she was irritated. "I told her not to tell you because I wanted to be the one to break the news to you."

"Well, it's done."

"I see. She had no right to interfere in my business."

"You sound like you are upset," I said.

"I don't like her," she admitted.

"But I thought you did?" I asked.

"At first I found her to be nice but my opinion has changed. Plus, I didn't want you to think I was jealous of her."

"Were you?" I asked, eager to hear her response.

She took in a breath and said, "That doesn't matter now."

"It matters to me. I wouldn't have asked if I didn't want to know."

"And if I said yes, Derrick, it's not going to change our situation."

I took a sip of my coffee before saying, "Kea, I asked you to marry me and you turned me down. You know I love you more than he does," I confessed.

"Derrick, I didn't come here to hear this. I came to tell you about my engagement to Jaquon. I didn't want you to find out from anyone else but just like I figured, Trinity told you. And look," she said, placing her hands on her chest, "I'm here anyway."

"Don't you think since you are here we should cut the crap? We both know this has nothing to do with Trinity. It has to do with you, me, and your messed-up decision to marry Jaquon."

"Messed-up?" she blurted.

"Yes, messed-up. You are ruining your life by sticking with him. You sat here months ago crying to me about him dogging you out. Now you want to make it a lifetime commitment with him?"

"Did you expect me to say no to him?" she asked.

"Damn right. You told me no. What's the difference between the two of us? What does he have that I don't?"

She couldn't answer that.

"How can you say yes to him when you still love me? You are fooling yourself, Kea."

"I love Jaquon," she tried to say with assurance but I knew she was lying.

"You love me too, Kea. That's why you couldn't come by my place to talk to me because you knew where our conversation would have led us," I said, reaching across the table and grabbing her hand. My hand enveloped her delicate fingers.

"You know if you would have come to my house, we would have ended up making love," I said, gazing at her tenderly. "Stop lying to yourself, Kea. You can't control the passion you feel for me, baby. You knew once you crossed the threshold to my place I would have kissed you. Then, I would have picked you up and taken you to my bed to make sweet love to you. Do you remember our lovemaking?" I asked, watching as she squirmed in her chair. Still she didn't pull her hand from mine.

"Do you remember the way I pleasured the softest part of you, the way my body felt on top of yours? The way the heat generated between us? And we could hardly breathe because we were so enthralled with one another's infatuation."

"Damn, girl. If you don't want him, I'll take him," the young woman who was behind the counter said as she wiped off the table beside us. I hadn't notice her but was annoyed she decided to interrupt our conversation.

"Do you mind?" I asked angrily.

"Excuse me," the young woman said, walking away, which allowed me to turn all my attention back to Kea.

She continued to say nothing. She fixed her eyes on mine. I knew she was imagining this in her mind. Just thinking about her getting turned on made me rock hard.

"I'm who you want. And I don't understand why you insist on living a life with a man who is going to end up disappointing you again."

"I'm so tired of people telling me he's going to disappointment me again and cheat on me. Why can't anyone be happy for me?"

"When true friends see someone we love running into the line of fire, we want to protect them from getting hurt. And, baby, Jaquon is going to hurt you."

"You sitting here acting like you love me so much," she said, jerking her hand away.

"I do."

"But that hasn't stopped you from sleeping with Trinity."

Her words stunned me. What was I supposed to say to that? "Yes, I love you, but I'm sleeping with another woman to help me get over you"? And she still didn't have a clue Zacariah was back in my home.

"You are sleeping with Trinity right?" she asked accusingly.

"Yes," I said hesitantly.

"But you love me," she bellowed.

"Yes, I love you but do you expect me to put my life on hold until you decide who you want? I thought you wanted me. All the signs were there. Then lately you haven't given me one sign that you could possibly change your mind."

"And I'm not."

"Exactly. If you didn't care about me anymore then why would you let the fact I'm sleeping with Trinity affect you?"

Again Kea said nothing at this point.

"You go back and forth and I just want you back with me. Hell, you are confusing me. Like now. We sat here and held hands. I know you felt the transference of my energy surge through you because your energy entered me. I felt your love. Even when you were gazing at me, I felt it, Kea. Can you sit here and say you didn't feel anything?"

Again nothing.

I sighed my frustration and continued to talk. "I have always been here for you. I have laid my heart on the line and ruined a friendship with a guy I've known since childhood for you. Now, you want to throw Trinity up in my face to justify why you are with Jaquon. Kea, all you have to do is give me the word and she's history. Tell me right now you want me and I will forget Trinity ever existed."

Kea lowered her head because she knew I would do that for her. She knew I loved her that much.

"Just say the words, baby."

She peered into my eyes.

"Kea, marry me," I asked her again. "Please, be my wife."

She stood abruptly, visibly shaken by what I was saying. "I have to go," she said.

"Oh. So you are going to run. When things get tough for you and you don't know how to handle it, you run."

"I'm not running. I have an appointment to meet with my pastor."

I squinted and asked, "You are going for marriage counseling?"

She nodded.

"Don't you think you need to wait until after the marriage because that's when you are going to need it?"

"I wished this could have gone better," she said, picking up her purse. "But I see this was a big mistake."

I stood, now upset myself. "The only mistake you are making is marrying Jaquon."

"But it's a mistake I have to live with. You so busy telling me about my faults, you better be looking at the snake lying next to you at night."

"What is that supposed to mean?" I asked.

"Something isn't right about Trinity, Derrick."

"You just mad because she let the cat out of the bag about you and Jaquon."

"True, but there is something else lying beneath the nice blue-eyed exterior she's putting on. I just pray once you find out what it is it's not going to be too late for you to leave her."

Chapter 6

Zacariah

How could Derrick think I would be stupid enough to believe that he and Kea were over? What was it that needed to be resolved now that hadn't already been determined? Didn't he tell me she chose Jaquon over him? Didn't she make her choice and she selected not to be with him? So why was he still pining over this chick? What hold did she have over Derrick? Did she have a pussy dripping gold or something? Hell, the way men seemed to be tripping over themselves to be with her, maybe I should have switched teams for a minute to see what the big hoopla was all about.

Don't get me wrong, I was happy when Derrick asked me to come back into his life. It was what I had been fighting for all that time. I did question if this was the wrong decision. And I say that to bring up Fabian. I really missed that man. I couldn't understand the feelings I was having since I knew I loved Derrick. Still, Fabian was tugging at my heartstrings.

He had been blowing my phone up but I kept rejecting his calls for fear it would look like I was up to my old tricks. It seemed like he wasn't letting up because my phone vibrated on the granite countertop and his name popped up on my screen for the fifth time today. I picked the phone up and debated answering it.

Swiping my finger across the screen I said, "Hello."

"Zacariah."

"Yes."

"Hey. It's me, Fabian. Are you okay? I've been calling you but you haven't returned any of my calls."

"Fabian, that was on purpose."

"Oh, okay," he said, sounding taken aback.

"Look, I think you are a great guy but the reason I haven't called you back is because I'm back with my boyfriend."

There was a slight pause before he said, "I see."

"I didn't know how to tell you."

"I understand," he said blankly.

"I hope you are not mad."

"No, I'm good."

"I appreciate everything you did for me. I really do, Fabian."

"I was happy to help you. I like you, Zacariah, and I hope you find the happiness I know you deserve."

Fabian was not making this easy. This was the reason why I liked him so much. "Thank you, Fabian."

"Don't get rid of my number, though. If you need me for anything, Zacariah, give me a call, okay?"

"Okay," I agreed and hung up the phone.

Was I making a mistake by letting him go? We couldn't be friends because I was afraid we would turn into friends with benefits. As fine as he was, I knew it wouldn't be hard falling into bed with him, especially since I wasn't getting any action from Derrick. He was depriving me and was giving all his goods to that trick Trinity. Was this another punishment he wanted to bestow upon me to see if I would resort to my old ways? So far I was managing to be good. I did wonder how long I would be able to deal with him giving me a taste of my own medicine. Kissing him made me want to rip his clothes off. But Derrick always stopped it before it went any further. I knew once I was back in the house, we were going to make love and things were going to be back to normal, as much as it could be with the ultimatum he gave me. To my dismay, Derrick put me in the guest bedroom. The guest bedroom! How could I have sex with him if I wasn't even in the same room with him?

One night I did sneak into his bedroom and slid under the covers with him. He was lying on his back with his left hand behind his head. I swear it looked like this man was posing for me. He looked so damn good. Looking down at the cover I could see his nightly hard on was at full attention and I wanted to feel that extension inside me. I slipped my panties off and thought about how I could do it. Should I climb on top of him and put his dick inside me? Or should I get under the covers and taste him to the point he couldn't deny me because my lips felt good to him? I decided to go undercover. I hadn't had the pleasure of having this man's dick inside me in any way in quite some time. So to taste him, it was amazing. Like old times.

Derrick moaned and woke up to my lips slurping his massive manhood into my mouth. He peered down at me and sighed. I smiled as I sucked and stroked him. He didn't bother to stop me. I was happy at this because he had stopped any type of advances I'd made before. I was in and knew I had made the right decision by sucking him before riding myself to a climax.

Derrick gripped my head as he pumped himself in and out of my mouth. I took all of him, happy I could make him feel as good as I used to.

"Damn, Zacariah," he said as his head began to swell within my mouth. I knew my man and I knew it was getting close to him releasing.

His strokes became harder and faster. He gripped my head tighter as his body stiffened, indicating he was about to cum.

"Oh, Zacariah." He called out my name and it felt good to hear him say it. I sucked him hard and deep until I felt the juices of his ecstasy gush into the back of my throat.

When Derrick let me go, I came up for air and lay on his chest. I looked down at his still-hardened dick knowing he was the type of man who could bust and keep going. I stroked his dick, priming it for when I could climb on top of it, but Derrick moved my hand away. He sat up, basically pushing me off his chest.

Sitting on the edge of the bed, he said, "You can go now."

"What?" I asked in utter shock.

Derrick turned to me and said, "Please, Zacariah. Go back to your room."

Was he serious? After I sucked him and drank down his juices, he was going to dismiss me?

"But, Derrick—" I tried to say but he interrupted.

"I'm not going to have sex with you, Zacariah. Not yet."

I never felt so used in my life. I'd been with plenty of men who had used me but this time it felt different. This time it came from a man I loved.

He must have seen the saddened look on my face because he said, "I'm sorry. I didn't mean to hurt your feelings but this is how I feel right now."

I didn't bother to argue with him. I wiped my mouth, climbed out of his bed, and left the room, pulling the door closed behind me.

Ever since then, I hadn't tried to seduce him. I couldn't stand to be disappointed again by him shunning me. And since then I had thought about calling Fabian up. I knew he would be down to have sex with me. But I didn't. Instead of using a real dick, I went and purchased me a fake one. That would have to suffice until Derrick came to his senses about dumping that trollop Trinity and only being with me. That was until Kea came calling. Just when I thought she was out of the picture, she found another way to inch her way back into Derrick's life. I just hoped whatever she had to tell him wouldn't lead to him making the ultimate choice of choosing her only.

Chapter 7

Zacariah

I rinsed the dishes from breakfast, trying to find something to take up the nervous energy I was having about Derrick now, probably sitting across from Kea discussing who knew what. Was I supposed to take his word and believe he was really sitting in some coffee shop? Would he believe me if I told him something like that?

I sloshed the water around a little too forcefully, causing water to splash up on my chest. The front of my shirt was soaked as I looked down at the wet spots clinging to me.

"Damn it," I yelled to myself.

I picked up the dish towel and wiped some of the dampness away. I didn't think it was a good idea to change my shirt yet. I wasn't finished cleaning the kitchen. If I would have used the dishwasher I would be dry right now, but no, I had to do things the hard way. Story of my life.

Here I was upset over Kea when the obvious person I should have been upset over was Derrick still being involved with the blue-eyed monster. Yes, I agreed to be cool with Derrick seeing Trinity. But now when I thought about it, I was a damn fool to agree to such a setup. Honestly, I didn't know if I could take this anymore. This trying to be a good woman to one man was getting old real fast. I hoped Derrick could see how much I was trying but I wasn't certain because I felt like our relationship was different.

This man made me his priority before. Anything I said went. Anything I wanted was given. Now, I sat around in a state I wasn't used to seeing him in. I thought he would be happy to have me back in his life, especially since I agreed to his crazy plus-one scenario. I had to wonder if this was his way of making me pay for when I was screwing around on him.

Yes, I was the woman in the house. I drove the cars and had access to his accounts again—well, the one he put some allowance in for me. But every Tuesday and Thursday night Derrick was with Trinity. He never stayed overnight but the fact still remained he was with her and I was not his priority.

I heard the beep of the door, indicating someone was coming into the house. I knew nobody was breaking into this house while I was here. They probably figured no one was here since Derrick's car was gone. He did tell me it seemed like somebody had been in his house but nothing was ever taken. The intruder must've figured no one was home today too but they were about to get a rude awakening.

Reaching into the dish drainer as quietly as I could, I pulled out the heavy frying pan I just washed and that I cooked bacon in earlier. With the makeshift weapon in my hand, I tiptoed to the kitchen entryway and stood to the side, waiting for the person to walk through the door so I could knock the hell out of them. My heart was pounding a hundred miles a minute waiting for the person to enter. I began to shake nervously as I waited uneasily, wishing I had grabbed a knife, too. The pan would stun the person while the knife would deliver the mighty blow. But it was too late now.

The footsteps got closer. I raised the pan up ready to swing. Whoever it was starting humming. What intruder hummed while they robbed the place? And it didn't sound like a man. It sounded like a woman. *Please tell me Derrick didn't give this trick a key to this house without letting me know and she is walking around here like she owns the place now.*

I continued to hold the frying pan up. *Maybe I should knock this trick out and get rid of her for good. Especially if she thinks she is going to have free range of this house.* When the person walked through the doorway, she turned, saw me, and started to scream. The way she grabbed her chest, I thought she was going to have a heart attack. And after I saw who it was, I almost wished she did.

"What in the hell are you doing here?" Derrick's mom screamed.

"I live here. What are you doing here?" I retorted.

"You live here?" she said, frowning and ignoring my question. "Since when?"

"Since Derrick and I made up," I said, walking over to the sink to place the frying pan back into the dish drainer.

Ms. Shirley looked me up and down like I was lying. I guess she was checking my attire out, which clearly proved I stayed here. I was dressed like I slept here with my mint green fleece bottoms and matching tank.

"My son has lost his ever-loving mind," she murmured.

"What did you say? Speak up. I didn't hear you," I said, hearing every word that fell out her self-righteous mouth and I didn't appreciate it.

"Where's Derrick?" she asked, dismissing my question.

"He's not here."

"So where is he?"

"I don't know. He had some errands to run. He told me he would call me when he was on his way home," I said, leaning against the counter and crossing my arms across my still-wet chest.

It gave me great joy to see the anger on his mother's face. I knew she couldn't stand me and was hoping I and

Derrick were over for good. But now she saw we weren't. I smirked at her uneasiness.

"You should have called before you came by. I think that would have been better. That way you could have saved yourself the trip, and the gas for that matter," I said smartly, not giving a damn about this woman's time or gas.

"I don't have to call. I have a key and can come by anytime I feel like it."

"But, does Derrick even want to see you?" I questioned.

She shot me a heated glare. I could tell the wheels in her old head were turning. I knew she was wondering if I knew about everything that happened.

She tried to play it off by saying, "Of course my son wants to see me. I'm his mother."

"Should he question that? I mean since he doesn't know who his father is. I'm just saying." Those words let her know I knew everything.

"Little girl . . ." she said, pointing her finger as she started walking toward me.

"First of all, Mama Shirley, I'm not a little girl. I'm a grown-ass woman who will be addressed as such."

"Humh, a woman you are not. Maybe a whore. But not a woman," she shot back.

"I guess you would know one, huh, since you don't know who your baby daddy is," I retorted. "It's evident, so far, three men's dicks have been up in you and one of them was a damn child molester. But you have the nerve to judge me."

She balled up her fist and walked away from me, pacing the floor. I knew I touched a nerve with her but I didn't care. This woman never cared about me. She wrote me off the day she met me. I was never good enough for her son. But look who was by his side now: me.

"You're still riding that high horse of yours. Too busy tearing me down to recognize the turmoil you've caused your own son," I told her.

She turned to look at me but didn't say anything.

"He told me everything. About how you had him believing your husband was his dad. Then you had him believe Mr. Hanks was his dad only to find out the DNA test results proved he wasn't his father either. What type of mother are you to put your own flesh and blood through something like that? Just because you were unsure didn't mean you had to withhold your doubt. Evidently, you had some," I said.

"You don't understand."

"I don't need to understand. Derrick does. As much as you dislike me and hate to see me with your son, Mama Shirley, I do love him. Yes, I have made plenty of mistakes. But you know what? I'm human. Just like you. I bleed, just like you," I said, pointing back and forth between us. "The only reason I started treating you like I did was because you treated me like I was trash. The way you looked at me and even talked about me did hurt me, even though I acted like I didn't care. I clearly heard you when you said many negative things about me when you thought you were whispering, and it was totally disrespectful. This was coming from a so-called Christian. I thought only God can judge me. And people in the church wonder why people like me don't want to come up in the church. It's because of Christians like you."

Ms. Shirley stared at me as I talked.

"You have never tried to get to know me or ask about my life. Immediately upon meeting me, your wall went up, blocking any chance for me to get to know you. This was the reason why I disliked you. As if I didn't have enough rejection in my life, I had to get it from the mother of the man I love."

Ms. Shirley paced nervously, not having anything to say for the first time ever.

"Well, now look at you. How does it go? You reap what you sow? Or is it what comes around goes around? Or is it people in glass houses—"

"I get it," she cut me off. "You don't think I've thought about all of that? I know what I've done. I have to live with my bad decisions each and every day. No one, not Otis, not Derrick, and especially not you know what I have gone through. Nobody would ever understand," she said, starting to cry.

"Again, Ms. Shirley, I don't have to. Derrick does," I found myself saying sincerely. "As much as we don't like each other, I want you to resolve things with your son. You two have what I never had with my mother. I didn't have the connection you guys have. Maybe when I saw it in the beginning of our relationship, it made me a bit jealous."

Ms. Shirley's eyebrows rose a bit.

"I know I'm also far from perfect. I didn't love your son the right way. But I'm trying to learn to love him the way he deserves to be loved now."

She nodded like she understood me. I didn't know if it was her emotional state or just the heartfelt look in her eyes, but Ms. Shirley was hearing me without rolling her eyes at me.

"I never wanted any beef with you. I got too many other problems in my life to be fighting with you. Heck, I'm competing with two other women for your son's affection," I said, frustrated.

"Two?" she asked, surprised, as she wiped the tears from her cheeks.

"Yes. Kea and Trinity."

She looked at me like she didn't know what I was talking about.

"You did know about them right?" I asked.

"I know about Kea but who is Trinity?"

Chapter 8

Trinity

Sitting in my car, I scooted down so Derrick couldn't see me spying on him. He had his back to the window. He had his head held down like he was sad. He shouldn't have been sad because he had me.

"Oh no. Why is she here? Why is Kea here to see my man? Look at her, thinking she's cute in her fuchsia sundress with matching shades on. She's pretty but not as pretty as me," I said, talking to myself.

When Kea walked to the table, Derrick practically broke his neck to get up and hug her.

"He's standing too close to her. Why are you touching her, Derrick? Why does the hug have to be so lingered? Let her go already," I screamed through the window, which was let up, like Derrick could hear me.

"Why is she touching my man? Now, I have to wash him. Now, I have to scrub her fingerprints off my man's body. How dare she think she can touch him like that?"

I couldn't believe Derrick was meeting with Kea. He told me he was going to the gym. This coffee shop didn't look like a damn gym. Unless there was a treadmill, elliptical, and some weight benches in the back, he didn't have a reason to be here. Why did he feel like he had to lie to me? After all I had done for him. He still chose to betray me and go running after this woman who didn't even want him. I'd been right by his side though everything and he still couldn't see I was the woman he needed to choose to spend the rest of his life with? He acted like we were friends. Couldn't he see we were beyond that point now? Friends don't sleep with one another. Friends go out to clubs and bars and lunches together and talk about everything. They don't end up in bed at the end of the night. Friends go their separate ways.

I rocked back and forth, like I was in a rocking chair sitting on a porch. I saw Derrick reach across the table and touch Kea and I began to rock faster.

"No, Derrick. No. Stop touching her. You're only supposed to touch me," I cried out angrily. "I'm your woman. You want to marry me."

I continued to rock.

"They are talking too long. I can't hear what they are saying. The enemy has put in soundproof glass so I can't hear what they are saying," I said to myself as I rocked. "At least I can see them. At least the enemy hasn't blocked my visual."

I saw Kea stand up. It looked like she was upset about something and this was a good thing. She was saying something but I couldn't make out what it was. Now Derrick was standing. Was he about to leave with her? Was he going to chase after this woman who didn't want him? His body language was uncertain. I couldn't tell if he was happy or angry. But Kea looked upset. Why? She was marrying Jaquon. Why be upset? Well, that was something to be upset about but she couldn't have Derrick.

Derrick stepped closer to her. What was going on? Out of nowhere there was a tap at my window. It was something long and black. The tap sounded again and I let down the window to see who it was.

"Ma'am," said the police officer standing back toward my driver's side window with his hand on his gun ready for anything.

"Yes, Officer."

"Is everything okay?"

"Yes, it is. Why?"

"Well, I marked your tires fifteen minutes ago and you were sitting in your car. I come back and you are still sitting here acting like you are agitated about something. Your time is up and if you don't move your car, I'm going to have to write you a parking ticket. Is there a reason why you are still here?"

"I . . . I . . . was waiting on someone but I will move. Can you give me a few minutes?" I asked nicely, trying to return to looking at Kea and Derrick in the coffee shop.

"No, ma'am, I can't. You've sat here your allotted time. If you stay here any longer, I'm going to write you a ticket."

This man was ticking me off. He was interfering with my investigation over a fifteen-minute parking space. The space didn't have his name on it. This city wasn't his, so why was he tripping? Didn't he have some other tickets to write instead of bothering me about why I was sitting here? *All these cars he could harass and he chooses to bother me.* If I wanted to sit here all day then that was my right.

"Ma'am. Are you going to move or do you want the ticket?"

In the midst of looking at the cop, I forgot about my main focus and that was Derrick. When I looked back at the window, both he and Kea were gone.

"Where did they go?"

"Ma'am?"

"Where did they go?" I asked in a panic.

"Who? Ma'am. Are you okay?"

I cranked my car and pulled off driving around in the direction Kea came from earlier. When I whipped around the corner, there was no sign of either of them.

"They couldn't just have vanished."

And then I saw something. I saw someone wearing fuchsia pink entering a store. A parking space was becoming available as I saw the reverse lights brighten. A car was to my left with their signal to turn into the space but I sped up to get to it first. I zoomed into the space before the car had a chance to turn into it.

The woman laid on her horn, throwing her hands up. With my window still down, I stuck my arm out of the window and held up my middle finger to her.

"You bitch!" the woman screamed. "You saw me waiting to pull into that parking space."

I jumped out of my ride yelling, "Who you calling a bitch, you old wrinkle-face hag?"

Her mouth opened wide like she couldn't believe I was speaking to her like that. What did she think, I was going to stand here and take her calling me a bitch? Please. She didn't know me. And if she didn't back the hell off, she was going to find out who the real Trinity was.

She got brave and yelled, "I'm talking to you, you rude ghetto whore."

"Ghetto," I yelled, getting angry at her audacity. Immediately, I thought about all the racial things I'd gone through in my past with both races not accepting me because I was either too dark or too light. My hair wasn't straight enough or it was too good of a grain. And now today, because I was recognized seen as black woman, this white hag decided it was fitting to call me ghetto.

"Okay," I said, bending down in my car. I searched for something, anything I could use on this woman. And there it was. I reached over and picked up a brand new bottle of Hennessy I bought for later because I knew Derrick liked it. It was still in the black plastic bag to conceal it. I snatched the bottle out of the bag and stood holding it like a weapon by the narrow neck.

I yelled, "I got your ghetto, bitch."

The woman's mouth flew open again. If she was really smart, she would have already pulled off. She was lucky I only had a bottle of Henny and not a damn gun to shoot her behind with.

The woman attempted to pull off but some pedestrians were crossing in front of her so she couldn't move. This gave me just enough time to get to her vehicle. She tried to let the window up but wasn't fast enough to get it all the way up. I swung the bottle of Henny, shattering her driver's side window. To my surprise, the bottle didn't break.

The woman screamed, "Get away from me, you crazy bitch."

I swung the bottle and shattered the back driver's side window and again the bottle had yet to break.

"I bet this will teach you to call another woman ghetto, or a bitch for that matter."

The woman saw she had clearance to drive forward and stomped on the gas. I swung at the car again and missed but regained enough strength to toss the full bottle of liquor at her car. The bottle landed perfectly into her back window, causing it to shatter also.

People always caused me to act out of my character. Why did I always have to be pushed to the level of proving I was no one to mess with? I turned to walk back to my vehicle and noticed some people watching what just went down. When I made eye contact with some, they quickly went about their day, probably figuring it wasn't wise to start with me too. And that was their best bet.

When I clicked the locks to walk into the store I thought I saw Kea walk in, I heard someone call out, "Ma'am."

I didn't bother to turn because I didn't think anybody was talking to me. But when the "ma'am" got louder, I turned to see the same officer who was at my window earlier coming toward me. He had his hand on his weapon like he was about to pull it out on me and get to cappin'.

"Ma'am, put your hands up."

"For what?" I asked in irritation.

"Because you are under arrest."

Chapter 9

Jaquon

I was running late and knew if I was not on time for this appointment, Kea would have my head. She called to see where I was and I lied and told her I was on my way, when I hadn't even left the apartment. I had to come home and change clothes first before I met her. I didn't want to show up in my work clothes. I really wanted Kea to see I was serious about this marriage and I was serious about her.

I rushed out of the door freshly showered and dressed in my Sunday best only to bump into Sheila. I swore it was time to move out of this building just to get away from her. I was getting sick and tired of every time I turned around, she was standing here. I thought she was waiting for me to leave so she could step out in the hallway to talk to me.

"In a rush?" she asked.

"Yes," I said coldly, trying to lock the door. Once I did that, I attempted to go down the stairs but she blocked my way.

"Will you move?" I asked irately.

"You look nice," she said, rubbing my arm, but I jerked back from her grasp. She giggled. "Where you off to so fast?" she asked.

"Marriage counseling."

She started to laugh. "Counseling? You really are trying to be this changed man for Kea, huh? But don't you know, Jaquon, that ain't going to help your raging sex drive?" she said, looking down at the front panel of my slacks.

"My sex drive is none of your concern."

"Well, it was the other week," she countered.

Here she was reminding me of the day she almost got me to come over to her place for me to almost hit it again. Luckily, fate stepped in and sent this woman, Trinity, to my door with her proposition. I knew if she never would have shown up, I would have buried myself deep into this whore.

"Look, Sheila, the other week was a mistake."

"It was a mistake that would have ended in mind-blowing sex if that woman hadn't shown up. Who was she anyway?"

"None of your business."

"You were with her long enough to screw her. I listened at the door to see if I heard anything, but I couldn't," she revealed.

"Are you stalking me?" I asked.

"Please, don't flatter yourself," she said. "If anything, you want me. And you've had me. I know you want some of this good pussy again," she said, walking closer to me.

"I'm getting married, Sheila."

"I've slept with married men before. I find it kind of exciting. You know the legal papers, and vows before friends and family, yet they come to see me when they want some excitement in there miserable relationship."

"Well, Kea is exciting and I'm not going to sleep with you anymore."

"Oh, you are going to, even if I have to blackmail you to do it."

"Blackmail? Please," I said, brushing her off.

"I'm serious, Jaquon. I don't like you, but I love what you have to offer," she said, walking up to me and grabbing my manhood. "Such an arrogant, low-down, dirty dog, but your sex is off the chain. I've been with plenty of men but none of them have made me feel like you did."

Knowing Sheila's reputation, I felt damn good about her compliment. It somewhat elevated my self-assurance for what I could offer in the bedroom. Regardless of that, I couldn't be with this woman anymore.

"You mean to tell me I can't get any more of this good—"

"Sheila, let go of me," I demanded, pushing her hand away, probably not convincingly enough. Her hands did feel good gripping my Johnson. The more I tried to push her off of me, the harder she gripped me, causing a slight pain to radiate in my groin area.

"Do you really want me to let go or do you want me to drop to my knees and take you in my mouth and suck you until you cum?"

Her words were like smooth lyrics being played at a jazz festival: relaxing and intoxicating all at the same time. Sheila backed me up against my own door. There was nowhere else to move. Plus, she still had me in her grip.

"You sure you got somewhere to be?" she asked seductively.

"Sheila, I'm flattered but this appointment is important," I pleaded.

"But what about me? It would be a shame if Kea found out about that woman with the blue eyes. It would also be a shame if she found out about you and me."

"I haven't been with you since I got back with Kea."

"She doesn't know that," Sheila said, unzipping my slacks. Her hands went inside my pants quickly and I didn't do anything to stop her. Her touch was warm and soft. She stroked my member, causing my right leg to tremble. I can't lie, it felt really good. Why did fate have to tempt me like this?

"Look, Sheila, please. I'll come check you out later. Just let me go to this appointment," I begged.

"Don't lie to me, Jaquon, because that wouldn't be wise."

"I promise. I will think of something, okay? Just let me get to this meeting and I'll holla at you later."

Sheila smiled devilishly. I thought she was going to let me go but she surprised me by what she did next. She whipped out my manhood, bent over, and put me into her mouth. I grabbed the base of the doorway and trembled at the wetness of her lips on my Johnson. She sucked me long and deep as her tongued cupped me. I hadn't felt this in so long and it felt amazing. I forgot Sheila had oral skills that could make the Pope lose his religion. I yearned for what I had been missing. I closed my eyes and enjoyed what she was doing to me until I realized I was outside. I looked around and wondered if anyone was watching. Did anyone see Shelia from across the way sucking me like she was hungry for the biggest link sausage she had ever had? Without thinking I grabbed the back of her head and pulled her into me. Just when I was on the verge of climaxing, she released her mouth from around my Johnson. I almost pushed her back down so I could finish.

She stood up, wiping her mouth with a smirk on her face. "Later, right?" she said, backing away moving toward her door. "I'll let you bust in my mouth then."

I couldn't do nothing but nod. My rock-hard Johnson was sticking out as it dripped with her saliva. She looked down at it and grinned sheepishly.

"You better not disappointment me, Jaquon, or there will be repercussions."

She went into her apartment and slammed the door in my face, leaving me panting for more. I couldn't believe what just happened. Sheila may have been a whore but she knew how to please a man.

"Kea," I said, remembering my appointment with the minister.

I pushed my extension back in the best I could and bolted down the stairs, hoping I wouldn't be late for this appointment; but I felt like I already was.

Chapter 10

Kea

"You are late," I told Jaquon when he came through the door of the church. I was waiting for him in the vestibule looking like an idiot because our appointment with the pastor should have started twenty minutes ago.

"I told you to be here at four o'clock. It's almost four-thirty. What have you been doing?" I asked angrily.

Jaquon shifted uncomfortably as he avoided looking Kea in her eyes. He glanced at the crucifix on the church wall and dared not to lie within the sanctuary. Thinking quickly, he responded to her question.

"Kea, I ran into some trouble, okay? I tried to get here on time. I'm here now."

I was ticked off and hated feeling this way since I was getting ready to go into this office and speak to the pastor who would be marrying us. I knew Pastor Wilson would see right through me, so there was no need for me to try to hide my mood from him when I walked in.

"Pastor Wilson is ready to see you now," his gorgeous secretary said and we both got up to enter his office. I watched as the woman, wearing a tight, fitted blouse and gray pencil skirt, twisted her way as she led us to the pastor's office. Her behind was huge. As wrong as it was, I wondered if this secretary was getting it in with Pastor Wilson. She looked like the type. Men slept with their secretaries all the time and she looked like a prime candidate for such a task.

I looked back at Jaquon to see if he was looking and he wasn't. He was looking at the pictures on the walls as we entered the pastor's office.

"Kea," Pastor Wilson said when he saw me. He came around the mahogany desk to give me a hug. "It's so good to see you."

"It's good to see you too, Pastor," I said, returning his embrace.

Pastor Wilson looked the same as he did when I was a little girl coming to church with Mama and Daddy back in the day. The only thing different was his hair had gone from solid black to a salt-and-pepper mix. He still had his mustache and beard, which he kept neatly trimmed; and he still wore his signature dark-rimmed glasses, which he always took off when he was about to give us a sermon that would bring us to our feet.

"Pastor Wilson, this is my fiancé, Jaquon Mason," I introduced them.

Pastor Wilson held out his hand and shook Jaquon's, saying, "It's good to meet you, son."

"Good to meet you too, sir . . . I mean, Pastor," Jaquon stuttered. He actually looked nervous. He looked cute in his black suit with grey and black striped tie. I knew this was probably why he was late for our meeting. I felt a little guilty now that I realized he was making great strides. Jaquon was trying hard to make this work.

"You two have a seat." Pastor Wilson gestured to the two black leather chairs sitting in front of his desk. He walked around and proceeded to sit down in his. Leaning forward with his elbows on the desk, he locked his fingers together and said, "It's been awhile, Kea."

"I know, Pastor," I said shamefully, knowing there was no excuse why I hadn't been coming to church.

"You were such a dedicated member of this church."

"I know," I said, remembering attending church every Sunday. This was my parents' home church and I grew up in this sanctuary. It was like home, so I didn't know how it was so easy for me to stray from here. I guessed life got in the way. And it didn't help my parents were no longer together.

"I am sorry to hear about your mother. It was indeed a shock to hear such a tragedy happened and that she was involved. Honestly, I knew she had problems, but none bad enough for her to want to take someone else's life."

Hearing Pastor Wilson say this brought back the feeling of me being an innocent child born due to a horrific event. But that didn't give Frances the right to make my life a living hell. Nor did it give her the right to pay someone to kill the man I would later find out was not only my neighbor, but also my biological father.

"If you only knew the entire truth," I said.

"I've been praying for Sister Frances."

I nodded, not knowing what to say. My mother was the last person I wanted to talk about right now. Not on a day when the focus was my marriage to the man I loved.

Pastor Wilson continued to say, "And to also hear she and Joseph are getting a divorce, this has to be hard on you," he said, leaning back in his chair with his hands resting across the small belly he had started to form.

"It's been difficult but Daddy has been there for me every step of the way."

"You all are in my prayers."

"Thank you, Pastor."

"Now, let's get down to business," he said, sitting up straight again. "You two want to make it official and get married."

I looked at Jaquon as we both nodded.

"And you two are sure you are ready to take such an important step?"

Again we both nodded.

He stared at us for a minute before saying, "Marriage is not to be taken lightly. I hope you two know what you are getting yourselves into."

"Pastor Wilson, I love Kea with everything in me," Jaquon said, shocking me by speaking up.

"Have you shown her you love her?" Pastor Wilson asked.

I immediately thought back to all the terrible things he had done, proving his love wasn't of pure nature when it came to being faithful to me. I looked at Pastor Wilson, who was staring at me. I knew he was examining me to see my reaction. He probably could tell by my body language the answer to his question was no. This man baptized me and had been a part of my life for as long as I could remember. So I knew he knew me.

"I have, but honestly, Pastor Wilson, I have done things to her in the past that have hurt her tremendously. I've cheated on her numerous times, but I have changed."

"'Thou shall not commit adultery' is a commandment that is not to be broken, son. So many don't take heed to the words of the Lord. If you think it's a possibility this will happen again, then you two don't need to wed."

"I know, sir, but I'm ready. I'm changing because I want Kea to be my wife."

Pastor Wilson sat back in his chair, again examining us. "My spirit is telling me you two do love one another, but there are some obstacles blocking your way. These obstacles can be hindrances to this marriage working."

Neither Jaquon nor I said anything. I didn't know what Jaquon was thinking but my thoughts immediately led me to Derrick. As much as I tried to convince myself that Jaquon was the one for me, I still had an inkling in the pit of my stomach that maybe, just maybe, Derrick was that man also.

"I'm not sure what these hindrances are but I think you need to give this marriage a little while so you two can work through some things."

"So are you telling us not to get married?" I asked, almost wishing he would say yes but also wondering why I felt this way all of a sudden.

"I'm not saying that at all. I just think there are some things you need to work through. Maybe you should have a long engagement. You don't have to get married immediately," he suggested.

"Pastor, I've known you for a long time and I feel like there's something you are holding back from me. Can you please just tell us? I will respect anything you have to say," I said eagerly.

"Kea, I feel neither of you are being honest with each other." Pastor Wilson hesitated before finishing, saying, "Or honest with yourselves."

Those words hit home. I almost gasped when he said it but I tried to play it cool. I looked at Jaquon, who grabbed my hand sincerely. I wondered what his opinion was on what the pastor was saying.

"I don't want you young people to rush into this marriage thinking love conquers all, because most times it takes more than love to make a marriage work. Now don't get me wrong, in a lot of situations it does; but by the same token you can't use loving one another as the glue you think will keep this marriage together. There is trust, honesty, knowing when to choose what battles to fight and if it's even worth fighting over, and it also takes give and take. You have to be a strong individual to endure marriage until death do you part."

"You don't think we are strong enough?" Jaquon asked.

"Only you know if you are strong enough. But let me tell you like this: the number one reason marriages break up today is due to infidelity. The second is money. Marriages are ruined every day because of these two things. We all know money is the root of all evil and sex can land you in a world of trouble, especially when you are going against your vows to have it."

I thought about Terry telling me to get a prenup, and I hadn't mentioned this to Jaquon. If he loved me, I felt he would sign it. *This could be a hiccup in our relationship that sends Jaquon into a rage because I know he's going to think I don't trust him. And if I don't trust him, then why am I marrying him?*

"And adultery. Whoa," he said, rocking back and forth in his chair. "Men and women are tested every day with the power of sexual advances. Jaquon, this would be especially hard for you because you are going into this relationship having cheated on her numerous times already. Now, I'm not saying you can't or haven't changed. I'm saying you will have to work extra hard at avoiding temptation. You also have to ask yourself why you haven't been able to be faithful before, when you had this lovely woman by your side. Why are you willing to change now? Do you think the devil is going to stop now that you are trying to become this man of faithfulness?"

Jaquon looked at him inquisitively, like he was considering what the pastor said.

"Kea, you have to ask yourself if you truly trust him enough to make him your husband. You can't have any doubt about his faithfulness to you. If you go into this thinking he's going to do it again, then you shouldn't settle and marry him."

His words cut deep. *Settle. Isn't this what Terry told me?* Was I settling? It sounded so different coming from Pastor Wilson. I had to question if this was God's way of confirming what Terry was telling me.

I looked over at Jaquon, who was staring at me now, I guessed waiting to see if I was going to respond. But I didn't have anything to say. So the pastor continued.

"So many women settle because they think they can change a man. Or they think they can't do any better than this man. No disrespect to you, Jaquon," the pastor said, waving his pudgy hand at him.

"I understand, Pastor," Jaquon said.

"Women and men are given warning signs before they go into a marriage. Most choose not to heed the warning signs."

I nodded, knowing that through all the years Jaquon and I had been together there had been major warnings signs, flashing bright red lights to stop and go the other way because danger was ahead. Still, here I sat ignoring what I knew in my heart was a big mistake. Again, I had to wonder why.

"If your mate is beating you upside the head and promises to change once you get married, then you need to think why couldn't this person change before the marriage. Vows said to one another is not going to make it stop. If someone constantly puts you down, then it's more than likely they will put you down after you marry. If a person is bad with finances, then more than likely they will spend up their money, leaving you holding the bag with all the bills. Marriage is not the remedy. You two see where I'm going with this?" Pastor Wilson asked.

We both nodded and my head was swimming with all kinds of doubt now.

"Just think about everything before you walk down the aisle before God to say 'I do.' The words 'I do' are supposed to be eternal and not to be taken lightly."

When the counseling was over, Pastor Wilson came back around his desk and gave me another hug. "I want to see you back in church, Kea."

"Yes, sir. I'm going to try."

"Try hard, too. And, young man, I want to see you with her," Pastor Wilson said, reaching his hand out to shake Jaquon's.

"Yes, sir," Jaquon said, smiling as he shook the pastor's hand.

When I walked out of that church, I felt the weight of a thousand uncertainties pressing down on my temples.

"What did you think about what he said?" Jaquon asked.

"I don't know," I answered, lying already and I wasn't out of the sanctuary five minutes.

"I think we are strong enough to do this, baby," Jaquon tried to convince me. He must have sensed I was considering backing out of this.

"I'm glad you think so."

"You don't?" he questioned.

"Honestly, no."

"Are you saying you don't want to marry me now?" he asked with a frown on his face.

"I'm not saying that," I said, backpedaling, wishing we weren't engaged at all. "I'm saying that maybe we should wait a bit."

"How long is a bit?" he questioned.

I started to get frustrated. Could he let my mind absorb the advice from the pastor before he started browbeating me about this marriage I didn't think he was ready for either? "I don't know," I said, aggravated.

"Why are you getting an attitude with me?" he asked.

"I'm not," I said, raising my voice slightly.

"See, now you getting mad."

"Look, Jaquon, can't you give me a minute to process what the pastor said? It's like you didn't take into consideration anything he was telling us."

"I heard him, Kea, but I feel like we can be that couple who makes it."

"Even with everything that has happened?" I asked.

"Yes," he said confidently. "We love each other and that's all we need."

How could he believe love was all we needed? Many marriages broke up with the two individuals loving one another. They just couldn't figure out how to make it work.

"Can you please just let me think on this a bit? That's all I'm asking you."

"Okay. I'll leave this alone for now. When you decide about our marriage, let me know," Jaquon said with an attitude and walked away from me, leaving me standing in the church parking lot alone.

And here it was: that large elephant in my brain I'd been trying to push out of my mind. The love I had for Jaquon was squashed quickly with the reservation brought back by my pastor's confirmation that this may not be the right move to make. Was I really ready for this? Was I ready to be Mrs. Jaquon Mason? Honestly the answer was no. Would I go with my heart, or would I go with what my mind knew all the time, and that's this marriage to Jaquon was a big mistake?

Chapter 11

Zacariah

One year ago, or better yet one hour ago, you wouldn't have been able to convince me I would be able to stomach being in the same room with this woman. I mean moments ago I was ready to hit her over the head with the frying pan even after I saw it was her. Now, I was sitting at the kitchen table catching her up on what had truly been happening.

By the time I went through everything that had happened in regard to losing my best friend and telling Ms. Shirley Derrick met this woman the night he found out the results of his and Kea's paternity test, she was flabbergasted. I also revealed, which shocked me, I had something to do with the false results. There was no need to lie for Derrick to tell her the truth later. I was getting too old to play games. So right now I was a work in progress and telling her my truth was a new beginning for us.

We had some common denominators but the one that brought us together was Derrick. We both loved him dearly.

"My son won't even talk to me," she said tearfully. "I know I've lied to him but I'm his mother."

"True, Ms. Shirley, but you are also the last one he would expect to betray him."

She paused, staring at me. "I never looked at it like that."

"You have been his rock, his world, and now his world has folded beneath him. Then dealing with me and our issues on top of everything else, it has broken him. I betrayed him. You have betrayed him and his dad betrayed him. And let's not forget his best friend Jaquon. Everything and everyone he knew to be true has disappointed him."

"I need to fix this. I came over here hoping I would catch him so I could speak with him."

"And you still can."

"I feel like when I'm looking at him, I don't recognize my own son."

"All of this has changed him dramatically—"

"For the worse," she interrupted. "I didn't raise him to treat women like this. How can he give you the ultimatum to allow him to sleep with you and this Trinity character? What's wrong with him?" she asked, which caused me to giggle. "And what's wrong with you to agree with it?" she asked seriously.

"I love him. Plain and simple. As you can see I've done a lot to get him back."

"I agree with you there."

"I will be his only woman one day. I'm just trying to be patient," I explained.

"Well if you ask me, and I know you didn't but I'm telling you anyway, something is not sitting well with me. As soon as I saw you, I thought my mother's intuition was answered."

I chuckled, realizing she thought I was the bad omen.

"But I still have this uneasy feeling. So it must have something to do with this Trinity person."

"I call her the blue-eyed monster."

"Blue eyes?"

"Yes, ma'am," I found myself saying.

"And she's a black woman?"

"She has black in her. I'm not sure what her nationality is. But from the looks of her, she's mixed with quite a few."

"You see, the more you talk, the more I know it's this woman I'm having uneasy feelings about," Ms. Shirley said, shaking her head with a worried look on her face.

The chime to the front door dinged as it opened, indicating Derrick was entering.

Ms. Shirley's eyes stretched as she looked at me. I reached across the table and patted her hand, knowing she was nervous about seeing her son.

When he entered, the look on his face told me how he felt.

Chapter 12

Derrick

How shocked was I to see Zacariah sitting down at the kitchen table with my mother having a cup of coffee. And neither of them were yelling and pulling each other's hair out. The both of them greeted me with smiles as both of them let go of each other's hand. I wondered if I was in the right house. I almost walked out and came back in again to make sure this was really happening.

Zacariah saw the confused look on my face. She got up and came over to me. "Hey, babe," she said, kissing me on the cheek.

"What's going on here?" I asked suspiciously.

"Your mom stopped by to see you," she said, turning to my mother, who looked like she had been crying.

"So why is she talking with you and why are you all not going at each other's throats?" I asked.

"We are past that now," Zacariah said.

"Since when?" I asked.

"Today, actually. We talked things out after we threw a couple of blows but we have recovered."

I looked at Zacariah, who glanced at my mom, who had a smile on her face. Was this really happening? The two of them managed to get along for more than five minutes? "Y'all are pulling my leg, right?"

"No, son," Mama finally spoke. "We have worked things out. I have to admit, the conversation in the beginning wasn't the best, but we came to some common ground. I misjudged Zacariah too quickly and she did the same with me as well. So here we are."

"Are you happy? I thought this was what you always wanted," Zacariah said.

"I did. I do. But . . . But . . . You know what? I'm not going to try to figure this out. I'm just going to take you guys' word for it and leave well enough alone."

"Good. Now I'm going to leave you to talk with your mother. You two have a lot to discuss," Zacariah said, walking toward Mama. She gently patted her shoulder and looked back at me before she left me alone with her.

For a moment the silence was deafening. I never had an instance with my mother that felt this awkward. It hurt me. I had always been able to go to her with anything. Even when I was a teen coming into my grown man status smelling myself and ready to plant my manhood in any girl who would allow me to do so, I talked with my mother about sex. Of course she wanted me to remain a virgin forever but my mother was one of those realists who knew, despite what she preached to me, I was going to sneak and do what I wanted to do. So when it came to sex, she advised me to be safe and wear protection at all times. I have to say I listened to that advice, which was why at my age I didn't have any children a woman could pin on me.

Thinking about how my mother had always been there for me made me feel fortunate. It hurt that our relationship reached this point. I could feel the tension build within me, which wanted to rise up into my mouth and spew all over this kitchen floor. But I maintained my dignity. What little I had anyway.

"Son, come over here and sit down," she said, patting the space that Zacariah got up from.

I listened and went over to the table and sat down. I pushed Zacariah's coffee mug away from me and leaned forward with my elbows on the table.

"Son, I have missed you."

"I've missed you too, Mama," I said back to her. I glanced at her when I said it but I couldn't bring myself to look her in the face. The anger I had toward her hadn't subsided much, because when I saw her, I saw deception.

"I know you are still angry with me, son, and you have every right to be. Because of me, you've had to experience a lot of things you shouldn't have."

"It's not the fact I had to deal with it, Mama. It's the fact you never disclosed information to me. Particularly, something as important as who my real father was," I said, grimacing.

"You are right again. That's why I'm here to explain. I should have talked to you when you came over but, son, I was dealing with things myself. When you told me the second set of results proved Mr. Hanks wasn't your father, that news sent me reeling. I was too embarrassed to talk about it. Do you know how that made me look?" she asked.

"My pain should have overridden you embarrassment, Mama."

"True, but I'm human just like you. As you can see I also make mistakes. There are things I would like to forget and there are things I wished I could change. I never thought our happy family would ever be destroyed."

"You mean you didn't think your secrets would ever surface," I said smartly.

Mama shifted uneasily. "Who wants secrets to come out, Derrick? Most times secrets are huge mistakes made that we want to forget about."

"But I'm a part of your secrets. And being part of your secrets makes me feel like I was also a mistake that never should have been found out about. So in wanting to forget about your mistakes, are you saying you wanted to forget about me?" I asked.

"No, of course not, Derrick. You are the best thing that has ever happened to me. You are the joy of my life. You can't tell?" she asked.

I didn't respond.

"Please don't twist my words, honey. As warped as things are now, we don't need to add more twist and turns to this."

"Did you come here today to tell me who my real father is?" I asked, rubbing my hands together.

Hesitantly, she said, "Yes."

I was not expecting that answer from Mama today. My stomach kind of fluttered when she said that. Here I was angry at her for not telling me who my father was and now I felt like I was afraid to know who he was.

Hesitantly I asked, "So who is he?"

"Son, this is difficult for me."

"Mama, just say it," I told her as my heartbeat increased.

She paused and stroked her hands over and over again. I could see how strenuous this was for her but I wanted answers. I wasn't going to give up until she gave them to me.

"His name is Gerald."

"Does he live here?" I asked, finally having a name, but wondering if she was just throwing a name out there to appease me.

"He doesn't live here. And before you ask he lives two hours away," she explained.

"And you know this why?" I asked, wondering how she knew this. Was she still keeping in touch with this man despite the fact that she was married to my father?

"I know this because your father is married to my sister."

I frowned at this revelation. This seemed to be worse than Mr. Hanks, the pedophile, turning out not to be my father. It took me a minute to process what my mother was trying to tell me.

"What did you say?"

"Your Uncle Gerald is your father."

I put my head down on the table. Mama rubbed my head, saying, "Son, let me explain."

"My uncle," I repeated, sitting up to look her in the face, making sure I was hearing her correctly.

Nervously she said, "I did believe Mr. Hanks was your real dad, which was why I kept in contact with him and sent him pictures of you all these years. Hearing he wasn't your father devastated me because I knew at that point there could only be one other possibility," Mama explained.

I looked up at my mother solemnly.

"Derrick, I didn't know how to deal or even tell you. That day when you came over, I knew Gerald was your dad. I couldn't compel myself to say that to you. Admitting that also meant revealing how trifling a woman I was for sleeping with my sister's husband."

I shook my head at this eye-opening conversation. Just when I thought things couldn't get worse, they did.

"Even at my ripe old age I didn't have the answers. I couldn't stand to see what my careless actions were doing to you."

"Does my uncle know about me? Well, I guess he does because he's family," I said.

"He does now."

"So you told him?" I asked.

"Yes. I spoke to him recently about everything that has come out."

"Does Aunt Henrietta know?"

Mama paused, and I nodded, asking, "She doesn't, does she?"

Mama shook her head.

"The secrets just keep getting better."

"Now you can see why I've had such a difficult time with all of this."

"Does Dad at least know?"

"Yes. I've been very open about myself, my life, and my secrets with your dad. I didn't want to go into another relationship withholding things from him. He has been the only person I've been truthful with this entire time."

"Well, that's good to know, because I don't know if I could take you telling me you cheated on Dad with your sister's husband."

"I met your dad right after I had you. Once we decided to get married, I wanted our marriage to not be a replica of the mess I made before I met him," Mama said.

"Now you see truth matters."

"I realize that."

"So what do we do now, Mama?" I asked.

"I don't know, Derrick."

"How is Uncle Gerald feeling about all of this? Because this has been dropped in his lap like it has mine," I said, leaning forward and putting my forehead on my fist.

"He was surprised, shocked, and happy. Then he got upset of course."

"Why, because I'm going to ruin his happy home?"

"Yes and no. I don't want you to think he doesn't want anything to do with you, because he does. He got upset because he feels like he's missed out on a lot of your life. Yes, he's played a major role by interacting with you as your uncle, but the realization you are his son has devastated him because he didn't get a chance to play that role in your life. Then, on the flip side, this news means we have to tell my sister if we want this to come out," Mama said.

"If," I said, chuckling. "Are you two placing the decision in my lap on where we should take this?" I asked.

"You make it sound so bad," Mama said, shifting uneasily again.

"It is, Mama. If I want to know my uncle as my dad, this will destroy our family. Their marriage is on the line because she doesn't know what you two have done. Then you and Aunt Henrietta's relationship may be destroyed also. And we haven't mentioned how this would affect my cousins, who are really my siblings. This secret would be like dropping a bomb in our family."

"I know, son," Mama said as tears streamed down her cheeks.

"But if I don't say anything and go on with the way things are, then everybody's happy little family remains intact, which is what you two probably want."

Mama leaned forward, placing her hand on my arm, saying, "Honey, I'm sorry for all of this." She dropped her head down and tried to get her composure. "I never meant for any of this to happen to you. You are my pride and joy. I hope one day you can find it in your heart to forgive me."

I looked at my mother, who stared at me with tear-filled eyes. She patted my arm twice and said, "Whatever you decide, I'm fine with. I don't care who it hurts, just as long as you are good with things."

Mama sat back and pushed her chair back. She said, "I'm going to get out of your hair. I've overstayed my welcome. I did what I needed to do and now it's time for me to go."

She stood to her feet and pushed her chair up to the table. Mama came over to me and kissed me on the top of my head. "I love you, honey."

She paused for a second, I guess to see if I would say the words back to her, but I didn't. She nodded and proceeded to walk away.

"Mama, wait," I said.

She turned to face me with more tears running down her cheeks. I got up and went over to her. I wrapped my arms around her, giving her a big hug. She began to weep as she accepted my embrace.

"I love you too, Mama. I hope you can forgive me for how I spoke to you the last time. There was no excuse for me disrespecting you."

She patted my back, saying, "It's okay."

Releasing from our embrace, I said, "I can't lie. This is difficult for me to swallow. I don't know what I'm going to do yet. I will let you know when I decide. But please know this: the two people who have been constants in my life have been you and Dad. No matter what decision I make, I'm going to always love and appreciate all you two did for me."

Mama nodded, and for the first time in a long time I felt like things were on their way to being restored.

Chapter 13

Trinity

"I can't believe you," my brother, Steven, said, walking into my apartment first as I followed him inside. He threw his keys to the couch and turned to me with his hands on his hips. "Arrested, Trinity? You got yourself arrested."

"The old lady popped off thinking it was okay to call me ghetto and a bitch. So I decided to show her how much of a ghetto bitch I could be," I said, walking around my brother to sit down on the sofa.

"Attempted battery. Destruction of property. And God knows what else. What were you thinking? Hold up," he said, holding both hands up to me. "You weren't thinking. This is a sure sign you are not taking your medication."

"Steven," I said, putting my feet up on the coffee table, "I'm so tired of you riding me about my medication. I'll take it when I feel like it."

"You will take it because you need to, Trinity. You don't have a choice."

"I do have a choice," I yelled to him.

"No, you don't. Can't you recognize you are headed down the same road that landed us in this town in the first place? Do I have to remind you of—"

I shot him a glance warning him to keep his mouth shut. I didn't want to talk about that and I was sick and tired of every time he felt like I wasn't handling life, he thought it was okay to keep reminding me of my recklessness. "Leave it alone, Steven," I challenged.

I loved my brother dearly but he always acted like he never made any mistakes. I was trying. Why couldn't he see that? Why couldn't he praise me when I was doing great in my life? He never saw any good I did. Regardless of how well I did, it was never acknowledged. Not by him. Not by my family and not by my parents. That's why they weren't here now.

I sat in silence getting angry at everything. Tears started to form in my eyes and Steven sighed, turning to the door with his hands on his head in frustration. "Don't cry, Trinity."

With his words the tears streamed down my cheeks. I didn't bother to stop them. I let them fall rapidly as the emotional toll of being who I was had taken a hold of me.

Steven turned and walked over to me. He sat down beside me and softly said, "Trinity, please stop crying. You know I don't like to see you cry."

I dropped my head into my hands and began to weep even louder.

"I'm just so tired of running, Steven," I struggled to say. "I've been running all my life I feel like."

"I know."

"Life has never been fair to me. Does God hate me? He has to, don't you think?"

"God doesn't hate, Trinity. People do. And, yes, the life we have had is a difficult one but look at us. We are still here. We still have one another to lean on. I know I'm hard on you but that's because I love you. I want nothing but the best for you, sis. I know you may not believe me but it's true. You are my world. I would do anything for you, including give my own life for you, Trinity."

I looked into my brother's face and saw his sincerity.

"You didn't ask for the life that was dealt to you but I want you to make the best of the life you have left, sis. Don't make the same mistakes. That's all."

"I guess you think one of my mistakes is being involved with Derrick."

Steven dropped his head before answering, "Yes."

"But why?"

"First, answer my question please. What were you doing downtown in the first place?"

I didn't say anything.

"You see. I know it had something to do with Derrick. I know you were following him. This is the exact thing you did before with the last guy you were with."

"But—"

"And to add more to this, you haven't been truthful with this man. Do you really think he's going to want to deal with you after he finds out about your past?"

"Who says he has to know, Steven? The only people who could tell him about my past are me and you. And I don't plan on telling him."

My brother looked down to the floor.

"Are you going to tell him about me?" I asked.

"I don't know, sis. As much as you want love, love sometimes doesn't want you. As soon as things don't go the way you want, you lose it. I feel like this man needs to know who he is dealing with."

"You are supposed to be on my side, Steven."

"Can't you see I am?" he asked.

"You are not on my side if you plan on telling Derrick about me."

"Look, I don't know what I'm going to do."

"Just leave things alone. Things are good between me and Derrick. I believe he is the one," I said confidently.

"Are you sure? Because the last guy you were with was 'the one' and he had a wife and three kids," Steven reminded me.

"I know."

"And the one before that was seeing you and another guy."

I nodded.

"And let's not forget about the one who got you pregnant and convinced you that having the baby would ruin things in your relationship. Then you found out later he was married also."

I was not happy with my brother reminding me about the men I'd chosen in my past. He acted like I blatantly went after men who were no good for me. I wasn't any different than any other woman looking for love.

"Your track record with men has not been good."

"But Derrick is different."

"Is he? Do you know this for sure? I mean he seems like a good guy . . ."

"He is."

"Looks can be deceiving, Trinity."

I wondered why my brother was talking this way. What was he trying to tell me that he wasn't? The next words out of his mouth let me know for sure why he was strong in his opinion.

"I've been following this dude."

My brother paused as he looked at me.

"And?"

"Derrick is living with a woman. Did you know that?"

His words cut like a hot knife through butter.

"You're lying," I told my brother, not wanting to believe him. "You're just telling me that so I can dump him. I can't believe you would stoop to such levels," I said, standing irately.

"I'm telling you the truth and, yes, I may have an ulterior motive for revealing this to you so you can get rid of him, but this guy has a secret woman he's keeping from you."

I walked out of the room, not wanting to deal with my brother as his words marinated within me. *Derrick wouldn't do this to me, would he?* And who could this woman be if my brother was telling me the truth? My brother usually didn't lie but today had proven that Derrick did. The only woman I knew Derrick wanted more than me was Kea. It couldn't be her since she was about to marry Jaquon. So who could this other woman be and why did Derrick feel like he could continue to lead me on like this?

This day just went from bad to worse. I didn't know how much more of this I could take. I loved Derrick with all my heart but I'd be damned if I was going to play second best to anybody forever.

Chapter 14

Zacariah

I finally got the courage to venture out and be my old self again. I'm not going to lie, I was afraid for the first time in my life. Being kidnapped, put in the trunk of a car, and barely escaping with my life caused me to have some nightmares behind the event. I could be lying six feet under if I didn't have the strength to escape. The fact that the person responsible hadn't been caught disturbed me also because I didn't know if this person would attempt to try this again.

I hadn't been back to the bar since that night I met this good-looking guy who, I believed, drugged me. This would have made it easier for him to exact his plan. But the more I thought about it, I didn't know if it was him at all. There were a lot of people in that bar that night. Hell, the bartender could have done it. I didn't know. Right now, in my eyes, everybody was a suspect. I was so on guard that I considered carrying a weapon around; but I was scared I would get trigger happy and shoot somebody for just looking at me wrong. So that idea wasn't a wise one for me.

Today, I was treating myself. I was going to get my nails and toes done. But first I had to get this hot mess on the top of my head done. By me staying in more I didn't have a reason to keep getting it done. I kept it in a ponytail. Putting on some jeans, and a T-shirt that read, Too STRESSED OUT AND NO ONE TO CHOKE, I headed to the salon.

All the girls spoke when I walked in. Julie, my stylist, had been doing my hair since my previous stylist, Hope, moved to Atlanta to take care of her sick mother. Julie was good but not as good as Hope. I couldn't wait until she got back but, until then, Julie had to do.

"Girl, I'm so glad you could fit me in today. Look at me. It's been weeks since I got my hair done," I said, pulling the scrunchie out of my hair and letting it fall to my shoulders.

"I was wondering what's been going on with you. You came to see me every week faithfully. But I guess after what you have been through, getting your hair done was the last thing you were thinking about," Julie said, parting the young lady's hair she was working on and combing it before sliding the strand through the flat iron. Smoke from the device rose in the air as I caught Julie eyeing me.

I frowned at Julie, wondering what she was talking about. Then I looked around the shop at some of the women sitting in here. I saw two leaning into one another, whispering something as they looked at me. When I made eye contact with one of them, she sat up straight, acting like I wasn't the topic of their conversation when it was clearly evident I was. The woman who was doing the whispering noticed me staring and sat up too. She picked up the magazine that was in her lap and began flipping pages like she was interested. I instantly got ticked off and I walked over to them.

"Zacariah," Julie called out but I never stopped my stride.

"Zacariah!" she called louder, but by now I was standing in front of the two women.

"Why are y'all talking about me?" I accused.

"What are you talking about?" the woman who was doing the whispering said with her skinny face contorted. She wasn't cute at all. With two teeth missing in the front and lips black like she'd been smoking on a crack pipe, I was ready to put her on a street corner and tell her to drop down and suck a dick.

"Evidently you were talking about me because your bug eyes were looking at me the entire time when your lips were moving. So I'm standing right here. Say what you need to say."

"Ain't nobody talking about you," the crackhead said. The other woman she was whispering to was smart enough to keep her mouth shut. She looked at the woman denying the accusations like she was going down for this one by herself.

"Okay. I'm going to let you have your lie today. But if I catch you running your mouth again and your eyes are in my direction, I'm going to come over here and handle you."

"Zacariah, get over here now. I'm ready to do your hair," Julie yelled.

I stood a few more seconds making sure the women, especially crackhead, understood. Neither of them said anything and I walked over to Julie to climb in her chair to get my hair done.

"Something is wrong with you," Julie said.

"You know I don't play. If she had something to say about me, then she should have come to me with it," I said, staring the woman down. She never looked up.

Julie turned my chair so my back could be facing those tricks.

"Why you do that?" I asked angrily.

"I got to do your hair, don't I?" she said.

"But you did that so I wouldn't see them."

"Zacariah, girl, you need to chill. I know you quick to pop off but this is my place of business. You can't threaten the people who come here to get their hair done."

"Then they should keep their damn mouth shut."

Julie ran her fingers through my thick mane and said, "I think you need a perm."

"I know I need one," I agreed, trying to calm down.

Julie draped the plastic cape around me and took out the small bucket of perm to begin adding the cream to my thick roots. She had to turn my chair back around to do this and when she did, she said, "Keep your mouth shut."

I eyed the women but saw one of them was gone. Unfortunately the crackhead one running her mouth was still sitting there.

"I try to get along with people but they like to try me."

"That's the way the world is," Julie said.

"Please, Julie, don't start preaching that crap because I don't care. That's the damn problem anyway. People quick to run their mouth behind your back but once you step to them, they get quiet as a church mouse."

"People can talk. That's their prerogative. You have to know the things that have been going on with you have been the topic of conversation lately."

"Oh really? What have you heard exactly?" I asked her, knowing she would have all the dirty details. Julie was like a channel seven news reporter and had the dish on everything around the city. I guess doing hair allowed her the perk of finding out the scoop. And since she revealed gossip had been spread about me, I wanted to know the real.

"Well, what I heard is that you and Derrick weren't together anymore and that he broke up with you for cheating on him. And I also heard you and Essence got down for some dollars."

I abruptly turned to face her as she looked down at me with surprise, holding the brush filled with relaxer in her right gloved hand.

"Who told you this?" I asked.

"Now, Zacariah, you know I can't reveal my sources. Then I wouldn't be able to find out more information."

I turned back around so she could get back to relaxing my hair, knowing Julie wasn't going to tell me anything. So I asked her, "Anything else?"

"Um hm. I heard you got beat down at Derrick's house by Kea and you were hospitalized with major bruises and a concussion."

Hearing her say that caused me to tense a bit as anger filled me.

"And I'm sorry to hear about your friend Essence getting murdered."

Hearing the word "murdered" instantly turned my anger that was building into sorrow. My eyes watered. I tried hard to hold back the tears I wanted to release. The thought of losing my best friend in such a tragic way devastated me every time I thought about her.

"Girl, you have really been going through it," Julie said, steadily applying the cream to my hair.

I couldn't say anything because she was right. I had been going through it and it didn't feel good that everybody knew my business. I missed Essence so much. I didn't realize how much I loved her until she was taken away from me. Now, I had no one.

Well, now I had Derrick and I hoped to keep him in my life forever. I thought I'd gotten rid of one obstacle in the form of Kea. Now it was time to get rid of another.

Chapter 15

Zacariah

I stood in the mirror and flung my newly styled hair around loving the way it moved. I ran my fingers through it and was happy because Zacariah was back in full effect.

"Julie, you did it again, girl. I love it," I said, turning to my left to look at that side and turning my head to the right to look at the other.

"I might not be able to do a lot but I know how to do some hair," Julie said, standing behind me, looking at her finished work.

"Can't nobody look as good as I do," I said, twirling, causing a few of the patrons to laugh. "I keep it hot all the time."

"But you ain't hot now. You not even lukewarm. And you damn sure weren't hot enough to keep Derrick."

Some women put their hands to their mouths in awe as Julie had succeeded in embarrassing me, which took me back to my ticked-off state of mind. "We went through a rough patch," I tried to say and Julie cut me off.

"Well, that patch must be filled with thorns," Julie retorted.

"Bitch, that's enough," I said, giving her the eye to shut her damn mouth. "How much do I owe you?" I asked, trying to keep my cool. I knew Julie and I were cool but she was taking this thing too far.

"It's sixty-five."

I reached into my purse and pulled out my wallet. I retrieved three twenties and one ten. I handed her the money, saying, "I'll see you in a week."

"Zacariah, I hope you are not mad at me," she said.

"No. I'm not mad," I said with sarcasm dripping from my voice with a hint of irritation.

"I didn't mean to tick you off," she said, holding her hands up.

"I told you I'm good," I said loudly. "I'm getting ready to go home to my man, Derrick," I said, making sure to stress his name so everybody heard me clearly. Especially Julie.

Her eyebrows rose.

"That's right. We are back together, for your information," I said smartly.

"But . . . You know what, never mind," Julie said, starting to walk away.

"No, no, no. Tell me what you were going to say," I said, curious.

"Why should I? I clearly made you mad by my last comments."

"I told you I was fine," I said through clenched teeth. "Now tell me what you were going to say."

Julie turned to me, putting her hands on her hips. "I heard Derrick has another woman in his life. I think her name is Trinity. So if you are back with him, then he must be seeing the both of you," Julie revealed.

Just the mere mention of her name sent chills through me as I remembered that blue-eyed trick. I wanted to melt into the tile within that shop. Again, it was one thing for me to know about him playing the field with me and Trinity, but everyone else knew too. I didn't like that at all because it made me look stupid. But I tried to play it off.

"Trinity is old news. He doesn't have anything to do with her anymore," I lied. "Besides, all she was to him was a quick lay."

Julie smiled, but her smile quickly faded when she peered at someone standing behind me. When I turned, the eyes let me know who she was. It was little Ms. Blue-eyed Monster herself, Trinity.

"So you think I'm just a quick lay, huh?" she asked, stepping closer to me.

"Yes," I said, nodding and standing my ground. "He doesn't want you. Truth be told he never did."

"I find that funny when he was lying next to me last night."

The onlookers oohed with her words. Julie walked over to get her next client, bringing an elderly woman to her chair.

I snarled at Trinity, who had this smirk on her face.

"Cat got your tongue? Oh no, wait a minute. Derrick had his tongue in my cat last night. That's what I meant to say."

Some of the women burst into laughter as they continued to listen intently. I knew these ladies were hoping for an altercation to break out as they chatted with one another.

"No, she didn't go there," one woman said.

"Yes, she did, girl. She put it all out there for everybody to see," another said.

My blood began to boil with her words. It was one thing to know the stipulation Derrick gave me when I got back with him, but it was another to have his other relationship flaunted for everybody to see and know about making me look like a damn fool.

"So before you go around making me look like some home wrecker, tell the story how it really is, because I'm Derrick's girlfriend," Trinity hissed.

"Like hell you are," I retorted, stepping closer to her.

"Ladies! Ladies! Not in this shop, please," Julie begged.

"You will never have what Derrick and I have," I told Trinity. "He loves me and only me," I tried to say convincingly but I really didn't know who had his heart. "You were just a side piece to keep him occupied until he asked me to come back into our home. Let me make sure you heard me. I said our home. I'm the woman under his roof and in his bed every night. If you are his woman, then why aren't you there? Looks like you are proving to be what I said you were and that's a quick lay."

I could tell my words affected her. She squinted her eyes as she boldly crossed her arms across her chest. Looking up like she was thinking, Trinity said, "And how many dicks did you climb on while you were with this man you love so much? We all know—well, at least I know—you cheated on Derrick most of your relationship. That's the reason why he kicked you out of his house in the first place. What was the story? Oh, I remember," she said, placing her finger on her chin. "Derrick told me you came home with some other man's juices running out that stank pussy of yours."

Women fell out laughing at Trinity's statement. Julie was caught so off-guard by what she said she pulled the elderly lady's hair she was working on too hard, causing the woman to yell, "Ouch."

"Oh, I'm sorry, Ms. Beatrice," Julie apologized, trying her best not to laugh at my demise; but, try as she might, the girl's teeth was hanging out her head laughing.

I walked up to Trinity until my nose was almost touching hers. "Look here, you blue-eyed tramp, I'm getting sick and tired of you and that mouth of yours."

For some reason Trinity didn't even flinch. She didn't step back. She didn't have one ounce of fear within her. She said, "Zachariah, right."

More women burst into laughter.

"My name is Zacariah."

"Oh, that's right. Look here, you," she said, pointing her little finger in my face but not actually touching me. "You may walk around like you got it going on, and you might have a few women scared of this bold illusion you like to put on like you bad or something, but I'm not afraid of you. I see the fakeness oozing from you. So don't front. If you stepping to me like you ready to swing then don't hesitate. I'm standing right here," she said with the coldest look I'd ever seen from a woman. I can't lie, for a minute her wicked demeanor shook me, but I couldn't let anyone else see that.

"I should ram my fist down your throat," I said through gritted teeth.

"Again, I'm standing right here mouth all mighty. Don't talk it, prove it."

I swung and punched that trick in her face and from then on it was a fight. Both of us were throwing punches and pulling each other's hair. Rods that were in her head were snatched out. She tugged on my just-done hair and then I felt both of us fall into one of the stations. The searing hotness coming from the flat iron caused me to scream in agony. I pushed Trinity back to get away from the pain but as soon as she realized what I was trying to do, this trick picked up the flat iron and tried to burn me again with it. She aimed it at my face but I blocked it and punched her in her face again, causing her to fall back into the station. Product was flying along with fists until a couple of the women decided to break us up.

Trinity looked at me, grinning, and I lunged forward to hit her again but the women holding me wouldn't let me go.

"Okay. That's enough," Julie said, bringing both of her arms between us. "I should call the cops and have both of you arrested. I tell you one thing, whatever is damaged, y'all are going to pay for it or else," Julie said, picking up some of the items that were scattered on the floor. "This doesn't make any sense," she spat.

The patrons definitely had something to talk about later. I was pretty sure we had already given them enough to yap about.

Trinity sneered and said, "This is not over."

"You damn right it's not over," I agreed, glaring back at her.

"Linda, I think I'm dry," she told her hairstylist as she walked over to her empty chair and sat down. "Can you please hurry up and do my hair? I need to look nice for my man, Derrick, later."

Her hairstylist looked at me to see what my reaction was going to be. Hell, the entire salon was staring me down to see what I was going to do. Trinity sat up boldly in the chair with her legs crossed and back straight as Linda removed from her head the rods that remained.

It had been a long time since I felt this humiliated. I mean the fight with Kea, yeah, I lost that fight; but the plus side of that situation was I was passed out, and didn't have to see the stares of everyone around me. I woke up in the hospital. Here, I was in the middle of a beauty shop filled to capacity with individuals who loved to talk.

When I turned to walk out of the shop, all eyes were still on me. My once-strong, bold demeanor had been brought down by some blue-eyed Bohemian woman who had my man. Had finally met a woman more cold than I thought I was. Something wasn't right about Trinity. This was just the tip of the iceberg concerning her state of mind and I knew it was a matter of time before she really showed how crazy she was.

Chapter 16

Trinity

I watched Zacariah the entire time she was in here. Talk about a hypocrite. She confronted those two females because she thought they were talking about her. Then she turned around and did the same thing by talking about me. So I gladly confronted her. She wasn't expecting me to be standing there. When she turned around and realized I was there, the look on her face was priceless. I practically saw the blood drain from her face. And as if that didn't give me pleasure enough, it gave me great joy making Zacariah look pathetic in front of everybody. Damn right I taunted her. I knew a trick like her was going to put her hands on me because she couldn't be upstaged by me. Punching that bitch in her face and trying to give her third-degree burns on her face made me feel exhilarated. As much as it pained me to hear she was back with my Derrick, I wasn't going to let her see it. I held my composure even though I felt like crying. Just the mere fact my brother was right ticked me off.

Still, Zacariah was a huge problem that needed to be dealt with and soon. I didn't know what it was with people thinking they could push me but it was getting to me. I was trying really hard not to let that side of Trinity come forward that would unleash a wrath no one had ever seen before. Well, not in this city.

After all that talk and fighting I still ended up with Derrick in my home. He came over to eat dinner with me tonight and he looked handsome as ever.

"Wow, baby, you look good," Derrick said, looking at my free-flowing, curly 'fro, which I had just had dyed auburn. I loved it. It made me look more mysterious. I was happy Derrick liked it too.

He came up behind me and kissed me on the cheek. "Dinner smells good," he said, holding me around my waist. His body felt so good next to mine. I turned to kiss him.

"I missed you today. What have you been doing all day?" I asked, wondering if he would tell me about his visit with Kea the other day; or, better yet, that he was back with Zacariah.

He let me go and went over to the table to sit down. He said, "I went and shot a couple of games of hoops. Then I went to my cousin's house and played the video games for a while. Besides getting your hair done, what have you been doing?" he asked, not coming forth with what I wished he would.

This upset me a bit but I tried not to show it as I stirred the sauce trying to calm myself. What I really wanted to do was pick this hot pot of liquid up and toss it on him for lying to me. That's when I realized I loved this man and I couldn't hurt him. I knew then I needed to take my medicine. My thoughts and the voices were becoming too much for me to deal with. I didn't want it to come to a point where I couldn't control them. Not like . . . Not like . . .

"Trinity, baby, are you okay?" Derrick asked.

"Oh, I'm sorry, baby. I was thinking about some things."

"Well, whatever it was, it took you far away from here for a minute. So are you going to tell me if anything exciting happened to you today?"

"As a matter of fact it did. Guess who I ran into today."

"Who?" he asked.

"Zacariah."

"Where did you run into her?"

"At the hair salon. She came in there talking junk about me and how she was back with you," I said, looking at his body language, noticing him squirm a bit. That was the squirm of someone hiding something.

"She doesn't stop," he said. "I told her I didn't want to be with her anymore."

Okay. Was he lying? Or was Zacariah lying? I really hoped it was her because if Derrick was not being forth-coming with me, I was going to lose it. We'd been upfront with one another from day one. Why was he lying to me now?

I said, "We had some choice words and it almost came to blows but . . ." I lied, knowing we did get into a fight.

"Blows. What? Y'all were about to fight?" he asked.

"She put it out there and I dared her to swing. Just like I suspected, she got scared and backed down," I lied again.

"I think I need to have a talk with her. She's taking this thing too far. You think she would have gotten the hint by now. We've been broke up for a while now."

"Well, she still has this illusion you are together and even said she was back in your house," I said, reaching into the refrigerator and pulling out a pitcher of sweet tea.

"She's living in la-la land. She can continue to dream but this will be one that will not come true."

There was a knock at the door and in walked my brother, Steven.

"I'm just in time," he said when he saw me putting the pitcher of tea on the table.

"But you can't stay," I told him, wanting this evening just to be about me and Derrick.

"Come on, Trinity, let him stay," Derrick said.

I shot him a look of disapproval but he never noticed as he got up to shake Steven's hand. *Really,* I thought. It wasn't like he and my brother were the best of buddies. What was all this brotherly love? Why couldn't he see I didn't want him here?

"Derrick, honey, I wanted to spend a quiet evening with just you and me," I said with a forced smile.

"Baby, we can do that anytime. Put a plate on the table and let your brother join us," he said, smacking my butt as I walked over to the cabinet. I did as Derrick suggested, not happy at all about it, and pulled out a plate for my brother. I gave my brother an evil glare, wondering what he was up to.

We began to eat and for a short time there was no talking, that was, until my brother thought it was okay for him to start some conversation. "So, Derrick, my man, you and my sister are getting close, huh?"

Derrick nodded, not speaking because he had a mouthful of food. I couldn't eat. I just moved food around on my plate wondering what was going to come out of my brother's mouth next. I didn't have to wonder long.

"Has my sister told you anything about our past?" he asked Derrick.

I shot him a look, wishing he would drop dead in that instant.

"No, she hasn't mentioned anything about her past to me. I find that funny since she knows so much about mine," Derrick said, looking at me.

"I didn't think my past was important since we weren't making our relationship official. Why divulge information to someone who could leave me any minute?" I said defensively.

Derrick was emotionless. He looked at Steven, who was looking at me.

"That may be true, Trinity, but we are still getting to know one another. I can understand your hesitation, but what could you tell me that would cause me to look at you any different? We are always going to be friends even if we don't work out," Derrick said.

I nodded, not saying anything.

"You've been here for me tremendously. Why wouldn't you think I would do the same?"

"Does 'Kea' ring a bell?" I asked scornfully.

Derrick shifted nervously at the mention of her name.

"She's getting married," he said unhappily. I could tell by the change in his expression that he was hurt. He was hurt over a woman who didn't want him and this angered me.

"But you still love her don't you?" I asked bluntly.

"Enough, Trinity," my brother said. "I didn't bring up this subject to start a quarrel between you two. You know why I'm asking him this and I told you—"

"And I told you I was going to do it in my time," I said, cutting him off.

Derrick leaned back in his seat, looking confused. He could tell I was upset and I knew what was coming next.

He said, "I think there is something more going on here. What are you not telling me, Trinity?"

And there it was. I peered at my brother, looking at him like, "Are you happy now?" Derrick looked back and forth between the two of us and I said nothing. I wasn't going to say anything. I wasn't ready to go there. Why couldn't my brother understand that and listen to me? He was a thorn in my side that needed to be removed. And tonight he'd shown me it was time to make him disappear.

Chapter 17

Jaquon

Here I was having just had counseling with Kea's pastor and I was standing in a hotel room with Sheila due to arrive any minute now. I knew my past consisted of me being a womanizer but right now I didn't want to be that person. I wanted to be faithful and didn't like for a woman to blackmail me into sleeping with her. Yes, months ago Sheila could have blinked an eye and I would have been over there banging her brains out. But her forcing me didn't feel right. I hated not having any control of the situation and regretted the day I fell into her lioness den of lust.

The door beeped and I knew it was her about to walk in. I wasn't ready for this. I was nervous and mad at the same time.

She stepped into the room like she owned the building, wearing a short black trench and white stiletto heels. "Well hey, boo boo," she said, strutting into the space.

I didn't say anything. I was mad I was even here. My lies had already started and I wasn't married yet. I had to lie to Kea to get out the house. It wasn't like she was talking to me anyway. I wanted to continue my conversation on what she thought about our counseling session with Pastor Wilson but she shut me down. As if Sheila could sense the tension from far away, she called me, and told me to meet her at this hotel at seven. I wanted to tell her no but knew that could have been the demise of my relationship with Kea. At the same time, I was happy to get away from Kea's glum mood. She acted like she didn't care where I went, just as long as I was out of her face.

When I told her, "I'm going out," Kea nodded. She didn't protest or even ask me where I was going. I'm not going to lie, I did feel some type of way about it. Any other time she was questioning me about where I was going.

"I will be back later," I told her, hoping she would say something.

The only response I got from her was, "Okay."

When I left her, I almost went back into our apartment to tell her everything myself. I wanted to put everything out on the table and admit I'd cheated on her with Sheila, and where I was really going was to see her because Sheila was blackmailing me into sleeping with her. Kea would have to see I was trying, and that coming clean was one of the first steps to making this marriage work. I would tell her this was my way of us starting fresh for our new journey together. Kea would have to understand what happened between me and Sheila was in the past and didn't matter now, because I was ready to make this work.

When I went to go back into the apartment to confess, Sheila's words halted me. Fear crept in and I decided to take the coward's way out. I turned to leave, keeping my secret meeting with Sheila.

And here I stood, looking at the woman who was going to make me betray the woman I loved yet again.

"You ain't happy to see me?" Sheila asked.

"Not really."

"Well, what about now?" she said, undoing her trench and letting it fall to the floor. My eyes scanned her half-naked body. She stood in a white satin bra and panty set. Her full breasts screamed to be released as they pushed themselves up high to be ogled.

Sheila posed for me, standing with her hands on both hips. She then put her index finger in her mouth like she was shy, asking, "Do you like?" in a flirty voice.

"Yes," fell out my mouth before I could catch it. I tried to think of Kea to help me resist what Sheila was going to do, but the vision of her brown sugar complexion glowed in the light like she had oiled her body down good for me.

Sheila smiled and walked over to me, saying, "Aren't you glad I got this room? I could have made you come to my place but I didn't want to risk us getting caught."

She was thinking but I wasn't right now. My body was the dog it was as her ampleness enticed me to full erection.

Walking toward me, Sheila said, "You see, I was looking out for you, babe."

I nodded like I was in a trance. As she stood close to me, she looked up at me seductively. Then she looked down. "I see you do like what you see," she said, grabbing my dick.

Her touch sent shivers through me. I closed my eyes, wishing I didn't have to do this but also glad I was about to do this. Thoughts of what she did to me earlier only made me weaker to her advances.

Sheila kissed me gently, transferring her fruity gloss to my lips. The first couple of pecks were soft and teasing. Each time she kissed me, she looked at me while her hands proceeded to unzip my pants.

I knew it was useless to try to deny her because it didn't work earlier. She had dropped to her knees to satisfy me, not caring about who was looking. Now that we didn't have any audience, all bets were down and she was getting ready to win this round.

She placed me in her mouth and quivers ran throughout my body. I swear I thought she was better than earlier today because this felt good. It was too good. My player status was getting close to being revoked, just on the simple fact I was on the verge of losing my load. Was trying to be this true, faithful man for Kea turning me into a punk? Before, a female could suck me for hours and I wouldn't bust until I got deep inside her, but now that I was a one-woman man, I didn't have anything to prove because the woman I wanted to spend the rest of my life with, I had.

I jerked Sheila's head away from mine to give me some reprieve to calm down before she was swallowing my seed. She looked up at me, smirking with saliva coating her lips. With her right hand she was still stroking me slowly. Sheila leaned in again and flicked her tongue across the head of my dick. She still looked up at me as I stared down at her. I knew she liked being watched. She took my head into her mouth and slowly pushed the length of me deeper inside her throat.

"Damn," I said, pushing forward until the base of me was pushed against her face. She had my entire dick in her mouth and didn't gag one time. She took this dick like a pro and it turned me on even more.

I pulled her away, again, not wanting to release. This time I pulled her hair to stand before me. Sheila loved when I handled her rough. Without saying anything, I picked Sheila up, causing her to squeal. With her legs around my waist, I gripped her butt cheeks and spread them to open up for me. Thrusting forward, my dick angled just right to enter her on the first attempt. She clamped onto the back of my neck and gasped with my entrance. Bouncing her up and down on my dick, Sheila assisted by leaning back and grinding her wetness into me.

"Give it to me, baby," she begged and I gave it to her. I pounded her hard and deep. She was so wet and juicy I could feel the splatter of her juices trickle down my leg.

"Oh shit," I said at the thought, making me swell within her.

"Yes, baby. I'm cumming," she told me as her legs tightened around my waist. She grinded vigorously into me, screaming with the explosion that was entering her.

I ruined her moment by dislodging myself. I went to put her down as she looked at me with an unsatisfied look. I knew what I was doing. *Just when you know the woman is about to bust . . .* Sometimes I did this, knowing this only strengthened her need to ride this dick.

"No, Jaquon," she said, standing as I placed her down.

"You want it. You work for it," I challenged her.

Sheila hurriedly pushed me down on the bed. I fell to my back and grinned at her eagerness. She climbed on top of me, lifting herself as she gripped my dick and guided it to enter her. Still wet, hot, and juicy, Sheila lowered herself and immediately began bouncing. My dick filled her cavity.

"Damn," she kept repeating over and over again. She felt good. I wondered for a moment how I could become a one-woman man when pussy felt this good. Even for a whore, Sheila had some good pussy.

"I'm cumming," she yelled as her pounds increased.

Pound, grind, grind, pound, grind, grind. This trick was answering the challenge. I could feel her walls constrict.

Pound, pound, pound, pound, grind, grind.

"I'm cumming," she screamed, breathing erratically.

The Jaquon I knew was back in full control. No cumming for me. I was going to dig Sheila out so good, it would be awhile before she was going to blackmail me into more sex. I hoped that would be the case because I didn't know how long it would be before my secretive transgression would come to light.

Chapter 18

Derrick

Trinity was cleaning up from dinner and seemed to be upset, which I knew her brother had something to do with. I didn't know exactly what upset her. Maybe it was the fact she didn't want to tell me about her past. I didn't know but I was going to find out. It was just me and her now. Her brother left and it was my chance to find out why she didn't want me to know about her past.

"What's up with you?" I asked Trinity.

"Nothing," she said frigidly. She didn't bother to look at me when she answered. Wiping the counter was more important to her than acknowledging my presence.

"So, why are you giving me the cold shoulder?"

"Derrick, I'm fine," she snapped.

"You are lying. Ever since dinner you seem like you have a stick up your behind."

She peered at me evilly. Never had she given me this look before but never had I spoken to her in this manner either. She turned, her left hand resting on her hip.

"Dinner was meant for me and you only. Not my brother making this a threesome."

"I like threesomes," I joked, hoping she would find the humor, but she didn't.

"That's not funny, Derrick."

"Come on, Trinity. Steven is your brother and has eaten dinner with us a lot."

"Exactly, Derrick. He's always eating with us. Maybe tonight I needed to talk to you about something and I didn't need him here interfering."

"You still can talk to me. He's gone now. Why are you giving me the silent treatment?"

She paused, staring at me like I was her enemy.

"Say something," I demanded.

"You've been lying to me," Trinity blurted.

"About what?"

"You and Zacariah. I know you are back with her."

"And how do you know this?" I asked, puzzled.

"One, she told me."

"You believe Zacariah."

"Two, I went to your house and that bitch was there."

"You checking up on me now?" I asked, surprised at Trinity's actions. This didn't sit well with me at all. Trinity knew from day one what we had was nothing but companionship for a moment. This would never be anything serious. I knew she'd told me she loved me but I didn't feel the same way about her. She should have figured that out when I didn't tell her I loved her back.

"You call it checking up on you. I call it finding out the truth. Another truth is I know you have met with Kea also."

Was she stalking me? This was getting a little eerie. *Or should I see this as her way of trying to be possessive?* Either way, I didn't like what was going on. If I wanted to be in a relationship with her, I would have asked her to be my girlfriend.

"Trinity, I told you from the beginning I didn't want anything serious."

"Not with me anyway."

"And you understood that regardless."

"So if Kea wanted something serious, as you say, would you go back to her?" Trinity asked.

Lying to her was the first thing I thought to do, but I decided truth was what brought us together and truth was what I was going to give her. Look where it had gotten me. Not telling her about Zacariah being back in my life and seeing Kea had caused Trinity to do things that were outside of what I was used to dealing with. But before I could say anything, she began to speak.

"Your silence is golden," she said, running her fingers through her wild hair.

"I didn't answer because I don't know what I would do."

"Do you still love her?"

"Yes," I admitted.

"Do you love me?" she asked.

"I have love for you."

"So that's a no," she said irately. She turned her back toward me and bent over on the counter, rubbing her face over and over again. I walked over to her and placed my hand midway her back.

"Don't touch me," she yelled, swinging back and smacking my hand away from her.

I stepped back at her reaction. This was a side of Trinity I hadn't seen before and I had to wonder if this was the true woman coming to the surface. I'd been fooled by women before with them only showing me what they wanted me to see, and this included my very own mother. Realizing I didn't have to deal with this anymore I said, "I'm going to leave."

I turned to walk out of the kitchen when Trinity spoke. "Just like that."

"Why do I want to stay here and deal with your attitude?"

"You shouldn't always run when times get tough, Derrick. That's how you met me in the first place, running from the fact you couldn't deal with sleeping with your sister," she spat, saying it like she wanted to hurt me.

That was a low blow that enraged me. I didn't tell her my business for her to throw it back in my face. But I guessed that's what women did when they got all up in their feelings and felt like somebody was treating them wrong.

"You know what? I'm done with you," I said, attempting to leave the kitchen again.

Trinity ran over to me and jumped in front of me, pushing me in the chest. "You don't have the right to leave."

"Don't put your hands on me, Trinity," I warned, knowing my temper. I was raised not to put my hands on a woman, but if she kept it up, I would have to touch her in a negative way that I knew could land me in jail.

"Look, Derrick. I'm sorry. Please don't leave me," she begged.

"I don't think it's a good idea to stay here with you."

"I said I'm sorry. You know I love you. I'm just hurt because you don't love me back. All you have to do is try," Trinity told me.

"You are an easy woman to love but when I see my future, I don't see you being a part of it."

Sadness captured her face. She stepped back from me as she stared blankly into my eyes. I wasn't going to let her empty blue eyes stunt me.

"I think this thing between us needs to end for good, starting now," I told her.

She shook her head and said, "Nope. We are meant to be together forever."

"I appreciate you being here for me when I was going though some things but I don't think I need to be with you anymore. I shouldn't have misled you into believing we have a chance with each other."

"You don't have the right to do this to me," Trinity said softly as water filled her eyes.

"Good-bye, Trinity," I said, stepping around her. I felt sorry for her but knew I was making the right decision. I proceeded to enter her living room to exit this place for good. This was crazy. I was getting the feeling she was crazy, too. I had never seen a women look at me like she did. If I wanted to deal with drama, I wouldn't have left Zacariah in the first place.

I could hear her saying something but I didn't stay to see what it was. I left her place, never looking back.

Chapter 19

Zacariah

"What are you doing?" Derrick's voice rang out, causing me to drop my paper plate of food to the floor. My two slices of pizza and a few wings I ordered from Pizza Hut tumbled to the floor.

"Damn it, Derrick. You scared me," I said, holding my chest.

He giggled and said, "I didn't mean to scare you."

"I see you find my fear funny."

"It is."

"No, it isn't. I didn't hear the ding of the security system beep like it usually does. You know that's how I knew your mama was coming up in here. It's like a warning and I didn't get that this time."

"I'm going to have to get that checked out. I guess I have gotten used to the sound so I don't hear it anymore."

"Well, I've noticed," I said, picking up my mess from the floor and putting it in the trashcan. "What are you even doing here?" Usually nights when Derrick went to see his side chick, he came rolling up in this house after midnight. I looked at the time and saw it was only 7:24 p.m.

"Last time I checked, this is my house," Derrick answered.

"That it is, but you know when you are with *her*," I said, not wanting to say the tramp's name, "you get in late. Is there trouble in paradise?" I asked jokingly.

"You can say that," he said, leaning against the wall.

"Oh. Should I get excited?" I asked.

"Well, I ended it with Trinity tonight."

Wiping up the residual mess from the hot wings and pizza with a damp paper towel, I paused at his statement. "Really," I said, not expecting him to say what he said.

"Yep. We are done."

I finished wiping up the mess and stood. I walked over to the trashcan, putting the dirty paper towel in it. Then I went over to the sink to wash my hands. I didn't bother to say anything as I still tried to process this information.

"So are you happy?" Derrick asked.

I ran over to him with wet hands and all and threw my arms around his neck. I kissed him on this cheek and asked, "Does this answer your question?"

"I think it does," he said, surprisingly wrapping his arms around my waist. Even though Derrick had allowed me back into his life and home, it seemed like the only one getting any type of affection was Trinity. He hadn't touched me intimately or tried to have sex with me since I'd been back in his house. So feeling his arms around me was a welcomed delight. I didn't want to let him go because I was afraid once we released one another, Derrick would continue his unemotional connection with me.

Placing his hands on my waist, signaling it was time for me to let him go, I reluctantly did so. His hands never left my waist as I leaned back and looked up into his handsome face.

He said, "You really do care about me, huh?"

I nodded my response.

"I have seen a major change in you, Zacariah."

"For the better I hope."

"Yes. I don't see you going out. You've toned down your way of dressing. You are cooking. And you've even made amends with my mother," he said like he couldn't believe

I could change. "This person standing before me is far from the Zacariah I met at church that day."

"I hope you like the new me."

"I'm loving the new you," Derrick said.

"I told you I was willing to do whatever it took to get you back in my life. Plus, I think it was time for me to grow up and get ready to settle down. When I was messing up, I didn't know what type of good man I had at the time. It wasn't until I lost you and saw you with Kea that I realized you were the man who was meant for me."

"You do understand I still don't trust you."

"I get that. Just because I've changed from the outside doesn't mean I expect you to accept the new me and forget about my indiscretions. I know that's going to take some time but I'm willing to wait."

"Are you really?" he asked with uncertainty.

"I am."

"And you didn't meet anybody while you were apart from me?" Derrick asked.

Fabian instantly popped into my mind. I wondered if I should disclose this man to Derrick. Lies were what made me lose him in the first place so I admitted, "I did meet someone."

His eyebrows shot up in surprise. "Have you seen him since you been here with me?"

"Yes."

Derrick let go of my waist.

"But not in the way you think, Derrick."

"How do I know that?" he asked.

"Because, I'm telling you."

"You've told me a lot in the past, too, and I believed you, and that got me looking like a fool."

"Have you ever known me to admit to something like this? I'm telling you about a man I did meet. That's far from the old me. Think about it."

He nodded in agreement.

"I could have lied like I did before but I didn't."

Derrick rubbed his face like he was getting upset.

"I told this guy I was back with the man I love. And that's you, Derrick. There was no hugs, no kisses, and not so much as a handshake."

"And homeboy took it in stride."

"Yes, he did," I said, remembering how much of a gentleman Fabian was. After I talked to Fabian that day telling him about me and Derrick, I felt bad I said what I said over the phone. So I called him up and asked him to meet me. That's when I explained why I asked to see him, because I thought it was disrespectful of me to end by cell phone what we had going on, and that he deserved better than that. He was sincere as usual and understood completely.

"And he let you go just like that?" Derrick asked.

"He had no choice when he knew I was in love with another man."

Derrick turned his back to me. I walked up behind him and wrapped my arms around his waist. I laid my head on his back. He didn't pull away. He didn't try to pry my hands from around him. Instead, he put his hands over mine.

"I love you, Derrick. You are the only man for me," I told him.

Derrick didn't say anything. He just stood and let me hold him. I didn't know what he was thinking. For a moment I second-guessed whether it was a good idea to mention Fabian at all.

Derrick pulled my hands from around him and this saddened me. That was, until he turned and wrapped his arms around me.

"I believe you, Zacariah."

"You do?" I asked as happiness captivated me.

"You are right. The old Zacariah would have never told me. Your answer to that question would have been no. But you stood your ground and told me the truth and I appreciate that."

I smiled and said, "Thank you."

He leaned down and kissed me gently. I gladly accepted his soft lips on mine. When he pulled away, he looked down at me and said, "Is there any pizza and wings left?"

I chuckled as I nodded.

"Because a brother is hungry."

"Then let's eat. And try not to scare me again so I won't have to throw away any more food."

Chapter 20

Derrick

When Zacariah told me she invited Mama over for dinner tonight, I was a bit upset that she didn't ask me first. I didn't bother getting mad because, for once, I knew Zacariah was coming from a good place. She really wanted me and my mom to mend our relationship; and what better way to do so than over food?

Dinner with Mom was well worth the work Zacariah put into making it happen. The only person missing was my dad, who was out of town on a fishing trip with his brother. So you know Mama was more than happy to come over and spend some time with me.

Zacariah went all out. She set the table with this crimson tablecloth and crystal flutes sitting beside stark white plates. She had some wine chilling in a tall wine bucket positioned beside the dining room table. She made it look elegant. Usually we ate at the kitchen table but tonight we took full advantage of our dining room.

We ate until we couldn't eat anymore. Zacariah really outdid herself with this pasta dinner. Mama wasn't a big pasta eater but she tore up the dish Zacariah prepared tonight. And I didn't think she did this to make Zacariah feel good. I really think she ate her food because she enjoyed it.

Mama leaned back in her seat, rubbing her belly, and said, "Zacariah, I was a little skeptical eating anything you cooked but I have to say that was delicious."

Zacariah smiled and said, "Thank you, Ms. Shirley."

"I ate too much. And that apple pie was amazing."

"Well, I didn't make that but I did prepare everything else."

"You did a good job," Mama said.

"You did good, Zacariah," I seconded Mama's compliment.

"This food has made me sleepy," Mama said, yawning.

The doorbell interrupted the dinner and each of us looked at each other. Zacariah shrugged her shoulders letting me know she wasn't expecting anyone, as Mama glanced at me.

"I'll get it. Excuse me," I said, wiping my mouth with the cloth napkin and pushing my chair back getting up to check the front door.

When I swung the door open, I was stunned in more ways than one. Gazing back at me was Trinity, beaming from ear to ear.

First I thought, *what is she doing on my doorstep?* But seeing her dressed in a white wedding gown with a sheer veil covering her face overshadowed that thought. She was holding a bouquet of flowers, which looked like she'd pulled them from someone's backyard. The stems were rubber-banded together but the roots of the flowers were still showing along with the dirt, letting me know these were freshly pulled. I mean she looked like she was standing at someone's alter in a church about to say "I do" to whoever she was going to marry.

"Hey, baby," she said, throwing her arms around me.

I was too taken aback to move. My reflexes made me hug her back as my mind tried to figure out what was going on right now.

She let go of me and looked up with a smile plastered on her face. "Are you ready?" she asked nonchalantly.

"Ready for what?" I asked in confusion.

"If you want to know, yes, Trinity, I'm with Zacariah now," I said, trying to snap her out of this false sense of her reality.

"I'm not marrying you, because I'm with her," I said, pointing at Zacariah.

This revelation caused Trinity to halt. "What?" she asked in a dazed manner.

"I never wanted to marry you. What we had was temporary. We are over and you need to get that through your head," I explained like I was talking to a child in the first grade. I hated to be mean but being nice wasn't working. I had to be harsh for her to understand I wasn't going to marry her.

"But . . . you told me you loved me."

I sighed, regretting ever speaking those words to her. I told her that because she said it to me. In the beginning, I refrained from speaking those words; but, one night, in the throes of passion, I regretfully said "I love you" to her. Little did I know she would take those words and run with them.

"I do love you but not the way you want me to," I said.

"So you lied to me?" she asked solemnly.

"Yes," I admitted.

Trinity looked around, gazing at Zacariah and Mama. "I told you always be upfront with me, Derrick," she said, defeated.

"I know. And I'm sorry for that," I apologized.

"Sorry doesn't cut it. You hurt me deeply. I love you more than anything in this world. I told you if you ever hurt me, I would make you pay."

I didn't remember any of that conversation. She was starting to make me second-guess myself. Was I the crazy one here or was Trinity off her rocker? Then again, I didn't ask her to marry me, either, and she was standing here in a wedding dress and uprooted flowers ready to walk down the aisle with me. Was this her delusional mind? It had to be.

"Don't threaten him," Zacariah said, coming up behind me, but I stopped her.

"Zacariah."

"Who does she think she is?" Zacariah said.

"The name is Trinity. And I don't threaten anyone. I make promises," she said coldheartedly. I thought Zacariah noticed this arctic demeanor and stepped back a couple of times. I really thought Trinity shook her. I knew she shook me.

Trinity proceeded to take the ring off her finger. She held it out to me and I opened my left hand to receive it. She leaned in and spit in my hand before dropping the diamond ring in it.

She glared at me and, without saying another word, Trinity hoisted her wedding gown up, turned, and walked away.

Chapter 21

Zacariah

"What in the world was that all about?" Derrick's mom asked with her hands on her hips.

"Ms. Shirley, that was Trinity."

Derrick was shutting the door as he held his left hand open, which was still filled with the spit Trinity decided to cast his way. The dumbfounded look on his face let me know he had no clue what this was all about. He walked over to the console table to grab a tissue out the box to wipe the liquid spew Trinity left behind.

"I need to wash my hands," Derrick said, walking toward the kitchen. We followed as Mama Shirley continued to talk.

"That girl had on a wedding dress, Derrick," Mama said.

"I know, Mama," he said, putting his hand under the automatic dispenser as a drop of hand soap dripped into his hand. He tapped the faucet with his wrist and the water came on. I was happy he had invested in this new faucet because I didn't want to have any germs from that crazy chick anywhere in this house. *Trifling heifer. Who spits on people anymore?* She was lucky Derrick didn't punch her dead in the face for that one. Spitting was the ultimate violation. I knew if she would have done that to me, the old Zacariah would have reemerged to administer the worst beat down ever.

Mama asked, "For what?"

"I'm still trying to figure that one out. She said she was coming to get me so we can get married."

"And where did she get that asinine idea from?" Ms. Shirley asked.

She didn't give me a chance to ask a question, which I was fine with because she was asking pretty much the same questions I was going to ask Derrick.

"She said I left this ring for her," he said, tapping the faucet with his wrist again to turn it off. He reached for a paper towel to dry his hands off.

"Well, did you?"Ms. Shirley asked.

"No!"

"Where did the ring come from?"

Derrick looked at me before speaking. "I got this ring for Kea," he said, drying the ring off, too, with the paper towel as he stared down at it.

Ms. Shirley looked at me. I was shaken by this news myself. I knew he had feelings for her but they had to be deeper than I expected for him to want to marry her.

"So, you asked Kea to marry you?" I asked sadly.

"I did but she said no," Derrick admitted.

"Is that why you took me back?" I asked a bit upset.

"Yes."

"Derrick, it was bad enough agreeing to your stipulation about seeing cray cray but now I find out I'm the rebound chick to cray cray and Kea?" I said angrily.

Derrick lowered his head, sighing. "Do we need to do this now?" he asked, looking at his mother.

"Why not now? Maybe she needs to know how confused you've been. I mean come on. What are you doing?"

"Not that I should have to explain myself to either of you but since I have to, both of you should know the reason why I am in this state of mind."

He paused, I guess waiting to see if either I or his mother was going to answer that question for him, but neither of us volunteered to do so. So he continued. "It's due to the decisions you both have made for me," he said resentfully.

Both of us stared at him in shame.

"Zacariah, you cheated on me, which in turn landed me in the arms of Kea and Trinity. And, Mama, you lied to me about my existence, which has made me unsure about anything in my life."

"I can't speak for your mother but how long are you going to make me pay? I've agreed to and done everything you wanted me to do and more, have I not?" I asked.

Derrick nodded.

"And now I got a crazy woman showing up in a wedding dress and uprooted flowers threatening you, which could also put my life in danger. But you want to still point at the finger at me. Maybe it's time you stand up and be the man we both know you to be," I said.

"You wanted an explanation for why I've been out of control and I told you, point blank. It wasn't meant to throw anything back at you. Just like you are trying to explain, Zacariah, I'm trying to explain," Derrick said angrily.

"Okay, you guys. That's enough. The both of you are getting caught up in something that has nothing to do with the status of where you are now. If there's one thing I've learned, it's deal with the situation and move on. Zacariah, you love my son, and, Derrick, you have to care for her because you've allowed her back in your life. Now, son, I don't agree with you playing both sides of the fence. Take it from me, it's not worth it. You should know this by what I've just revealed to you about your real father."

Derrick shifted uneasily.

"You two need to decide if you want to make this work but in doing so, you have to eliminate anything and anybody that's going to interfere with you guys making this relationship work," Ms. Shirley explained.

"But, I made my choice," Derrick said.

"You sure about that?" Mama asked.

"Yes," Derrick said confidently.

"And you are choosing Zacariah, is that right?" Ms. Shirley asked.

Derrick looked at me and said, "Yes. Like I told you before, Zacariah, I'm done with Trinity."

"But what about Kea?" I asked, still thinking that at any moment, if Kea wanted him back he would be more than happy to take her back.

"I'm done with her too," he said.

A part of me didn't believe him, but it felt good to hear him say that. All I could go on was his word.

I smiled and said, "Okay."

"So there it is. Problem solved. Let's continue to enjoy this evening," Derrick said.

"I think I'm ready to call it a night. This mess got me feeling some type of tired. Are you taking me home?" Ms. Shirley asked Derrick.

"You can stay here if you like," I suggested, looking at Derrick to see if this was okay.

"Oh, no. I have interfered with you all enough."

"You are not interfering. We would be happy if you stayed," I said.

She looked at Derrick to see what he thought. He said, "Mama, you know you are always welcome to stay."

"But I don't have anything to sleep in."

"I can run to the house and grab you something," Derrick suggested.

"You don't have to do all this."

"Mama, it feels good that you are here. So please stay and let us wait on you. I don't mind doing this for you."

"You sure?" Ms. Shirley asked, looking at me.

Both me and Derrick smiled and said yes.

"Well, since you guys insist," she said, smiling gleefully. "But I think I need to ride with you home, because you don't know what I might need tonight, or tomorrow for that matter."

Chapter 22

Trinity

I sat outside Derrick's house across the street, watching his home. The lights in the living room were on. I wondered what he was doing inside with her.

"Spsssssss. You need to handle that ASAP. Who do she thinks she is taking your place in his home? That's supposed to be you in there," the whispered voice said.

I looked over into the driver's seat and saw the figure I hadn't seen for quite some time. I didn't know if it was my rage that brought her back or if it was because I had stopped taking my medication. Either way I knew I was in trouble. I could never resist what this person told me. Then again I came to realize I wanted to do the things the voice suggested. It always made me happier.

I looked over into the driver's seat to see her staring back at me. She hadn't aged much. She was about the same age as me. We grew up together but I seemed to have retained my looks more than she had. She looked like she could be the sister I never had.

"Trinity," she said slowly, "handle your business, girl. There's no need to be mad. Just get even. Take your position back in his life."

I nodded because she was right. I was supposed to be the one by Derrick's side, not Zacariah. The nerve of him, thinking he could leave me for her. What did she have that I didn't? Clearly it couldn't be her personality or her trustworthiness, because her lying to him and cheating on him was what landed him in my bed in the first place. Now he acted as though he wanted nothing to do with me. I was the one who was there for him and he seemed to not give a damn. He kicked me out like I was last week's trash. And I would be no one's trash. Zacariah was responsible for Derrick leaving me and she needed to be dealt with once and for all.

Eventually, the lights in the living room were turned off and the house went dark. But all of a sudden his garage door opened and I saw Derrick's car leaving. I wondered where he was going but figured he was taking his mom home. I wasn't about to follow him. I had some other business to attend to.

The voice whispered, "You know what you have to do, don't you?"

I looked at her and nodded.

Getting out of my car, I walked across the street and entered into his yard. Going around the side of his house, I opened the wooden fence and entered his backyard. Pulling out the spare key I made from Derrick's keys awhile back, I slipped the key into the lock and turned. The lock clicked and I entered slowly. The security system didn't beep as I crossed the threshold and I was happy that they hadn't gotten this fixed. Really there was nothing to fix. All I did was unplug the battery from the keypad and then located the main box, also unplugging the main box he kept in his basement. I knew one day this would come in handy. I just didn't know it would be this soon.

Derrick never gave me a key, even though I hinted around this a couple of times, but he ignored my request. So I took it upon myself to get a copy made. On days when I knew he wasn't home, I came over and hung out in his place. I would eat some of his food, take showers, and sometimes put on a shirt he'd worn just to smell the essence of him. There were a couple of times I would lie in his bed and masturbate to his scent, pretending my fingers was him inside me. I wanted his home to be my home. But that day never came. And now with Zacariah here, it never would. It wasn't until our little run-in at the salon did I find out they were back together. As soon as I left the salon, I went straight to his home. I knew neither of them was home by looking into the garage and not seeing either of their cars sitting in the parking spaces. I made my way in and went straight to the bedroom to find her clothes in the closet next to his. It took everything I had in me not to set the entire place on fire. But I was able to restrain myself. I knew one day I would be able to get revenge and that's when I came up with the idea to disarm the security system.

I crept through the kitchen. The room smelled like someone had cooked dinner. I peeked into the oven to see if anything was in there and there was nothing there. I looked in the microwave and saw nothing there either. And then I checked the fridge to see containers filled with food. Reaching in, I opened one to see a medley of vegetables. I saw an apple pie, a bottle of wine, some bottled water, a Pepsi, and a long dish filled with some pasta. I reached in the long dish and pulled out a piece of pasta to taste it. It was amazing. Looking at Zacariah, I didn't think she could cook, but this was actually good. They say a way to a man's heart is through his stomach; and the fact that she was trying really hard to take my man by enticing him with food and probably sex infuriated me.

I slammed the door closed. I tiptoed my way through the dining room to see no one moving around still. The house was completely dark but the moonlight helped to navigate me to my destination. I entered the living room to see this space empty also. I proceeded to go up the stairs. Passing by the main bathroom, I headed to Derrick's bedroom. I wanted to see if this bitch was in my man's bed.

The door was cracked. I could tell through this narrow opening that no lights were on in the room. I pushed the door as slow as I could, hoping it wouldn't creak with the movement; and with luck on my side, it didn't. I stood in the doorway and looked around the bedroom until my eyes landed on Derrick's bed located in the middle of the room. Zacariah was sound asleep. All nuzzled and tucked nicely under the covers that Derrick and I used to make love on. Seeing her there enraged me.

I approached the bed at a snail's pace. I could hear her breathing softly. She was in a deep sleep and looked peaceful as the covers were pulled tightly around her head. She was almost covered completely but a bit of her hair was peeking from beneath the sheets. Little did she know I was about to bring her the ultimate nightmare. Stepping even closer until I was finally standing over her sleeping body, I lifted the weapon I came in with and swung it like I was trying to get a home run.

This was a home run for me and I was about to win the game by getting rid of the competition. Over and over and swung the bat at her head. Blood splattered everywhere. The covers became saturated and so did I as I swung until I got tired of swinging. I was going to make sure this bitch was dead for good and that there was no chance of her ever coming back.

Once I was done, I stood over her body and stared at the blood-drenched covers. She didn't scream. She didn't yell. She didn't make a sound when this was happening. There was no fight at all and I was a little bit upset because this was so easy. I wanted to see her struggle to live as I took her life away from her, but I didn't get that pleasure.

I wiped the residue of her blood mixing with my sweat from my face. I panted trying to catch my breath. I was now closer to getting my man back. I had to see the late Zacariah one last time so I could leave. I reached down and pulled back the cover, but what I saw almost made my knees buckle beneath me.

Chapter 23

Derrick

Police sirens cut through the darkness like a hot knife through butter as the noise indicated a tragedy within my home. My house was swarming with police and paramedics as I sat on my couch in my living room wondering who could do something like this. An officer was talking to me but I didn't hear anything he was saying. I got back up and went up the stairs to go back to my room to make sure I saw what my eyes viewed, but the police tape was blocking me from entering my room again.

"Sir, please go back downstairs. You don't need to see this," an officer said.

Tears streamed down my face. "I just want to see her again," I urged.

"I'm sorry but that's not a good idea."

I broke through the police tape and rushed over to the bed, falling on her. "Mama, please come back to me," I begged.

A couple of officers tried to pull me off of her, dragging me out like I was the assailant who murdered my mother. I pushed the younger officer off of me, causing him to tumble back. But the veteran one grabbed me, twisting my right arm behind my back as he slammed me against the wall. My face was pressed into it as tears continued to stream down my face.

"Please, don't hurt him," Zacariah yelled as they tried to restrain me.

"Derrick, we know you are upset but you have to let us do our job. Please don't risk getting an assault charge," the veteran officer told me, trying to give me a break in my time of sorrow. "I know this situation is painful but we are here to assist in finding out who did this to your mother."

"Please, listen to him, Derrick," Zacariah cried out.

"Now, I'm going to let you go," the officer said, releasing me slowly.

He stepped back. The young officer I pushed had his hand on his weapon, but the veteran officer shook his head at him, letting him know it was okay.

"Let me take you to the bedroom down the hall," the veteran officer suggested and I walked as if I were in a trance.

I was in hysterics as they sat me down on the bed in the guest bedroom. Zacariah came running over to me. She wrapped her arms around me. She didn't say anything. I don't know if there was anything she could say that would make me feel better about this situation.

I opened my hands and looked at the crimson hue covering me. I looked down at my blue and white striped button-down shirt, also covered in crimson. It was my mother's blood. The only thing that kept running through my mind was the fact that I couldn't recognize her. Her face was so bad damaged that she was unrecognizable.

"Who could do this to her?" I asked.

"I don't know, sweetie," Zacariah said through her cracking voice.

I looked over at her and saw her wiping tears from her eyes. And I broke down again. I wept uncontrollably and fell to my knees, wrapping my arms around her waist. She held me close, rocking me as if I were her child. I screamed my pain and the more I screamed, the more it hurt.

We weren't gone that long from my home for all of this to happen. Who could have done this? Was this an intruder? And if so, why did they have to kill the first woman I ever loved, my Mama?

Chapter 24

Kea

"Kea, we have to go," Jaquon told me when he entered the bedroom to throw his shoes on.

"Go where?" I asked, frowning at him. I was comfortable in my bed watching television and didn't feel like moving. That was, until I heard the next sentence fall out of his mouth.

"It's Derrick."

When he said that, I flung the covers back and jumped to my feet. Seeing the urgency in Jaquon's movement I asked, "Jaquon, what's wrong?"

"Zacariah called me and said I needed to get over there immediately and that it was bad."

"She didn't tell you why?"

"She was too upset to talk. I told her I was on my way."

"So how do you know it's concerning Derrick?" I questioned.

"Because, the two of them are back together."

When Jaquon said that, it took the wind out of my sails.

"Back together. How? When?"

"They have been back together for a minute. I heard about it in the street."

"I think the street is wrong because . . ." I said, pausing. I was about to let Jaquon know I had just met with Derrick and he didn't mention anything to me about being back with Zacariah. If anything, the only person I knew about him dealing with was Trinity.

"Because what?" Jaquon asked, looking at me curiously.

"Because, I thought he was with Trinity," I said, playing it off.

"From my understanding he's seeing both of them. It's been so bad that Zacariah and Trinity got into a fight the other day over the situation."

I had to wonder where in the hell had I been to not know any of this was happening. But as usual I was always the last to know anything.

Changing the subject, I asked, "Why does Zacariah still have your number?"

"Kea, I don't know."

"You still seeing her?" I asked.

"Look. Do you want to stay here and argue or are you coming with me?" he snapped. "Because if it's arguing, I'm going to leave you here to talk to your damn self."

Jaquon grabbed his jacket and rushed out of the room. For a second, I wasn't going to go. I was going to let him go by himself but a part of me wanted to make sure Derrick was okay. So I grabbed my jacket also and rushed to catch up with Jaquon.

When I saw all the police cars and ambulances when we pulled up to Derrick's house, I knew it was bad. My heart plummeted into my stomach because I was scared something real bad had happened to Derrick. We both jumped out of our car and ran to the scene. A couple of police officers stopped us from entering the house.

"I'm sorry, but you can't enter the house."

"Please. We have to go in there and see my brother," Jaquon said. "Please, tell me Derrick is okay."

"Sir—"

"What happened?" Jaquon asked urgently.

"Sir, I can't say."

And that's when we saw a body bag being wheeled out on a stretcher. I didn't know who it was. If it wasn't Derrick, I had to wonder, was it Zacariah? My stomach continued to churn because I thought Derrick had finally lost it and killed her.

"Please, let us in," Jaquon continued to plead.

"I'm sorry, sir, I can't do that."

Jaquon pulled out his cell and dialed a number.

"Hello, Zacariah. Look. Come get us. We are right outside. They will not let us through," he said.

Now he had her number. Maybe I was overreacting. He could have gone into his call log and found the number to call. Either way, it still didn't sit well with me.

Moments later Zacariah appeared, coming outside, and I could tell she had been crying. She made eye contact with me but didn't say anything.

"Officer, please let him through," she begged. The officer looked around before he lifted the police tape and let Jaquon in, but he quickly placed it down, leaving me on the side to not enter.

"I'm with him," I said, pointing at Jaquon.

"She said him," the officer told me.

Zacariah looked at me for a moment and finally said, "Please allow her to come through also."

I could tell she didn't want to let me through. The officer lifted the tape and I entered. Jaquon followed Zacariah closely and I lagged behind.

"What happened, Zacariah?" Jaquon asked as we entered the house.

"She's dead."

"Who?" Jaquon asked.

"Ms. Shirley."

Jaquon stopped dead in his tracks. He grabbed his head in disbelief and said, "Zacariah, please tell me you joking right now."

"I wish I was," she said through her tears. Still we said nothing to one another. "Come on," she urged.

We proceeded to the living room, where we saw Derrick sitting on the sofa, covered in blood. He was staring blankly ahead, like he couldn't see anyone around him.

Jaquon stopped and looked at him and he began to break down. "Derrick," he called out.

Derrick turned slowly and looked at Jaquon. His head dropped and his shoulders began to move as his weeping ensued. Jaquon dropped to his knees beside him and embraced Derrick.

"I'm sorry, man," Jaquon said, crying himself. "I'm so, so sorry."

Tears streamed down my face also. I couldn't believe any of this was happening. And who knew the tragedy of this event would have the four of us together?

"I'm so sorry," Jaquon kept saying.

Derrick laid his head down on Jaquon's shoulder and wept more than any man I had ever seen.

I walked over to Zacariah, who eyed me as I approached. "How did this happen?" I asked.

"We don't know. We went to get her some clothes because she was staying the night here. Then we went to the store to get some things for breakfast in the morning. When we came back, Derrick went to check on her while I put away the groceries, and that's when I heard Derrick scream. I ran upstairs to see what was wrong. And when I walked into that room . . ." She paused, shaking her head. "It was so bad."

Derrick sat up off of Jaquon, who got up and sat down beside him. Jaquon had his hand around Derrick's shoulders and said, "Man, I can't believe this. She was like my mom too. And despite everything we've been through, Derrick, I'm here for you, man."

Derrick nodded.

"Where's Pops?" Jaquon asked.

"He's been called. He had gone on a fishing trip with his brother," Zacariah answered, walking over to sit beside Derrick. She stroked his back. When Derrick felt her touch, he sat up and looked at her lovingly. She grabbed his hand and he wrapped his fingers around hers. She was the woman by his side to get him through this tragic time and I felt some type of way about it. Jaquon turned to look at me, I guess to see what my reaction was. I looked at him, hoping he didn't see my envy rise at their connection.

I hated that she was here acting like she belonged. And for once she looked as though she did. Zacariah wasn't dressed like the whore we all knew her to be. She was toned down and seemed to be a bit humble. I still couldn't figure out why Derrick didn't bother to tell me that he allowed her back into his life. I went to reveal my wedding to him but he failed to reveal him getting back with her. I had to admit I was upset by this. And it was in this moment I realized for sure that I still loved Derrick with all my heart and I wanted him back in my life.

Chapter 25

Trinity

I tapped on Steven's door with my open hand and watched the transference of blood on the door. I looked at my hand, not realizing I had so much blood on me. I began to sob. I rubbed both my hands on my dress to get the crimson off. I turned to see if anybody was behind me and there was no one, thank goodness. If they would have seen me, they would have thought it was me who was wounded.

I banged on the door again, this time using my fist, trying to get my brother to answer the door.

"I'm coming," I heard him yell.

When Steven whipped the door open, he said, "What is . . ."

He paused, cutting off what he was about to say once he saw me. He jerked me into his place. He then stepped outside, looking around to see if anybody saw us, and then he came back in, slamming the door.

"What have you done?" he yelled. "And why are you in a wedding dress?"

"I . . . I . . . I . . ." I struggled to say.

"Spit it out," he yelled.

"I was going to get married."

"To who?" he asked.

"Derrick, but he wouldn't marry me. So I . . . I . . . I . . ."

"Trinity, no," he said, grabbing his head. "Not again. I told you I couldn't do this again." He ran up on me and grabbed my shoulders, shaking me violently.

I crumpled beneath his grip and said, "I'm sorry, Steven."

He pushed me away from him and began pacing angrily back and forth across the room. "Tell me what you did," he demanded. "Tell me who you hurt this time."

"I killed Derrick's mom by accident," I admitted with the voice of a small child.

His face contorted like he couldn't believe what I was saying. He said, "By accident."

"Yes, it was an accident."

"How do you accidently kill somebody, Trinity? You can accidently trip. You can accidently curse. But accidently killing someone doesn't happen. Does that really make sense to you?" he asked, pointing to his temples.

"I meant to kill Zacariah. I thought it was her in the bed but once I pulled the cover back, I saw it was his mother."

I was scared Steven was going to explode on me as he roared out loud. His outburst probably could be heard next door but I didn't bother to calm him. Steven went over to the wall and punched it. I watched as his fist went through the sheetrock, which easily gave way to his anger. Moving away from him, I maneuvered to the other side of the room.

Steven leaned forward with both hands on the wall, looking down at the floor.

"I'm sorry, Steven," I apologized again.

He turned to face me. He didn't approach me though. He glared at me with so much hatred.

"Please don't be mad at me," I said gloomily.

My brother went over to his black leather chair and sat down. He leaned back and looked at me furiously without speaking.

The room was so quiet. I couldn't stand it. "Say something," I said.

"What is there to say, Trinity?" he asked.

"Say something, anything."

"I'm too busy trying to wrap my mind around you putting me in this situation again," he mumbled, shaking his head.

I attempted to walk toward him but he held his hand up to stop me and I halted.

"Go to the bathroom and clean yourself up," he said, looking at my disheveled appearance.

I did as he said and proceeded to his bathroom. I peeled off the blood-drenched clothes and got into the shower. Standing under the water as hot as my body could stand, trying to get the blood off of me, I cried uncontrollably about my mishap. I looked down and let the water cascade over my hair and run down my body. I watched the remains of blood disappear down the drain.

"You did what you had to do," the voice told me.

Responding, I said, "But I got rid of the wrong person."

"And it's better because this may give you more of a reason to be by his side. You'll get another opportunity to take Zacariah out," the voice said.

My eyes were closed as the voice spoke to me. I was afraid to open them and see her standing in the shower with me. I needed to deal with what was going on now before I could think about taking out Zacariah.

The shower curtain opened and I jumped, startled by the movement, only to see my brother standing there. He tossed a towel to me and said, "Hurry up. We have to go." And then he walked out.

I cut the shower off and stepped out to dry myself off. I saw Steven had put on the vanity a pair of drawstring jogging pants and one of his big tees. The bloody dress I had taken off was gone, along with all my underclothes.

The only thing left were my shoes, which weren't covered much with blood since the big, bulky gown had covered them. I put the clothes and shoes on. I looked in the mirror at my freshly washed 'fro and combed it back, putting a rubber band around it, positioning it atop my head. I didn't look like I had committed murder at all now.

When I walked into his living room, I saw that Steven had a suitcase sitting by the door.

"What is this?" I asked.

"I told you we have to go."

"Go where?" I questioned.

"We have to leave town, Trinity."

"But—"

"No buts. You killed Derrick's mom. It's probably all over the news right now. We have to leave. What if somebody saw you?"

"They didn't," I said.

"But what if they did?" he argued. "For goodness' sake you left his house in a white wedding gown covered in blood. The wedding dress alone would draw attention to yourself but to have it splattered with blood was a neon sign saying, 'hey, look at me. I just committed murder,'" he said.

I didn't respond. Maybe Steven was right. I did rush out of Derrick's home and I wasn't paying attention to my surroundings. All I knew was I was trying to get away as soon as possible once I realized I had killed the wrong person. Still the fact of the matter was I didn't want to move again. I was tired of running. And then that meant I did all of this for nothing. Even though I killed the wrong individual, I was still determined to get Derrick back into my life.

"I'm not going anywhere, Steven," I told my brother.

He halted and asked, "What?"

"I said I'm not going anywhere. I'm staying here to take care of Derrick. He needs me," I said, going over to his oversized leather chair to sit down.

Steven grimaced and said, "You have truly lost it. Do you think Derrick is going to want you once he finds out you killed his mother?"

"He's not going to find out," I stressed.

"You can't keep getting away with murder, Trinity."

"I thought I was killing Zacariah."

"Like that's better. You told me you weren't going to do anything like this again. Do you remember?" Steven asked.

I nodded.

"What about Marlin and Harvey and Reginald? You stalked them and threatened them also. Then there was Rashad, who you hit with your car. The only reason you got away with that was because he died."

"It was an accident."

"Accident my ass, Trinity. You meant to hurt him. You may not have counted on killing him but you knew what you were doing."

"He was cheating on me."

"He was married. You were the other woman. You knew that going in."

"He told me he was separated. But then he went back to her without telling me. How was I supposed to react?"

"You were supposed to act like normal people and walk away. Man, how many times am I supposed to protect you from yourself, Trinity?"

"I didn't ask you to protect me, Steven. You took that role on yourself," I snapped, tired of my brother making me feel bad about everything.

"If I didn't protect you, you would be in jail right now. And the more I think about it, maybe you should be. Maybe I should be the one to turn you in for all your crimes, because I'm sick of this."

"You wouldn't," I said nervously.

"Why not? Then the burden of having to look after you will be lifted off my shoulders once and for all," he explained.

I did not like where this conversation was going. Steven couldn't do this to me. He wouldn't. But once I looked at him, for the first time ever, I saw he was considering it.

"I'm your sister," I spat.

"You can't keep destroying families like this. Way too many people have gotten hurt by you. You promised you wouldn't do anything like this again after—"

"After what?" I interrupted.

He glanced over at me and said, "After you killed that little boy."

"You know what, I don't have to stay here and listen to you take me down memory lane of things I've done. I told you it was an accident."

"There you go again telling me it was an accident. In your own words you told me you wanted to scare this woman into leaving Marlin, one of your other so-called loves. All that woman was trying to do was go home after grocery shopping but you had to taunt her."

"I tapped her car with mine, that's all. I didn't make her speed up."

"She was trying to get away from you. Here was this crazy woman hitting her in the back, trying to run her off the road. What you weren't counting on was her speeding to get away from you. And like the Trinity I know, you sped up too."

"Only to scare her," I explained, standing with my arms crossed.

"You scared the woman so bad that it caused her to get hit by a tractor trailer. Her son was in the back seat and got ejected from the car, killing him."

"That was her choice to run. She should have taken precautions knowing her son was in the car."

Steven sighed as he rolled his eyes. He bit his lip in frustration as he began to pace again. "I'm playing babysitter to a grown woman who should know better, especially if she's taking her meds like she's supposed to."

I didn't say anything.

"You are not taking them are you?"

"I don't like the way it makes me feel."

"You have schizophrenia. You are crazy, Trinity."

"No, I'm not," I yelled.

"Okay. You're sane. That voice that convinces you to do these things is just a figment of your imagination that you can control, huh?" he asked.

"I'm not crazy," I told him, also trying to convince myself of this.

"That's why all these people are dead. They didn't die by being bludgeoned by you, and poisoned, and being hit by a car and—"

"And fire," I revealed.

"Who died in a . . . ?" And my brother paused.

We looked intently at each other for a moment. He took three steps back like he was losing his balance.

"You?" he asked. "Please tell me you didn't."

"They kept riding me."

Steven squatted with his hands over his face, still staring at me. He said, "You killed Mommy and Daddy too."

"They tried to keep me away from Wayne. You know he was my very first love."

"It was for your own good. He was a married man too, Trinity."

"Still. They had no right."

"You were too young to understand. They were trying to protect you," he yelled. "They loved you."

"But I loved Wayne."

Steven stood to his feet. He shook his head and said, "I'm done. I am so done with you."

"What do you mean?"

"I can't let you hurt anyone else. This has to end," he said, walking toward the door.

"Steven, please. You can't do this to me. I need you," I said, giving him an opportunity to change his mind. "Please, let me cook you something to eat. We can talk about this over some good food," I said, running to his kitchen and opening his fridge to pull out some eggs and bacon. Putting the items on the counter, I saw Steven enter. "I'm starving so I know you have to be also."

"Trinity, I love you, but this has to stop," he said regretfully. Then he turned to leave.

"Steven, come on. You can't do this to me."

He said nothing.

I began to panic. I couldn't believe my brother was turning his back on me like this. Looking at the items I pulled out for us to have a wonderful breakfast, I saw a butcher block filled with knives.

"You know what you have to do," the voice in my head said.

"Steven, wait, please," I yelled as I snatched the biggest knife from the block and jogged to the living room where my brother was putting on his jacket.

"Please, don't do this," I pleaded one last time, trying to give him an opportunity to change his mind. I had my hands behind my back so he couldn't see the weapon. I didn't want to hurt my brother, but if I had to, I would.

"It's over, Trinity," he said sadly as he turned to leave.

I walked up to my brother and plunged the knife in his back. He froze and tried to turn to face me as I pulled the knife out of him. His eyes were stretched wide when he turned to look at me. Then he looked down to see the knife I was holding, which was dripping with his blood.

"Trinity," he struggled to say.

I plunged the blade into his abdomen three quick times before he grabbed me. His knees buckled, causing him to tumble to the floor on his back. Steven looked up at me. He coughed and blood spewed from his mouth as he struggled to breathe.

Kneeling down beside him I said, "I couldn't let you ruin everything."

A tear rolled down the side of his face. I took my finger and wiped it away before I plunged the blade into him again.

Chapter 26

Kea

I hated when the phone woke me up from a sound sleep. It just made for a day of everything going wrong and I hoped today wasn't going to be one of those days. My cell rang again and I nudged Jaquon to answer it for me since it was on his nightstand charging. But he was dead to the world. He slept so hard, I think an earthquake couldn't rattle him enough to wake him.

I sighed my irritation, reaching over him to answer, "Hello."

"Kea," a woman's voice said.

"Yes. And who is this?" I asked, looking at the time. It wasn't even six in the morning yet.

"I can't believe you don't know who this is," she said.

I rubbed the sleep from my eyes and tried to concentrate on the voice but I was too tired. I was sleeping so good. All I could think about was going back to sleep. It was a cool morning and I loved this type of weather, as I snuggled under my fleece sheets enjoying my restful slumber.

"Kea, are you there?" she asked.

"Yes. Yes, I'm here. I'm just trying to wake up. Do you know what time it is?"

"Kea, wake up and talk to me. It's me, Emory."

"Emory?" I asked in shock. "Are you calling me from California?"

"Yes."

"If it's five forty-five a.m. here then it's . . ."

"Two forty-five here."

"What are you doing up so late? Did you just come from a party or something? Are you drunk?" I asked.

She giggled, saying, "No, Kea, I'm not drunk. I couldn't sleep and decided to call you."

"And this call couldn't wait until I woke up," I said groggily.

"You are my sister. I had to hear your voice," she said weirdly.

I sat up in bed now, trying to get my wits about myself. Jaquon hadn't budged at all with my talking and continued to snore next to me. I pulled one of the pillows from under him and placed it over his face to drown out his sound.

"Emory, what's going on?

Emory got quiet. I wondered if she hung up.

"Emory," I called out.

"I'm still here," she said through a cracking voice.

"Sis, what's wrong?"

"Kea, I'm just tired. I'm so tired. I thought marriage was supposed to make things better, but it's worse."

"What do you mean?" I asked, having some clue. My mother, Frances, told me about Aaron cheating on Emory, and how she should stay because he had money. That was typical for Mother. Stay and deal so you can live well, not once thinking happiness overrode money most times.

"I'm ready to pack my things and leave him," Emory admitted.

"Then why don't you?" I asked.

"Because, I love him. And I know that sounds crazy after what he's done to me but he's still my husband. I wouldn't have my daughter if it wasn't for him."

For a moment I forgot about Emory having the baby. She gave birth to a baby girl, who I couldn't wait to meet.

"The baby is only a few weeks old, Emory. You haven't been gone that long."

"I know, and it's been the worst few months of my life. You know it's bad when living here with Aaron is worse than us growing up with Mother."

I had to laugh at that. It was like she was reading my thoughts because I thought our life with Mother was horrible. "Do you want me to fly to California, pack you and my niece up, and bring you both back home with me?"

"No."

"I would love to hold my little niece. I know she's beautiful," I said.

"Yes, she is. I can't wait for you to see her. I could have texted you a picture but I wasn't thinking," Emory said.

"It's okay. You are a new mother."

"I'm sorry for not calling you much at all," she said, sounding like she was about to cry.

"Well, that works both ways. We've been so caught up in our own lives that we've completely disconnected."

"I don't want that for us, Kea," she said.

"Me either," I agreed.

"I thought moving far away from Mother was going to be a good thing. I never once thought about losing you and Daddy. Now I need you all more than ever and you all are thousands of miles away from me."

"We can be seconds away if you let me come out there to get you. You know you are more than welcome to stay with me. And you know Daddy would love to see his baby girl and grandchild."

"I know he would," Emory said.

"So do you want us to come?"

"No. I'm thinking about coming home. California is nice and everything but it's nothing like home. It's just not my cup of tea."

"So you are leaving Aaron?" I asked.

"I'm going to have to before I kill him."

Her words shocked me. "Kill" was a strong word. I knew Aaron had to be doing something terrible if she was thinking about killing him.

"Don't do that," I told her.

"It would serve him right for cheating on me all the time. He thinks because we got married and he's giving me the life so many women would die for, I should turn the other cheek and allow him to sleep around."

"Typical man," I said, thinking I was possibly looking into the future of my own marriage if I decided to make it legal with Jaquon.

"He's been bold enough to take these women to social events for the word to get back to me. He would deny it but then I would see pictures he'd taken plastered in the local newspaper here."

"Wow."

"He's even had other women in our home, Kea, in our bed."

"No, he didn't."

"Yes, he did. But tonight I caught him. I walked in on him lying on top of some floozy and he had the nerve to tell me to get out until he got done."

"No, he didn't!" I yelled, causing Jaquon to stir a bit. I was amazed at how our lives were similar.

"Kea, I lost it. He wanted me to excuse myself while he finished. Needless to say their sex was cut short because I tried my best to cut him."

I started to laugh.

"Aaron thought I was a weak bitch but I showed him. He had this machete mounted on the wall. I went over and snatched it off the wall. Aaron was so into this whore, he thought I had abided by his demand and left the room. How surprised was he when I started slicing at the sheets that covered their naked bodies."

"Emory, no, you didn't."

"Yes, the hell I did. Aaron hopped off that woman so fast holding his hands up for me to stop."

I laughed at this story and tried to picture my innocent, quiet sister going on a rampage, swinging a machete.

"The woman started screaming. She was too scared to move. But I didn't want her. I wanted him. I ran around that bed and Aaron jumped onto it, stepping all over the woman to get away from me. I kept swinging the blade, nicking his skin a couple of times. He screamed in pain but it only fueled me more to continue to go after him. The closer I got to him, the lower I was swinging because I was trying to cut his dick off."

"No, you weren't, Emory," I said, now in tears from laughing.

"I had that man scared for his life."

"Is he alive?" I asked through laughter.

"Unfortunately, yes. He managed to lock himself in our master bathroom until I calmed down."

"Where is he now?"

"He's still in there."

"You got the man still locked in the bathroom?" I asked, shocked.

"Yes, and I'm going to sit outside this door until he can explain to me why he insists on cheating on me," Emory said.

"Where's the woman?"

"I let her get her clothes together and leave, but not before getting her ID and cell phone number. I told her if she called the cops I was coming after her next, and if I couldn't get to her, I had people who owed me favors who would."

"And she believed you."

"Yeah, she believed me. That trick knows nothing about me so she doesn't know what I am capable of. Money around here talks and the only advantage I have is having money by being Aaron's wife. And you best believe I've stashed some away for a rainy day."

"Well, this sounds more like a storm."

"Emory, baby, listen to me," I could hear a faint voice calling out in the background.

"Is that him?" I asked.

"Yeah, that's him. I guess he's ready to come out and talk."

"Are you going to let him?"

"Not sure yet."

"Do you still have the machete?"

"Yes, and I'm prepared to use it," she said confidently.

"Emory, put the weapon down before things get really ugly. He's not worth going to jail over," I heard myself say as I remembered Terry telling me the exact same thing months ago. Boy how things turn around.

"I'm not going to hurt him much. I just want to cut his dick off and put it in his mouth for him to choke on it," she screamed loud enough for him to hear.

I laughed. "Girl, stop scaring that man."

"He should have treated me better."

"Come home, okay?" I told her.

"I think I'm going to do that. I miss you all so much," she said coolly.

"When should I expect you?"

"I'm going to try to catch a plane tomorrow. If I can't, I will let you know what flight I get."

"Let me know so I can meet you at the airport."

"Okay."

"And, Emory, I love you."

"I love you too, Kea," she said through tears, causing my eyes to fill with tears.

"Let that man go."

"I'll think about it."

With that we hung up the phone. It was now after six and the sun was slowly peeking from the horizon. I was too alert to go back to sleep so I crawled out of bed and went to the living room to watch some TV.

Chapter 27

Kea

If it weren't for my dad today, I wouldn't have come to court to see the fate of my so-called mother, who was convicted of conspiracy to commit murder. In my mind, she deserved whatever she got. The entire trial, from what Daddy told me, consisted of her being the victim and this thug was lying on her. Of all the individuals in the world, why would this young guy point his finger at her saying she paid him to kill Mr. Hanks? The irony alone with him being the man she hated most was enough to make her look guilty. But Mom couldn't see it. Again, she was Frances Fields, a prominent figure in her community who didn't have so much as a parking ticket. She was so busy trying to be something she wasn't that she couldn't see she was a charlatan. She had committed forgery on her own life and was too conceited to see it.

When Mother was walked into the courtroom, she was dressed in one of her best suits looking like she hadn't spent one day in jail for the crime she had committed. Mama looked my way and didn't so much as smile at me. Her glance was cold and heartless; but why would I expect anything different from the woman who never wanted me in the first place, and made it known most of my life how she didn't care for me? I wanted to get up and walk out right then. But when I saw the concerned look on my father's face, I knew I had to stay.

"All rise," the bailiff said as the judge entered the court-room. As much as I liked watching Judge Judy and Judge Mathis, this felt different. I felt anxious, which could be attributed to my mother being the defendant in this case.

"You may be seated," the bailiff said and everyone in the courtroom sat down.

I looked over at Daddy, who still looked worried. I knew this was because he still loved Frances despite how heartless she'd been to him. Isn't it always like that? A good man always ends up with a woman who never de-served him in the first place. Looking at my father's gray hair let me know the life he'd led should have been better spent than him spending it with a woman who could toss him away like yesterday's trash. I knew he stayed for me and Emory. Thank God he did because I don't know where I would be now. Still, I hated it had to be at the cost of my father's life.

"Frances Fields, you have been convicted of conspiracy to commit murder. Do you have anything you would like to say to the court?" the judged presiding over the trial asked.

She looked at her lawyer before saying, "Yes, Your Honor. I would like to speak."

"Address the court," the judge said.

"First, I would like to say the verdict that was decided for me was erroneous. I'm totally appalled the court trusted in the word of some thug with a vast criminal background, where I have been an upstanding citizen. But here my image has been tainted with this guilty verdict. It's true I knew the deceased. He was the man who raped me as a child; but why would I want to exact revenge on this man after thirty years have passed? The decision is preposterous. Again, you decided to trust in the word of a low-life thug. I do ask with this absurd verdict, you recognize a wrong decision has been made and give me the sentence of time served."

I know I looked on with my mouth wide open. Was my mother serious? She basically called the court idiots. Frances was serious as a heart attack. Even standing before the judge who found her guilty, she felt entitled to be released. She had not learned one thing and still acted like everyone owed her something. She truly believed in her sick head the world should bow down before her and give her what she wanted. I shook my head in disbelief. I looked over at Daddy, whose head was hung low as Frances spoke. He had to be thinking the same thing but I wasn't about to ask him what he was feeling.

"I'm innocent, Judge, so please release me at once," Frances said confidently.

The judge paused. Then he shuffled some papers around before he said, "Thank you, Mrs. Fields. The court has heard and acknowledges what you had to say. Now, I'm going to render my sentence."

Daddy reached over and grabbed my hand. Even though Frances was my mother, I truly despised her for all the things she'd done to me. Still, a small part of me didn't want to see her sentenced to a lot of years in prison, knowing there was a possibility she would die in there.

"With the charge of conspiracy to commit murder, I hereby sentence you to twenty-five years in prison," the judge said.

My eyes closed, knowing this was not what Mother, nor my dad, wanted to hear.

"What?" Frances said, shocked at the time given. "After all I've said. After all I've been through. Living among criminals and people who are well beneath my stature, you sentence me to twenty-five years," she belted.

"This sentence is to start immediately with time served counted toward the years assigned to you," the judge said.

"You can't do this to me," Frances yelled.

Mother's attorney tried to calm her but she jerked her arm away from him, saying, "Get your hands off of me, you pathetic piece of shit. I want all of my money back," she yelled at him.

"Frances, be quiet," Daddy stood and told her.

"You shut up, you worthless excuse for a man," she said, glaring at Daddy.

"Order," the judged yelled, banging his gavel to get control of his courtroom.

Frances ignored him and said to Daddy, "This is not your life on the line here. This is mine. If you cared, you would have convinced her to get me the best lawyer money could buy. But just like your selfish daughter, you refused to help me," she spat, now glaring at the both of us.

Her words angered me. My mother lived the life of luxury due to the career of my dad. He gave her everything she could ever want, only for her to file for divorce, still expecting Daddy to bow down and let her have everything. But Daddy was no fool. He fought and got the majority of the assets because he earned it. She had shown the court, just like in court during their divorce proceedings, what type of conniving woman she was, which was why she was left with only enough to pay for the court-appointed lawyer given to her. She'd used him long enough. And now she had the audacity to stand here and accuse him of not caring about her.

It was at this point I decided to put my two cents in. I wasn't planning on saying anything to this woman I hated to call my mother but I had to come to my dad's defense.

Standing, I said, "Don't you stand there and accuse him of never caring about you. He's here today and has been here for you this entire time."

"To gloat," she said. "He took everything away from me."

"You took everything away from yourself. If you weren't so busy trying to push the ones who loved you away, you wouldn't be in the position you are in now," I replied angrily. "You deserve every bit of what you are getting. The mental and physical abuse, the lies and the cruelty to others, you deserve this fate. And you have no one to blame but yourself."

"This coming from the monster's daughter," she spat. "That rapist got everything he deserved," she yelled.

"And if you let the faith you claimed you had be the driving force to you moving forward, you would have let that man answer to God without taking his fate into your own hands," I retorted.

"Order! Order in the courtroom," the judge yelled again, banging his gavel.

"I'm Frances Fields," Mother said.

"Bailiff, take the defendant away," the judge demanded.

"Why am I getting punished for getting rid of trash?" she yelled. "He deserved to die."

And there it was, finally, her confession. I think she was so delirious with the sentencing, she didn't care what came out of her mouth now.

"That bastard raped me. Why am I being punished?"

Tears began to stream down her face and for the first time in my life, I saw my mother's stoic demeanor crumple before me. This was the woman I wished I saw coming up, the genuine person who had a pain that lasted her lifetime. She could have gotten help for what happened to her. I never once condoned what Mr. Hanks did to her. No child should ever go through what she went through. Still, she didn't have to bury it so deep to the point she was too busy trying to be this person who never existed. All of it was a fraud. And now that her world had been taken from her once again, the real Frances stood before us. This Frances represented the child who also wanted her mother to save her but didn't, and Mother wept like she'd never cried before.

"Please. You have to understand," she said as the bailiff struggled to remove my mother from the courtroom. She became combative. Another police officer came to assist the bailiff in restraining her. The officer grabbed both my mother's wrists and twisted her hands behind her back, slapping handcuffs on her.

"Please. Don't take me to jail," she pleaded. "I don't belong there."

The police officer pushed Mother to the door, leading her to her life behind bars.

"Please, help me. Help me," she yelled as she disappeared behind the now-closed door.

Daddy sat down and began to sob. He couldn't contain his emotions anymore. I sat down next to him and put my arms around him, watching tears stream down his face. The verdict was final and I knew from that day that I would never see my mother again.

Chapter 28

Jaquon

Kea was surprisingly upset when she called to tell me her mother had been sentenced to twenty-five years. I expected whatever sentencing given to her mother wouldn't affect Kea since she had written her mother off. I guess the point still remained this woman was her mother, and, despite the fallout they had with one another, Kea still cared for her.

"Babe, are you sure you are okay?" I asked sincerely.

"I'm good. I'm glad it's finally over."

"How's your dad?"

"He's saddened by the verdict also but we are getting ourselves together. Emory coming home today makes this day better than it has been. We are almost at the airport to pick her and the baby up."

"Well, if you need anything, call me. I'll be here waiting for you all to get home," I said.

I hung up the phone and tossed my cell on the bed as I remained stretched out watching the ball game that was on. As much as I loved Kea, I was glad I had this time to myself. Even though I had taken off today, which was not in my nature, it seemed like I would be busy entertaining when really what I wanted was to spend the day relaxing. I didn't have long before company would be in our home so I was taking this moment to get my thoughts together and unwind before I had to play host with Kea.

I still felt shook. The death of Derrick's mom did something to me. She was in a sense my mom, taking me in when my mother wasn't there like she should have been: hence, the friendship that connected me and Derrick like brothers. Seeing his state of devastation was too much for me to even bear. I cried along with him as I mourned the senseless murder of Mama Shirley too.

Who in their right mind could do that to her? What could she have ever done to make somebody want to take her life? I knew something wasn't right about this picture. I had to wonder if her death had anything to do with what'd been going on within this past year: Essence being found dead, Mr. Hanks being killed, and now her. This was too coincidental. Three deaths so close together when it seemed like I hadn't lost one person within the last several years. This was a lot for me to handle. I knew if I felt the way I did, Derrick had to be feeling ten times worse.

I smiled when I thought about the last time I saw Mama Shirley, which was two weeks ago. No one knew I visited her. Not Kea and definitely not Derrick. Despite the collapse of our friendship, I still felt like it was my duty to drop in and see how she was doing even though my visits had become few and far between due to the events that had transpired.

"It's good to see you, son," she said, embracing me with that motherly hug she always gave me.

"Hey, Mama Shirley," I said, smiling at the nickname I called her sometimes.

"You've become a stranger around here," she said, playfully hitting me on the arm.

"Well, you know, I've been busy."

"Jaquon," she said, giving me a look to tell her the truth. She was always good at reading me. "Did you forget who you were talking to, son?"

I smiled and replied, "Okay. You got me. I stopped coming by since my argument with Derrick. I was afraid he would be here and I didn't want any confrontation. Plus, I didn't know how you felt about me after, you know," I said, feeling ashamed about my part in what had happened between me and Derrick.

"Derrick does not run this over here. I'm grown and too old to let the troubles you two are going through to make me choose sides."

"I figured you would be on his side since Derrick is your son," I admitted.

"And you are like my son too. Jaquon, I love you like I love him. Yes, I gave birth to Derrick and raised him but we can be mothers to children we didn't have. I may not agree with what you two do but nothing will ever change my love for you."

Hearing Mama Shirley say that made me feel good. I felt bad for ever having any doubt that she would treat me any different and I should have known better.

"Now don't get me wrong, I don't condone what has happened. You were wrong, but Derrick was wrong too. I've been praying for you two to resolve things."

"I tried, but you know how Derrick is," I said.

"Yes, my son is stubborn just like me," she said, giggling.

"I don't think he will ever forgive me. Our friendship is done."

"Jaquon, you must not know the God I know because He can fix anything. And if you don't know Him, you need to get to know Him," she said to me with more confidence than ever. "Are you going to church, boy?"

I chuckled and said, "No, ma'am."

"Well, that's one of your problems. You need to go listen to the Word so you can get filled up to deal with all that's out here. You've let them streets lead you down a path of confusion."

I nodded, agreeing with her. I said, "I'm trying to do the right thing now."

"I can tell something has changed you. I take it that something or someone is Kea?" she asked.

"Yes. She's agreed to marry me."

"She has?" she asked, surprised.

"Don't sound shocked," I said jokingly.

"Well, you know I am. After all the women you cheated on her with."

"How do you know . . . ?"

She gave me a look that caused me to stop talking.

"Jaquon, I know you. You've been a ladies' man since I've known you. You could never turn down those fast-tail females, and I told you—"

"'If you keep messing with those fast-tail women, you're going to get something you can't get rid of,'" I said, completing the sentence she'd always told me during my time with her.

"Exactly. I'm not telling you this to preach. I'm telling you this because I love you."

I smiled and said, "I know, Mama Shirley. You know I love you too."

"I'm going to keep praying for your and Derrick's situations. I pray you two get back to being the friends you used to be. But let me tell you one thing: all the secrets should be out in the open so you two can move on now."

What Mama Shirley didn't know was not all the secrets were out in the open. Derrick still didn't know I could have gotten Zacariah pregnant and that she had an abortion because she didn't know whose baby she was carrying. I never wanted kids but I knew Derrick did eventually. The fact that Zacariah could have gotten rid of his child would destroy not only Derrick; it would destroy any chance of us ever being able to reconcile our friendship.

Mama Shirley's last words I remember so well were, "It's going to take time because, like I told you, my son is stubborn as a mule. But don't give up on him, Jaquon. The day is going to come where he's going to need you."

And as always, Mama Shirley was right. The day did come where Derrick needed me. I hated it had to be at the cost of Mama Shirley dying. Who knew that would be the last conversation we would have? I was happy I was able to tell her I loved her. And I was happy I was able to hear she loved me too. If God would let her come back to me, I would give up Kea, Derrick, and my own life, to have her back here on this earth. That's how much I loved her. Remembering what she said to me brought tears to my eyes. I swiped at the tear that rolled down the side of my face. I heard the buzz of my cell phone, letting me know someone was calling. When I picked it up, I didn't recognize the number.

Answering, I said, "Hello."

"I see you are alone."

"Who is this?" I asked.

"It's Sheila, silly. You don't know my voice by now?"

"How did you get my number?" I asked heatedly.

"I have my ways," she said.

"Don't be calling me. What's wrong with you? What if Kea would have been here?"

"But she's not. I know this because I watched her leave. So come open the door and let me in."

"Are you serious right now?"

"Of course I am. I want some more of that big dick."

"I told you the last time, it was a one-time deal."

"Says you, but I didn't agree to that."

"I'm telling you it was."

"Are you sure about that? Don't make the next time I'm knocking at your door be when Kea is there," she threatened.

I didn't say anything.

"That's what I thought. Now if you are not comfortable with me coming over there, then come to my place and do me. My door will be unlocked for you. All you have to do is let yourself in so you can get in this wetness. I'll be waiting."

Sheila hung up the phone. I gaped at the television, upset I was allowing this trick to continue to blackmail me. I knew Sheila wasn't going to let this go. If I didn't get a handle on this real soon, my relationship with Kea was going to be over. Not only did I need to figure out a way to keep Sheila's mouth shut, I also need to figure out how to tell my best friend I had another secret to reveal to him.

Chapter 29

Jaquon

The last place I wanted to be was in Sheila's place again. It was too close to home and that was the reason why we chose the hotel before. I didn't want it to be obvious I was hitting Sheila off. I walked out into the hallway, looking around to see if anybody was outside to see me make my way across the hall to her place. No one was. I sighed my relief. I didn't want anybody saying anything about us having an affair.

Just like Sheila said the door was unlocked. I entered her place, still looking around, making sure no one noticed me entering her apartment. The living room was dimly lit as usual. Sheila had blackout curtains that always kept her space dark. If I didn't know any better, I would swear she was allergic to the sun or something. Even though she was a known whore, she did keep her place looking neat and smelling nice. Candles were lit and the space smelled like apple pie.

I entered the space deeper and didn't see her anywhere.

"Sheila," I called out.

"Back here," she responded.

I proceeded to her bedroom and entered a space I hadn't been in before. The room was very nice, also dark like her living room. A black comforter covered her king-sized bed and candles were lit in this space, along with a lamp on her side table next to her bed. Sheila was sitting on the bed. And between Sheila's legs was this caramel-skinned woman eating Sheila out. Caramel's bone-straight long hair was swooped over her right shoulder as she pleasured Sheila, who seemed to be into what she was doing. I cleared my throat to let them know I was standing here. Both took a moment to notice my presence.

"We started without you. I hope you don't mind," Sheila said.

"Why do you need me if you have her?" I said, pointing at the woman who was looking me up and down seductively.

I said this trying to act like I didn't want to be here and that seeing them didn't turn me on. But seeing Caramel getting her eat on did arouse me. One woman in bed for me was great but two was twice the fun and double the pleasure. I had been with two women at one time before and I would be lying if I said I didn't enjoy it because it was a mind-blowing experience. My dick immediately became erect seeing the two of them getting it on. Plus it was a fact that Caramel was gorgeous. Sheila definitely had great taste in women.

Caramel dove her head back between Sheila's legs and Shelia leaned her head back, moaning as she propped herself up on her elbows. Caramel inserted two fingers inside Sheila and this sent her to higher levels of pleasure. I didn't move. I couldn't. My dick was saying, "Man, you better get in that." But my heart was telling me to go back home and be there for Kea, her dad, and her sister when they got home. If Sheila wanted to tell Kea, then I was going to let her. I would stand my ground, proving the love I had for Kea did outweigh my urge to fall victim to being blackmailed to do what I loved, which was having sex.

Sheila bucked as a climax hit her.

"Yes," she said, gyrating her hips into caramel's face. Caramel feverishly penetrated and licked Sheila to her climax. Moments later, caramel came up for air and smiled at Sheila, who fell to her back, panting at the explosion she just experienced.

"Come over and join us," Sheila demanded.

"I'm good. It seems like you are too. So I guess I can go now," I said, still trying to find a way to get out of this before it was too late.

"Jaquon, you know you want us," she said, looking over at me as she came down from her climax.

I didn't say anything. Sheila looked at my pants and saw my dick was erect. She smirked and sat up on the bed. Then she made her way to me. Pressing her naked body against mine, she gripped my hardness.

"This is what we want," she said.

I looked over to see Caramel sitting on the side of the bed rubbing her center as she gazed at me. I knew just from seeing her hands between her thighs pleasing herself, my dick got even harder.

Sheila stroked my dick from the outside before she started unbuckling my pants. This was when I should have pushed her away to tell her to do what she had to do because I was not going to sleep with her again. That's what I knew I should be saying, but my body was doing something different. My body was betraying me. My body tingled from her touch and became aroused by what she was doing.

She pulled my jeans down around my ankles and then did the same to my boxer briefs. My dick protruded forward and she smiled at its girth. She grabbed and stroked it a few times before dropping to her knees to do what she did best. She easily took me into her mouth and down her throat, causing my legs to tremble with pleasure. Sheila stopped sucking long enough to finger for her friend to come over and join her.

"Jaquon, this is Samara. Samara, this is the infamous Jaquon."

"Nice to finally meet you," Samara said to me.

I didn't respond. What was I supposed to say? "It's nice to meet you too" as she stood in front of me naked also? Her breasts were not large but her body was bangin'. Where she lacked in breasts, she damn sure made up for in her ass.

"Can you help me with this?" Sheila asked Samara.

"I would be happy to," Samara said, dropping to her knees next to Sheila.

Both began licking and sucking my dick as Sheila stroked my balls. This felt so damn good. I looked down at the both of them and Samara stared up at me as she took the length of me into her mouth. My dick glistened with her saliva as she bobbed back and forth taking me deep as Sheila took me into her throat. Sheila licked my balls and both of them slurped me closer to my climax. I didn't know how much more of this I could take. I gripped both of their heads, clenching a handful of their hair between my fingers. I could feel my dick swell with satisfaction. I was about to cum and it was nothing I could do about it. Samara increased her sucking as her hand assisted in stroking me.

Coming up for air, Samara said, "That's right, baby. Cum in my mouth."

Hearing her say that was like a signal to release. As soon as her mouth returned to sucking me, I gripped the back of her head and shot my load into her mouth and down her throat. She swallowed all of me. Sheila, like the hungry trick she was, pushed Samara off so she could also taste my sap.

I was good now. I could go home but knew like the freaks they were and like the man I was, I was going to dig the tricks out.

"Damn, he's still hard," Samara said like she was surprised my extension was still standing for some attention.

"Girl, I told you this man right here got dick for days. You can still feel the aftermath of this man's dick penetrating you days later," Sheila said with a giggle.

They were talking like I wasn't here. Yet both of their hands were on my dick ogling it like it was a masterpiece in a museum. They really knew how to make a brother feel good about himself.

"I can't wait to ride it," Samara said.

And as gorgeous as she was, I couldn't wait to get my dick inside her.

Samara bit her bottom lip as she stood to her feet. She grabbed my hand to lead me over to the bed. I had to take small steps since my jeans and boxers were still around my ankles. Once I was at the bed, Samara pushed me onto my back. Sheila reached down to remove my shoes and jeans.

"We don't need any restrictions," Sheila said.

Samara climbed on top of me eagerly ready for me to penetrate her. She reached beneath her and angled my dick for entrance. Sliding down, she sighed, saying, "Damn, this is big."

"But he feels good right?" Sheila asked.

"Hell yeah," Samara responded, slowly moving her hips back and forth.

Her pussy was tight, almost virgin tight.

"Oh, he feels good," Samara complimented me again.

"Told you the brother would make you switch teams again."

"Switch teams," I said as Samara tightened her walls around me.

Sheila lay down beside me, rubbing Samara's breasts as she bounced up and down on my shaft. Sheila proceeded to say, "Samara has never had a real dick inside her. She was gay but was curious and I told her you would be the perfect one to break her in right."

I looked up at Samara, who smirked as she moved her hips back and forth vigorously. I felt her walls tighten again and her head fell back. She began to move faster and screamed her way to an organism. From her moves, I would have never thought she hadn't ridden a man's dick before. I guessed when any woman got a taste of my manhood, her body's womanly instinct took over to ride me like a champ.

"My turn," Sheila said to Samara as she leaned up. Samara struggled to climb off my still-erect dick. I could feel her trembling but didn't have time to pay any attention to her before Sheila was climbing on. What a difference a pussy makes. I almost pushed Sheila off me and told Samara to climb that tight pussy back on. But when Sheila began clenching her walls like she did, you would have thought a hand was inside her tugging away at my dick.

Sheila winked at me as she too rode her way to multiple organisms. Samara lay beside me and took my right hand to put between her saturated thighs. She pushed two of my fingers inside her. I watched as both women got off to me. Damn this was good. As much as I hated cheating, the fact of the matter was I enjoyed having sex with both of these women.

Chapter 30

Kea

I could not believe I was carrying my little niece as we made our way into my apartment. Emory was right behind me and Daddy was following her, carrying her suitcases.

"Jaquon, we're here," I called out but he didn't say anything.

I put my niece down in the sofa. I looked at her sleeping soundly and had to smile at how angelic she was.

"You guys get comfortable and make yourselves at home. I'll be right back," I said, jogging to the bedroom.

"You haven't said nothing but a word," I heard Emory say as I looked back to see her plop down on the sofa next to her daughter. Daddy put her suitcases down beside the chair and sat down also.

When I entered my bedroom, I saw Jaquon was not there. This was puzzling since his car was still outside. I wondered where he could be. He told me he was going to be here when we got here. Nevertheless I wasn't going to worry about him right now. Today had been a long day and now I was going to enjoy my sister and niece.

Joining my family in the living room, I said, "I'm not quite sure where Jaquon is. I guess he'll be here in a bit."

I sat down beside the baby, who was still sound asleep in her chair. I stared at her and marveled at how beautiful she was.

"I know you want to hold her," Emory said.

"Please, can I?" I asked like a little kid begging for candy. "You know I've been yearning to hold her since I saw her at the airport."

Emory turned the seat toward her and unbuckled the baby. She squirmed a bit as Emory removed the straps from around her tiny body. Emory reached in and picked her up. She began to stretch as Emory handed her to me.

"Oh my goodness," I said, taking her into my arms. "She's so tiny."

My little niece had a head full of jet-black curly hair. She was lighter than Emory, probably taking after her father, but that was all she got from him because she looked just like my sister.

"This makes me want to have a child," I confessed.

"You say that now but wait," Emory said. "As soon as that baby cries in the middle of the night, you may change your mind."

"It can't be that bad," I said.

Emory stretched her eyes at me, saying, "I thought that too until Ms. Thang woke up every two hours. Don't you see the bags under my eyes?"

"Emory, you look fabulous. I don't see any bags under your eyes."

"I forgot. You can't see them because I've covered them up with concealer."

I giggled at my sister, realizing how much I missed having her with me. She really did look good. Even though she'd been stressed out by her cheating husband, she maintained that flawless appearance she'd always had since we were teenagers. Her hair was still long, almost hitting the middle of her back now. She wore a pink Juicy Couture jogging suit and some UGGs. Even my niece had on little baby UGGs.

"I'll get up for her," I said, rocking her.

"And you can have that job tonight. I would love to have one night of uninterrupted sleep," she said, lying back on the sofa."

"What did Aaron say about you leaving?"

"What could he say? He was just happy to be alive," Emory said.

"I can't believe you, Emory. That's not you, threatening that man like that," Daddy said.

"When someone hurts you like he did me, Daddy, another person takes over your body to handle things. I'm not going to lie; I really wanted to kill Aaron."

"But he's not worth it," Daddy said.

"I know that now. But in that moment all I could see was him having the audacity to bring some slut up in our home, in our bed to have sex with her like he couldn't have cared less about what time I arrived home."

"You did the right thing in coming home," Daddy said.

"That's right and we are happy you are here," I agreed.

"Can I hold my grandchild?" Daddy asked, coming over to me. I wanted to say no but this was his first grandchild. I felt like grandfathers outranked aunties, so I handed my niece over to him. Daddy took her into his arms and went over to the chair and sat down.

"Can I get you guys something to drink? Are you hungry? We can go out to eat or we can order in. What would you guys like to do?" I asked.

"Sis, after that long plane ride, I want to put my feet up and relax," Emory said, snuggling deeper into the sofa. She picked up the blanket I kept on my couch and covered herself with it.

"We can do that too," I said, smiling at her.

"Y'all don't have to order anything for me. I think I'm going home," Daddy said, cradling his granddaughter.

"Why?" both Emory and I asked in unison.

"Just like you said, Emory, it's been a long day, sweetie. This old man is tired."

"You are not going to stay and eat something?" I asked.

"No. No. I can pick something up on the way home," he said.

Daddy didn't seem himself but I didn't want to push it. I knew it was because of the verdict the judge handed down earlier today for Frances. He still loved her despite the fact that she filed for divorce. Even from jail she was determined to make his life hell. Daddy couldn't bring himself to sign those papers. I thought divorcing her was great. But this was his wife, the only woman he'd ever loved. I didn't know if the love was reciprocated to him like the love he gave. The only person Frances loved was herself, and maybe Emory.

"Daddy, are you okay?" Emory asked, noticing his somber demeanor also.

"I don't know," he said sadly, staring down at the little one. "Things have been difficult to deal with lately. And Frances getting sentenced today was a blow. I need some time to come to grips with everything that has happened."

"Daddy, I'm not trying to tell you what to do and I'm only saying this because I love you. You have to move on from her," I said.

He nodded.

"I know that's easier said than done but you have a lot of life left. You can mourn for a little while but make sure you get back up and enjoy life. I hope you start dating again and everything," I suggested.

He smiled and said, "I'm just heartbroken that's all. I never knew my life could change so dramatically in such a short period of time, you know."

"I do," I said, feeling the same way.

"I do too. Look at me. I'm sitting on my sister's couch with my new baby running from a man I just caught in bed with another woman," Emory said.

"All of our lives have been complicated lately," I said.

"You ain't never lied," Emory agreed.

I looked at her with a frown.

"What?" Emory asked.

"'You ain't never lied.'"

"What's wrong with that?" she asked.

"'Ain't.' When have you started saying ain't? The Emory I'm used to would say 'you have never lied.'"

"Well, that Emory is long gone. This is a new version of me."

"I hope a better version, but I'm not sure with you saying 'ain't,'" I joked.

Emory hit me playfully, saying, "Real funny."

"I'm just saying."

"This Emory believes in herself. I'm tired of people thinking they can control me. First, it was Mother. Then, I meet a man just like her, in a sense. I would have never married that man if it weren't for Mother," she said angrily. "I married him because she made me think I had something. And I thought I did but I was blinded by love or what I thought love was."

"Who knows? Maybe Mother wanted your husband for herself, no disrespect, Daddy," I said.

"None taken."

"Well, she should've married him. For me, the shades are off. I see everything clearly now," Emory said.

"Look at you," I said, snapping my fingers. "Little Ms. Emory has grown up."

"I had to, especially for my daughter. I don't want her to think it is okay to have a man treat her like her dad treated me. I want her to be stronger than that," Emory explained.

"I'm amazed by you, sis. I'm glad to see you have come out of your shell."

"It wasn't by chance. Aaron cracked that shell open. I didn't want to be left to suffer. So I had to put on my big-girl panties and start to love me."

"I'm proud of you, Emory," Daddy said. "It sounds like you are on the right path."

"I hope so. I feel like I am. I'm ready to move on and start living. And it doesn't hurt that I have a little bit of Aaron's money to help me get my start," my sister said, giggling.

"How much money do you have?" I asked, being nosy.

"Two million," she admitted.

My mouth fell open. "Two million, Emory?"

She nodded.

"Does he know you have it?" I asked.

"Yes, he knows."

"And he was cool with that?"

"He gave it to me. Plus that's chump change to Aaron. Remember, his family is rich."

"I knew they had money but not like that."

"Kea, they have Oprah Winfrey money if that tells you anything," Emory said.

"No wonder Mother wanted you to get with him."

"Exactly. She wanted to get her hands on some of that money too," Emory admitted.

"I'm still surprised Aaron gave you anything," I said.

"Well, after he saw the videotape of him with the woman I caught him with, he didn't have a choice."

"Videotape?" Daddy asked.

"The man runs a multibillion-dollar cooperation and was too dumb to realize we had security cameras in every room in the house. Even the bathrooms had cameras. Our home was so secure, a burglar would be an idiot to try to get into our home. Anyway, the security footage caught his acts of infidelity."

"Yes, that man is an idiot," Daddy said, putting the baby up on his shoulder.

"But didn't it capture the incident after you caught him?" I asked, wondering if he could use that against her in court.

"He could if he had it. Somehow the video footage didn't catch that part," she said with a smirk.

I smiled, saying, "You slick little thing, you."

"What? I don't know what you are talking about," she said, winking at me.

"Are you going to divorce him?" I asked.

"Yes, I am. There is no prenup either."

"Yes. That man is really stupid," Daddy said again.

"So you are going to rake him over the coals with the tape?" I asked.

"I'm not going to hurt him that bad," Emory admitted.

"I would. After all he's done to you, you catching him cheating. I can't believe you are not going to let him have it," I said excitedly.

"I've already contacted a lawyer who has a copy of this footage. All I'm asking for is alimony, child support, and this startup money to get me started. Even though Aaron is a prick, he does love his daughter. I know he will take care of her and make sure she has everything she needs. All I'm asking for is a few thousand a month for me."

"You are better than me," I said, leaning back, crossing my arms.

"There's no need to cause more friction."

"Emory, you are making me more proud by the second," Daddy said.

"You have grown a lot. Luckily Mother's ways didn't rub off on you because if it was her . . ." I paused.

"She would have owned his company before the ink on the divorce papers dried," Emory finished my sentence as we laughed together. It felt good laughing with my sister. It felt good being with my family, despite how this day started. It was ending wonderfully.

Daddy stood with his granddaughter nestled in the crook of his neck. He walked over to Emory and leaned forward to hand her the baby. "Girls, I'm getting ready to go," Daddy said.

"You sure you don't want to hang with your daughters, Daddy?" Emory asked.

"I'm sure. I just need some time to myself tonight. I promise we will get up tomorrow," Daddy said, putting his hands in his pocket and pulling out his car keys.

Emory stood with her daughter cradled in her arms. She went over and hugged him, saying, "I love you, Daddy."

"I love you too, honey. It's good to have you home."

I walked Daddy to the door and embraced him also. I told him, "It is going to be okay. We are strong and we bounce back easily."

Daddy kissed me on the cheek. He opened the door to leave. When he did, that's when I got the shock of my life. I had just found Jaquon. And he was exiting the apartment of my neighbor across the hall. Our eyes met and I knew the day, which was ending great, was now ruined by the fact that Jaquon was up to his old tricks.

Chapter 31

Jaquon

Talk about bad timing. When I turned and saw Mr. Fields standing in the hall with Kea in the doorway, and both of them were glaring at me, I knew I was done. My secret was about to be exposed and I was going to catch the hell of my life. I wanted to kick myself for not looking through the peephole first to see if anybody was in the hallway. I guess too many climaxes took all the blood flow from my brain, causing me to do some stupid things. And this mistake I knew was going to cost me plenty.

"Jaquon, what are you doing coming from Shelia's place?" Kea asked me suspiciously.

"Ummhhh. Ummhhh," was all I could say. Again, no blood flow to my brain.

Mr. Fields shook his head and said, "Kea, sweetie, I will see you tomorrow."

"Okay, Daddy."

Mr. Fields looked at me angrily before he made his way down the stairs, leaving me to deal with the wrath of his daughter.

"Are you going to answer my question, Jaquon?" she asked.

"It's not what you think."

"It's not what I think? Wow. We are going to do this again. The 'not what I think' comment, really. That alone is an admission of your guilt. So you're sleeping with her?"

"There you go accusing me again. Shelia needed some help with something," I lied.

"With what? Her pussy," Kea blurted. "Did you dig it out real good, make her scream your name?"

"Yes, Kea. Shelia wanted me to fuck her so I did. And yes, she did scream my name," I admitted but saying it in a sarcastic way.

"Are you seriously standing here telling me this right now or are you playing with me?"

"Does it matter? You are going to think what you want to think regardless of what I say."

"What do you expect me to think? You said you were going to be here when I got here and you weren't. I knew you hadn't gone far since your car is right there in the parking lot. Now when I escort my dad to the door to leave, I see you coming from the biggest freak's apartment. So, you tell me, what am I supposed to think? You were over there hanging drapes?" she bellowed.

"Think what you want to think. I don't care," I said, stepping to her to enter our place.

"How are you going to act like you mad at me?" she asked with an attitude.

"Why shouldn't I be? You've accused me of cheating, so what else is there to talk about?" I said, hunching my shoulders. "Please move."

Kea surprisingly stepped to the side to let me in. I walked past her and entered the living room to see Emory sitting on our sofa holding her new baby.

"Hey, Emory. How are you?"

"I'm good, Jaquon. I guess you are feeling better since you just released yourself, huh."

"Really. You just got here and you are going to start in on me too."

"Kea is my sister. I never thought you were good enough for her."

"Why? Because I don't have a lot money like your rich husband?" I asked.

"No. It's because you used to cheat on her. And now that I know how that feels, I think my sister should leave your cheating behind for good."

I looked at Kea, who was still standing in the doorway, looking at us arguing. "You know what? I'm going to our room to chill. You two have fun catching up," I spat, leaving them to talk more crap about me.

I went into the bedroom and slammed the door closed. I sighed heavily, leaning forward with my hands on my knees, happy to get away from Kea. I don't know how I did it, but I made Kea look stupid for a moment. All that talk I was doing was me winging it. This was buying me time until I figured out what I needed to do next. I expected Kea to follow me into the bedroom but she didn't. Things were silent until I heard what sounded like pounding. I stood, trying to figure out where that noise was coming from. I heard the banging again and realized it was Kea across the hall banging on Shelia's door.

"Bitch, open the door," Kea screamed.

I exited the bedroom and I ran into the living room. Emory was still sitting on the sofa like nothing was going on. I glared at her as she smirked at me as I passed by her.

Going out into the hallway I asked Kea, "What are you doing?"

"I'm trying to ask your little whore what you were doing over there," she said, anxiously shifting from one foot to the other.

Why couldn't she just come into our apartment to deal with this? She had to take it to Sheila. This scared the living crap out of me because I didn't know what Sheila was going to say. She could get angry at the way Kea was coming at her and tell her yes, she was screwing me. I had to think of something before this escalated into something I couldn't deal with.

"Kea, let's go inside and talk," I said, gripping her arm to pull her into our apartment, but she jerked her arm away from me.

"I'm not leaving until she opens this door and tells me what's going on," Kea said, banging on the door again.

"This is crazy," I said, almost pleading with her to stop.

"No. You are crazy if you think I'm going to believe anything that comes out of your mouth."

"Okay. If you think I'm lying, then deal with it. You don't have to ask her anything."

Kea turned to face me and asked, "Are you scared of what she's going to tell me?"

"Of course not," I lied.

Kea turned back to Sheila's door and banged again, yelling, "Open the door, trick."

The door swung open and Shelia stood there wearing a pair of jogging pants and a cut-off tee. "Why are you banging on my door like the po-po?" she asked with a scowl.

"Why are you fucking my man?" Kea asked furiously.

"What are you talking about?"

"I just seen Jaquon leaving your spot."

"And?" Shelia said, crossing her arms.

"And?" Kea said, giggling. "And, what was he doing over here?"

"I needed his help unclogging the toilet."

"Oh, I bet you he was unclogging something," Kea said.

"Think what you want to think, Kea. That's the truth," Sheila said calmly.

I could see now Sheila wasn't trying to out me at all. She had my back.

"Do you know what the truth is?" Kea asked, getting up in Shelia's face.

"First of all, step back up off me," Sheila warned, dropping her hands down by her sides like she was getting ready to swing on Kea if she had to. "I'm not disrespecting you and you damn sure not going to get up in my face and think I'm supposed to take it. Now back up off me before this talking we're doing escalates into something I don't think you want."

Kea didn't budge at first. She glared at Sheila. But Sheila didn't back down either. She stood her ground and gave Kea a look like "do what you need to do."

I turned to see Emory come up behind me. She was standing in our doorway with her arms crossed now like she might jump in this.

"Can you get your sister please?" I asked.

"She's doing fine," Emory said, also glaring at Sheila, who glanced back and forth between the two of them.

Kea took a step back and Sheila crossed her arms again.

"Now, like I told you before, Kea, Jaquon was over here trying to help me unclog my toilet. Whether you want to believe that or not—"

"I don't," Kea said, cutting her off.

Sheila giggled, saying, "Believe what you want to believe. The proof is in the mess I have in my bathroom. I couldn't figure out how to stop the water from running. So I asked him to come and help me. If you don't believe me, then come in and see for yourself."

"Okay," Kea said, pushing past Shelia like she said to come right in.

I eyed Shelia, wondering what she was doing. She didn't give me a hint of anything. We both followed Kea until we were standing in front of Sheila's guest bathroom. Water was everywhere. The carpet was wet right outside the bathroom door and Samara was on her knees surrounded by towels, trying to soak up the water.

"Jaquon, thank you for helping us fix this. If you hadn't, the apartment downstairs would have flooded," Samara said.

Kea looked at me like she couldn't believe what she was seeing. Hell, I couldn't believe it either. They just helped me get away with screwing them both. I almost smirked but tried to keep my face looking upset so Kea could feel bad for thinking I slept with Sheila.

"Do you believe me now?" I asked her, trying to make her feel worse.

"You see. I told you, Kea. We couldn't get that valve behind the toilet to turn. We needed him to try before this mess got worse. He was able to turn the water off and unclog the toilet. Now we just have to clean this mess up before the neighbors below start complaining," Sheila said, laying it on real thick.

Kea looked bewildered. Then she glanced at me with a disappointed look. She turned away from me quickly, trying to hide her expression, but it was too late. I saw the look and a slight twinge of hurt she had. Was she hoping I cheated on her? And if she did, why? The only reason I could think of was this being her way out, her answer to not having to marry me. Hearing Kea's voice snapped me out of my thoughts.

"Look, Sheila. I'm sorry," Kea apologized. "I thought—"

"I know what you thought. I also know what you think of me."

Kea didn't say anything.

"It's okay. You can think what you want. It's not going to change me or the life I lead. So, if you two could excuse us, we have some cleaning to do," Sheila said, giving us the cue to leave her place.

Kea walked away and I followed, but not before glancing back to see Sheila wink her eye at me. As much as I couldn't stand her, she definitely came through for me today. I was busy trying not to get caught when I should have been trying to figure out what Kea's look was about and if all of this was even worth the trouble if she didn't want to be with me.

Chapter 32

Zacariah

I hated funerals. I know there is not one person who likes them. I had only been to one in my entire life and that was my dad's. My dad wasn't the best parent, but he still was my father and him dying affected me. Seeing Derrick in the pain he was in was hard for me because it took me back to that day.

Ms. Shirley's funeral was beautiful. There was singing and praising and the preacher preached a marvelous tribute for her. Still, the entire time Derrick sat there unemotional. Not moving. Not crying. Not saying anything. His zombie-like condition scared me. All I knew to do was be by his side through this. It felt good I could do something for him for once. But the fact that he hadn't said much of anything since the night we found his mother did make me wonder what he was thinking. I knew he was devastated but after his breakdown that night of the incident, Derrick said and did nothing. All he did was sleep. I did manage to get him to eat something but it wasn't much. He wanted to be left alone, which was the opposite of what he needed right now in my opinion.

Jaquon and Kea showed up to the funeral walking in with the family right behind Derrick and his father. He was devastated also but he showed it. Jaquon wept like a child when he saw Mrs. Shirley's coffin. Kea was by his side and cried along with him. We glanced at one another a few times but nothing was ever said. That was fine with me. Losing Ms. Shirley let me know there were more important things to deal with than spending time battling with someone who didn't matter to me anyway.

The unfortunate thing that happened at Ms. Shirley's funeral was that creepy Trinity decided to show her face as well. Seeing her made my blood boil. I don't know why she thought it was fitting. It wasn't like she knew Ms. Shirley. Derrick's mom didn't have a clue who she was. Yet, Trinity was here at her funeral. I knew why. She was hoping she would be the one to console Derrick today. How surprised was she to see me by his side. And I made sure to give her a look like "what now, trick?" She glared at me but I'd been hated on all my life. She was irrelevant and I would treat her as such.

Trinity showing up at the funeral was one thing but showing up her face at Derrick's parents' house was another. Ms. Blue-eyed Monster marched in like she owned the place. She searched the space, speaking and nodding to individuals like she knew them, until she found who she was looking for.

"Hi. I'm Derrick's girlfriend and I want you to know how sorry I am for your loss."

No, this trick didn't. Did she just say what I think she said? His girlfriend? I swear I almost sauntered across the living room and snatched that bitch up by her kinky hair. The nerve of her calling herself Derrick's girlfriend, and for everybody to hear, too.

Derrick's dad looked at her with a frown as he searched the room for me. When his eyes landed on me, he saw I was watching everything with a scowl. I hoped the look on my face also let him know I would not do anything here in his home to disrespect him, or Derrick for that matter, on a day like today. But if Trinity tried anything, I would have to handle my business.

"Thank you," was all Derrick's dad could say. He immediately tried to get away from her. Maybe he felt her evil presence too. I knew this trick was crazy. For her to introduce herself as Derrick's girl proved it, especially since everyone knew I was who he was with.

My thoughts were quickly interrupted when Jaquon approached me. Kea was by his side and she looked at me. Still we didn't say anything to each other.

Jaquon asked, "Zacariah, where is Derrick?"

"He's in his room in the back. You want me to take you to him?" I asked.

"No. I know where it is. Kea, I'll be right back," he said, leaving Kea standing before me.

"So," I said.

"So. How has Derrick been doing?" Kea asked clumsily.

"He's not good," I said, trying to be nice. I was trying really hard to change my image and be this new Zacariah, and being cordial to Kea was a great start.

"I guess he's lucky to have you."

She guessed. I didn't know if Kea was trying to be funny or trying to be nice. I couldn't tell, but I was not about to break bad with her. I didn't know what it was with us and funerals but this was getting old.

"Hello, ladies," a voice said.

Just when I thought things couldn't get any worse, the blue-eyed monster reared her ugly head. She came over smiling from ear to ear like we were friends. Both Kea and I looked at her like she was crazy. And neither one of us decided to speak either.

Trinity nodded. Then she said, "The proper response, ladies, would be to say hello back to me."

"Why are you even here?" I asked.

"I'm here for my man," Trinity retorted.

"I thought Derrick was with her," Kea said, pointing at me.

"He is," I said, sneering at Trinity.

She waved her hand like she was dismissing me and said, "Zacariah's temporary. Derrick is really with me."

I giggled at this deranged heifer. Kea looked at me and a smile came across her face. I swore this was the first smile Kea had ever given me.

"Is there something funny?" Trinity asked, looking back and forth between me and Kea.

"Yes, you're funny. Derrick dumped you, in case you didn't get the memo. Or did you forget? As a matter a fact, he dumped you twice," I reminded her. "Did you return that wedding dress you wore to his front door when he declined wanting to marry you?" I asked smugly.

Trinity's smile wavered and Kea continued to snicker at this nutty woman.

"We are getting married," she spat.

"In your dreams, boo boo. Go find your own man, okay? Because Derrick doesn't want you," I told her.

"This woman really is crazy," Kea murmured to me.

"What did you say?" Trinity snapped, looking at Kea.

"I said things are starting to get a little hazy," Kea answered cynically.

"That's not what you said. You two are standing here, the both of you having had a good man and not even realizing it."

"I have him, sweetie, so let's get that straight," I said, but Trinity continued her tirade, ignoring what I said completely.

"Both of you have screwed him. But neither of you have him. So you two have lost out," Trinity said, glaring at us.

"Trinity, you better leave before things get ugly," I warned, sitting down in a nearby chair. I sat back, crossing my legs, and my arms across my ample chest.

"Derrick came to me when you cheated on him. And you turned out to be his sister," she said nastily, turning her nose up at Kea. "Even after finding out different, you still chose a loser for your husband-to-be."

"Watch your mouth, Trinity, before somebody closes it for you," Kea snapped back.

"Poor little innocent Kea. I always thought you were dense. Too foolish to realize the man you are getting ready to marry is starting everything off with secrets and lies."

I frowned, wondering what Trinity was talking about. Kea shifted uneasily as Trinity continued and dropped a bombshell that left Kea speechless.

Chapter 33

Kea

I don't know what happened. The next thing I remember was some men in suits holding me back from something. I looked down to see Trinity lying on the floor. She was holding her mouth as blood spewed from her busted lip. Zacariah was standing at the side with a "you deserved that" look on her face.

"Calm down," one of the men said to me as he held me back from jumping on Trinity again.

"What is with you and fighting?" I heard Zacariah ask me. "I understand why you did it, Kea, and to be honest I'm happy you punched her in her face because she deserved it. But this is Derrick's mom's house. You really need to calm down," Zacariah urged, trying to talk me down.

For once I agreed with Zacariah. This wasn't the time or the place to handle Trinity. I loved Derrick's mom and dad and didn't mean to disrespect their home or family like this. But Trinity got to me. I mean she really pushed a button that flicked a flame within me, which sparked a fire that turned into an inferno, which created an explosion resulting in me knocking her to her ass.

Trinity picked herself up off the floor with the help of one of the guests. "I see the truth hurts, huh?" Trinity said.

"And if you keep running your mouth, I'm going to hurt you again."

"Don't you know it's against the law to threaten someone? Can somebody call the police please?" Trinity asked coolly to no one in particular. "I want to have this woman arrested for assault and battery."

"No, Trinity. You need to go," Zacariah demanded.

"Not until the police get here."

"This is not the time," Zacariah said.

"Then talk to her," Trinity said, pointing at me. "All I was doing was telling Kea her so-called engagement with Jaquon is based on a lie. She was the one who got mad when I told her the ring she's wearing was bought by me."

"Liar," I roared.

"Ask Jaquon. I took it to him the day I saw him coming from your neighbor's apartment."

Was she serious right now? Hearing her say that did stun me because I was wondering how she knew about Sheila. Trinity had to be telling me some truth since I, myself, saw Jaquon coming from her place the other day. Was he fixing something for her then too? And if Trinity was telling the truth about that, was she also right about this ring?

"Them two sure did look buddy-buddy. If I was you, I wouldn't allow them to be friends because I got the impression the two of them were sleeping together."

"That's enough, Trinity. Please leave," Zacariah insisted, pushing Trinity toward the door.

"What is going on in here?" Derrick asked, entering the space with Jaquon following him.

"Hey, babe," Trinity said, running over to Derrick, trying to plant her lips onto his.

Derrick quickly pushed her away, asking heatedly, "What are you doing here?"

"What's wrong, honey?" she asked obliviously.

Derrick grimaced. He looked at everyone standing around watching. He also noticed the two men still holding me. Jaquon walked over to me and told the men, "Let her go."

The men did as he said and I quickly tried to brush the wrinkles out of my clothes.

"Kea, what's going on?"

"You tell me, Jaquon. Kooky right here told me the ring I'm wearing was given to you by her. Is this true?" I asked angrily.

Jaquon looked around and saw everyone staring at us. "Kea, let's not do this here," he said, caressing my arm.

I jerked from his grasp and said, "No. Answer me. Did she give you this ring?"

"No," he finally answered.

"Why are you lying, Jaquon?" Trinity retorted.

"I'm not lying. Can somebody please escort this woman out of here?" Jaquon asked. "We do not need this disruption on today of all days."

"I can prove it," Trinity said, reaching into her purse and pulling out a slip of paper. Jaquon's eyes got big as saucers as he watched her do this. Trinity walked over to me and handed the slip to me. I looked at Jaquon and everyone else before reading what she gave me. I was looking at a receipt showing the ring, the price, the payment, and Trinity's name at the top of the sales receipt along with her signature at the bottom.

"Then how can you explain this?" I said, pushing the piece of paper into Jaquon's chest. He looked at it and I could have sworn the blood drained from his face.

"How could you?" I asked him. "You embarrass me again," I said.

"Kea, I can explain."

"If Trinity is right about this, then why shouldn't I believe this crazy bitch when it comes to her seeing you and Sheila together? To me it looks like you are back to your old ways."

"No. Look. Don't listen to her. What we have is good."

"Well, it seems to me what we have is based on a lie."

I looked over at Derrick, who was watching along with everybody who just came to support this family in their time of loss. And yet again my life was put in the spotlight, showing how naïve I was to believe Jaquon could be the man I wanted him to be.

"Derrick, I want to say I'm sorry to you and your family," I apologized, looking at him and his dad as I tried to hold back my emotions of being disgraced again.

Derrick's father nodded along with a few other family members, but Derrick didn't react at all. I couldn't read him. To me, he looked like an empty shell.

"Can we please not do this here?" Zacariah asked. "Trinity, you have to go."

I was surprised Zacariah didn't include me, telling me and Jaquon we had to leave also.

"You are the one who needs to leave. Isn't that right, Derrick?" Trinity said, trying to hold his hand; but Derrick snatched himself from her clutches.

"Get the hell out this house," Derrick said through gritted teeth to Trinity.

"But—"

"Get out," he yelled.

Trinity jumped when he screamed and she stared at him like she didn't understand what he was saying. "But, Derrick—"

"How many times do I have to tell you I don't want you? I'm with Zacariah now."

Hearing Derrick say that wounded my already-aching heart because I knew there was a time when he wanted me. Trinity looked at Zacariah along with me. Zacariah stood back, looking at Trinity with a smirk on her face. I knew this was a huge victory for Zacariah, in more ways than one. Now everybody knew who Derrick was with. Jaquon went over to Trinity and grabbed her by the arm.

"Let me go," Trinity yelled, snatching herself from his hand.

"Can somebody call the cops please? We have someone trespassing on private property," Derrick said.

"Are you serious right now?" Trinity asked, staggered by his statement.

To prove how serious he was, Derrick walked over to the coffee table and picked up the phone. He dialed a number and said, "Yes. Can I have an officer come to the address of 555 Brandon—"

"Okay," Trinity blurted. "I'm going to leave."

Derrick looked at her and halted finishing his address to see if she was serious. Trinity looked around the room at everyone.

"You all will be sorry."

Trintiy exited out the door and as soon as Derrick saw her leave, he said, "Never mind. The trespasser has decided to leave." And Derrick hung up the phone.

Chapter 34

Derrick

Not that this day wasn't bad enough, I had to deal with drama being brought into my parents' home. I felt like since Mama wasn't here, all hell was starting to break loose. The nerve of Trinity thinking she could waltz herself up in here after I told her we were done. What was it with her? Why couldn't she understand what we had was over? She needed to leave me alone.

I thought about talking to Mama about my problems but that's when my gut began to ache when the reminder that she was no longer here for me to talk to came to my mind. I closed my eyes, trying to choke back the tears and heartache I felt knowing I could never hold her again. I would never see her smiling face again unless it was in my dreams. And to think I wasted all those weeks away from her, being mad at her because I demanded answers concerning who my father was. I had just gotten her back in my life and someone took her from me.

I sat in the chair in my old room and looked out the window. I could hear the crowd of people who came over to hang out with Dad but I wasn't in the mood. I appreciated them coming to my mother's funeral and supporting us in our time of sorrow, but after that they could have gone home.

I heard a knock at the door and looked at it opening slowly.

"It's me," Zacariah said, still dressed in her black dress and black stiletto heels. "Do you want something to eat?" she asked.

I shook my head.

"Is there anything I can get you?" she asked.

I shook my head again.

"Babe, you have to eat or drink something."

"I told you I didn't want anything," I snapped.

Zacariah dropped her head, bringing her hands in front of her and clasping them together. "Okay. I'm sorry. I will leave you alone," she said, turning to leave.

"Wait," I said.

She halted and turned back to face me.

"Zacariah, I'm sorry for yelling at you. I didn't mean to," I said.

"It's okay."

"No, it's not okay. I'm having a hard time dealing with all of this. My mother is gone and the fact that somebody was bold enough to come up in my house and murder her ticks me off."

She sat down on the bed and didn't say anything as tears began to well up in my eyes again. I didn't think I'd ever cried as much as I had within these past few days.

"Who did this? Was it meant for me? Did somebody want something I had and Mama got in the way?" I asked, throwing random questions out there that had crossed my mind a hundred times.

"Babe, you are going to drive yourself crazy thinking about this. Let the police try to solve this."

"They are not going to do anything. This is going to be another unsolved murder of a black person they don't care anything about. They haven't solved the murder of Essence, so why should I think finding my mother's killer would be any different?"

"You are right," Zacariah said sadly, probably thinking of her best friend. Maybe I shouldn't have mentioned her. I really wasn't trying to upset Zacariah because of the grief I was dealing with but the truth was the truth.

"This was my mother," I said, struggling with my words.

"You know your mother wouldn't want you here being unhappy. You know she's in heaven wishing nothing but the best for you," Zacariah said. "Your mother loved you with everything she had and she wouldn't want to see you in pain like this, sweetie. And I'm not saying this to say you shouldn't feel anything. I just don't want you to let anger and vengeance be what drives you from here on out, babe."

I looked at Zacariah, who looked so sincere in what she was saying. Again she was amazing me. I found myself truly falling back in love with her a little each day. Especially within these past few days with her helping every way she could to make this easier for me and my dad to deal with.

"Thank you, Zacariah."

"It's no problem," she said with a reassuring smile.

There was another tap at the door and I sighed loudly.

"I'll see who it is," Zacariah said, getting up from the bed and going over to the door and opening it.

"Hello, is Derrick in there?" a male voice said.

"Ummmm," Zacariah said, looking back at me. "I don't think he wants to speak to anybody right now."

"Zacariah, it's okay. You can let him in," I told her.

Zacariah stepped back to allow Uncle Gerald to enter my room.

"I'll give you two some time to talk," Zacariah said, leaving the room and closing the door behind her.

I stared at my uncle, who stood there with his hands in the pockets of his black slacks. He had taken off his matching blazer. His red tie popped off the white button-down shirt he wore.

"How are you doing, Derrick?" he asked.

"Not so good," I admitted.

"Shirley was a wonderful woman and she will truly be missed."

I cut my eye at him and said, "And from what I understand you really know how wonderful she was."

"So she's told you?" he asked.

"She sure did. And I can't even be mad at you," I divulged. "I can be mad at what you two did but I can't be mad at you because you didn't know."

"Derrick, if I would have known—"

"You would have, what, left my aunt? You would have left my cousins to raise me and be with Mama?" I asked mockingly.

"I don't know what I would have done. The man I was then and the man I am now are totally different. So, I can't say what I would have done," Uncle Gerald said.

"Are you here trying to play dad now?" I asked.

"I can never replace your father. He has done a wonderful job raising you, Derrick. How can I expect the right of such a title when I haven't put in the work that required me earning it?"

"How could you do this to Aunt Henrietta?"

"Son—"

"Don't call me son," I snapped.

Uncle Gerald held his hands up, saying, "I'm sorry. I didn't mean it like that. What I was going to say is I made a mistake."

"So I'm a mistake."

"I'm not saying that."

"Then what are you saying? My mother was a mistake? You slept with her but that's all it was, just a fling, a roll in the hay, a—"

"Derrick, watch what you are saying to me," he inter-rupted. "I'm still your uncle."

I stood in rage and said, "And now I know I'm your son."

"Keep your voice down," Uncle Gerald said, holding up his hands and looking back at the door like he was expecting somebody to burst in after hearing what I said.

"Why? Why should I? You scared this little secret is going to mess up your happy home?"

He didn't say anything.

"Maybe the family needs to know what type of dog you are."

"If you feel like they should know, then come on. Let's go tell them right now," he dared me. "But please know we are at the home of the woman who agreed to sleep with me, too. Keep in mind we just buried her today, so do you really want to do this?"

I walked over to my uncle and snatched him up. I pulled his shirt so tight in my grasp that I pulled the shirt from being tucked into his pants. "Don't you talk about my mother."

"Derrick, you better let me go."

"Or what?"

"Or it's going to be some furniture moving up in this piece," he warned. "I don't think you ready to disrespect your mother's house, but if you keep disrespecting me, that's exactly what's going to happen."

He was right about disrespecting Mama's home. Her home had already been disrespected enough with the melee of Trinity coming here and the quarrel between Kea and Jaquon. I let go of my uncle and pushed him back. He fixed his shirt and tucked it back into his pants, getting himself together again.

"Let's get back to what we were talking about. Do you really want the last memory of your mother, to her sister, to be the fact that your mother and I slept together creating you?" he said, pointing at me.

I didn't say anything.

"What happened between us was over thirty years ago and I haven't cheated on your aunt since," he admitted.

"Why are you explaining this to me? It's not like I'm going to believe you. You cheated once; why wouldn't you do it again?"

"Because I loved your mother first, that's why," he revealed.

I looked at him, wondering what he was talking about.

"I loved Shirley. I loved her from the first day I met her but at the time she had someone in her life. I'm not going to lie; I didn't let that stop me. I let her know I wanted to be her man and I cared for her. But she never gave me the time of day."

"So you thought it was a good idea to be with her sister and marry her. What was Aunt Henrietta, a substitute?"

"No, Derrick. When I got with Henrietta it was years later. When I married her, I did love her. I still love her. But at the same time old feelings came flooding back for your mother at the time. Despite the life I was trying to make with Henrietta, a part of me still yearned for Shirley."

I sat down and tried to soak up the information he was telling me. This was a lot to take in. Uncle Gerald came over and sat on the edge of the bed.

"Look, Derrick, what me and Shirley did was wrong. It never should have happened. I can't say I regret it because I loved her. And look at what we created in love. That's you," he said, pointing at me. "It's true I didn't know you were my son, but the fact that I can look at you today, when Shirley is no longer here, and know you are the blessing that came from us, I have to be proud of that."

I couldn't say anything. I sat back in the chair and stared out the window as he talked, wishing I had Mama here to be a part of this conversation.

"I told you the decision to let this secret out was your choice. But please think about how it's going to affect everyone."

Uncle Gerald got up from the bed and headed toward the bedroom door. "All I ask you to do is think about it before you make a final decision. As your uncle, I still love you. And despite the fact that I'm your biological father, Derrick, please know I know my role here and I will be your uncle forever."

With that Uncle Gerald left the room. It wasn't five minutes before Zacariah was coming back in.

"Are you okay?" she asked, standing in front of me.

I leaned forward, grabbed her around the waist, and let the pressure of today spill in the form of tears into her stomach. She rubbed my head lovingly, saying, "It's okay. You are going to be okay."

Chapter 35

Jaquon

One minute I was in the room with Derrick, ready to confess the secret of Zacariah being pregnant and having an abortion because she didn't know if it was mine or his, and the next minute we heard a commotion in the living room. Was that a sign for me not to reveal this secret? I took it as such, especially with the evening turning out to be so bad for me.

I shook my head as I turned the corner getting closer to our apartment. Without looking at Kea, I could feel her glaring at me. She was piercing a hole through my head. She probably wanted to put one in it for real. I acted like I didn't see her looking at me. She hadn't said anything since we were in the car and I was glad because I didn't want to hear it. I continued to make my way home. The sooner I got out of this small space with Kea, the better.

As soon as we pulled into the apartment complex parking lot, Kea hopped out of my ride. She slammed my door, pissing me off since the freaking passenger side window shattered. She had to hear it but she kept walking and never looked back. I leaned forward, putting my head on the steering wheel, trying to stop myself from jumping out and smacking the hell out of her. Kea hopped into her ride and sped off.

I sat in my ride, not wanting to get out because I didn't have the energy to move. This day was terrible. I thought my life was supposed to get easier when I tried to change for the better, but it seemed like the more I tried to be this improved person, the more disastrous things happened. Life being a playa was so much better for me than this trying to do the right thing crap.

My cell phone rang and it was an unknown number.

"Yes," I yelled into the phone.

"Testy, aren't we," Sheila's voice said.

"What is it with you? Do you have a tracking device on me?"

"No, silly. I'm looking out my sliding glass door at you."

I looked up to see Sheila standing in the large glass pane waving at me.

"Why don't you really make things obvious?" I said, wondering who else was watching.

"Do you need to relieve some tension?" she asked.

"I'm not coming up to your place, Sheila. You can forget it. Kea already suspects we have something going on," I said, remembering Trinity trying to blow my spot up.

"We can go back to our usual destination."

I thought about it, and you know what? I was down for it today. Why not? I did need to relieve some tension and Kea wasn't here to give it me. If anything, she was causing more stress by making me figure out how I was going to get my window fixed.

"Meet me in an hour," I blurted. I could see Sheila smiling from ear to ear. Without hesitation, I put my ride in reverse, backed out, and proceeded to our spot.

It was two hours later and me and Sheila were lying next to one another in bed. She was right. I did relieve some tension and felt better already. Lying back with both hands behind my head, I looked up at the ceiling thinking about everything that happened today.

"What are you thinking about?" Sheila asked, facing me with her head propped up on the palm of her hand as she rubbed my bare chest.

"I'm thinking about Kea."

"After this good pussy, she's who you are thinking about?" she asked.

"She is my fiancée, Sheila."

"And?" she said.

"And we need to stop doing this," I said.

"You know you don't want to, Jaquon. You keep coming back for a reason."

"I keep coming back because you are blackmailing me."

"I didn't have to twist your arm today," she retorted. And she was right. I willingly came without so much as blinking an eye. "I didn't flood my bathroom to help you not get caught for nothing. By the way, you owe me some money. I need new linoleum floors laid in the bathroom."

"Why do I have to pay you?" I asked.

"Because, I saved your behind, that's why."

That she did. I wondered if it was worth it. *Should I just let myself get caught and deal with the consequences that are to come?* I mean, they were coming sooner or later anyway. At least if my secret affair was out, I wouldn't have to worry myself about trying to hide it.

"Why did you do all that for me anyway?" I asked Sheila.

"Well, I like the sneaking around. It excites me. Call it living on the edge. I don't know. But I knew if you got caught, you would end this with me."

"You're right."

"And let's just say I'm not ready for this to end," she said, stroking my chest. "I was watching everything go down through the peephole that night. I knew I had to figure out something and taking bowls full of water and throwing it on my bathroom floor was what I thought of."

"You thought quick on your feet," I said.

"I had to. Do you know how many women I've had altercations with? Lies have saved my behind many of times."

Curious, I asked, "Why do you sleep with other women's men?"

"Well, most times I don't know the man has a significant other until his crazy wife or girlfriend calls my line wondering who the hell I am. After so many times of getting accused when I had no clue they were involved with someone else, I decided what was the difference? Men lie. The married ones lie. The single ones lie. And I'm always the one caught out there with my pants down low looking like the whore in the end. So now I play the role fate has assigned to me."

It boggled my mind that I understood where Sheila was coming from. I could relate in a way. If you constantly get accused, then why not be what you are being accused of? Yes, I'd cheated on Kea. But as soon as I tried to be faithful and got home late or didn't answer my phone, she always thought I was with another woman. I got tired of the questions and that's why I continued to do my thing. I was accused of doing it anyway. I might as well get something out the deal for being innocent and still thought of as guilty.

I asked Sheila, "Do you think you are settling?"

"What you mean?" she asked.

"I mean you are not a bad-looking woman. Why put yourself out there like that?"

"Who's going to love me, Jaquon? I know what people say about me. I'm a whore, a slut, a tramp, and even a prostitute. This is a small area. As soon as a guy hears my name, they instantly think 'freak.'"

She was right.

"I didn't ask for the title nor was it my intention to be a home wrecker. But you know what, I don't care anymore. I have to forget about what everybody thinks of me and love me regardless," she said with finality.

"Do you think you are really loving yourself if you are degrading yourself by sleeping with all these men? You have decided to be what people label you as even though you said you don't care what people think. In actuality, you want to prove these people right?" I asked, looking at her taking in what I was saying.

Sheila rolled to her back and looked up at the ceiling. Tears began to stream down her face and she wiped them away. I turned to my side and propped my head up in the palm of my hand.

"I didn't mean to make you cry," I told her, using my index finger to wipe her tears away.

"It's okay. I've cried before and I'm pretty sure I will cry again," she said, choking on her words. She pulled the white sheet around her naked chest.

There was a silence between us. For the first time I saw a side of Sheila I hadn't seen before. This was not the woman who acted like she had it together and loved herself some men. The woman lying next to me was a woman who just wanted to be loved.

"I didn't ask for this life, Jaquon. All my life I've been judged because I was the preacher's daughter."

"Preacher?" I asked, flabbergasted by her revelation.

"Yep. My dad is a pastor of a church."

Hearing Shelia say that caused my stomach to drop. Before jumping to any conclusion, I asked her a question.

"What is your dad's name?" I asked nervously.

"The church knows him as Pastor Wilson."

Chapter 36

Jaquon

Was life all about making mine difficult? Of all the women I'd been with I had to end up being blackmailed by the freak-a-leak from across the way who happened to be the daughter to the pastor who was counseling me and Kea before our marriage. I was ready to pack my bags and move away for good. After Sheila revealed that to me, I think I checked out. I heard her talking but none of her words were penetrating the ones echoing loudly in my head. *Pastor Wilson is her dad.*

"Jaquon, are you okay?" Sheila asked, looking over at me.

"Uhmm. Yeah. I'm good."

"You sure?" she asked.

Hell no, echoed in my mind but I managed to say, "Yeah, I'm cool. Go ahead and tell me what you were saying."

She turned back to look up at the ceiling and continued her storytelling.

"Can you believe I'm a preacher's daughter?" she asked jokingly.

"No. Not really."

She chuckled. "It was hard, too. I always had to dress to impress but appropriately. All my skirts and dresses had to come below the knee. And I better not show up to church with no stockings on my legs," she said. "I couldn't go out to certain places and I damn sure couldn't go to any parties. A pastor's daughter doesn't conduct herself like that or else I would be reported to my dad and the church folk would think less of me."

Sheila shook her head in disgust as I listened. "I never understood this about church folk when they were supposed to be the ones helping me and not casting stones at me. They were the ones who turned their backs on me," she admitted.

"What happened with you and your dad?" I asked curiously.

"He pretty much disowned me," she confessed.

"Why?"

"Because I lied and snuck out to this party."

"A party got you disowned?" I asked.

"No, the sex I had with this boy, which got me pregnant, got me disowned," Sheila admitted.

"Whoa."

"Whoa is right."

"So you have a child."

"No. I ended up having a miscarriage. I guess Daddy was so ashamed by what I did and what the consequence ended up being from me having sex before marriage that he prayed my baby away."

"You believe that?" I asked her, hoping a minister wouldn't wish death upon no one.

"He might as well have. He wished for the problem to go away and so he got his wish," Sheila said as more tears streamed down her face.

"He couldn't forgive you?" I asked.

"He claimed he did but the way he treated me after that was so bad that he might as well have disowned me. He became stricter than ever but then acted like he didn't want to deal with me. Every look given to me was one of disappointment and disgust. But in church on Sundays, he played the father who loved his daughter and could turn the other cheek in a second. That only proved to me he was the biggest hypocrite of them all. I got tired of trying to mend our relationship and faking like things were okay when it wasn't. So I left. He didn't want to acknowledge me as his child so I ran away pretending like I didn't have a father."

"When was the last time you talked to your dad?" I asked, intrigued by this side of Sheila.

"It's been over five years. That's crazy, right? Especially with him being in the same city as me," Sheila said.

Hearing that kind of soothed my worry about Sheila being Pastor Wilson's daughter. All I needed was for her to tell her dad about the man she was with, only for him to put two and two together and figure out I was the same man who was getting married to another member of the church.

"Sometimes I want to call him but . . ."

"But what?" I asked.

"I'm not sure if he will talk to me."

"Why do you think that?"

"I know my dad is not proud of me. If the streets know me as this whore, then I know the word has also gotten back to him," she said, turning to look me at me.

What was I supposed to say, "Go and talk with your dad"? I wanted it to be another year or more with them not talking because I was afraid our affair would come out. Call me selfish but I was. I was working too hard at hiding this so-called affair to let the beans be spilled now. I felt like I was in a barrel of water with several holes and my objective was to plug each hole up. The more holes, the harder it got. Right now, I was in a hard position.

On my way back home I realized Kea hadn't tried to call me. I hoped when I pulled up into the parking lot,

I wouldn't have a repeat of Kea making it rain with my belongings again. To my delight, the complex was not littered with my things. And the reason why was because Kea's car was nowhere in sight. She hadn't made it home yet.

I wasn't going to worry about her. She was probably over at her dad's house telling him and her sister Emory what happened today. I guessed that was something else they could hold over my head in order to convince Kea I was not the man for her.

As I made my way into the apartment and turned to close the door, I realized I couldn't. Something was blocking the door from closing completely. I looked down to see a foot placed between the door and the frame. I opened the door, wondering whose foot this was.

"Trinity."

"Surprise," she said with the spookiest smile I'd ever seen on anyone's face.

What I should have done was close the door in her face but I asked, "What are you doing here?"

"I need your help."

"With what?" I asked, stunned that she was here and had the audacity to ask me for anything after she caused the problems between me and Kea earlier. But I wanted to hear what she had to say. Regardless, I had already made up in my mind I wasn't going to help this nutty bitch.

"You need to help me get Derrick back."

"What?" I asked, wondering if she was serious right now.

"Zacariah has brainwashed him."

"Brainwashed?" I asked.

"Yes. She did something to him to make him not want me anymore."

"You know what, Trinity, something is wrong with you. You are on your own with this one," I said, trying to shut the door, but she pushed it.

"Jaquon, please," she begged.

Opening the door again, I sighed my frustration and asked, "Why do you think I would help you after what you did? You basically destroyed my relationship with Kea."

"She treated me bad and I wanted to wipe that smirk off her face."

"You doing that also affected me. But I guess since you and Derrick are no longer together, you don't want to see anybody else happy."

"That's not true," she retorted.

"The reason why you gave me the ring in the first place was to keep Kea away from Derrick, right?"

Trinity nodded.

"But you didn't count on Zacariah," I said, giggling.

"She tricked him," Trinity said.

"And what do you think is going to happen now?"

"What do you mean?"

"You ruined what Kea and I had."

She looked at me with a puzzled look on her face like she didn't comprehend what I was trying to explain.

"Who do you think Kea will run to now that she doesn't have me?"

"Derrick," she said like the light bulb suddenly went off, clueing her in.

"Exactly, but it's not my problem anymore. Good luck with your love life because I know Derrick will not be a part of yours anymore," I said.

"You have to call Derrick and ask him to come over here so I can talk with him."

"He's better off without you," I told her.

"Jaquon, please. Do this for me," Trinity begged.

"You have a good evening," I said, trying to shut the door on her again but she stuck her foot back between the door and the frame again.

Frustrated, I swung the door open and said, "If you don't leave, I'm calling the—"

Chapter 37

Trinity

All Jaquon had to do was help me get Derrick back. I didn't think that was difficult. He and Derrick were back in good standing so he could have called him over here to talk with me. But he wouldn't help me.

"Get help," Jaquon struggled to say.

I looked down at his bloody body and said, "Now you want me to help you, when all I asked you to do was help me. Why? Why should I help you?"

"Please, Trinity, help me," he struggled to say.

I kneeled down beside him, and plunged the blade into him again. Jaquon cried out as his body tensed from the blade tearing into his flesh.

"Is that the type of help you want?" I asked, removing the blade.

Lying on his back, Jaquon moved from side to side like he was trying to get up but I pushed him back to the floor.

"Now, will you help me?"

"Yes," he said.

"Okay. That's what I'm talking about. I don't know why you couldn't do this from the beginning," I said, tapping his cheek with my hand.

I stood to my feet and looked around the apartment trying to locate the phone. I had mine, but I knew when Derrick saw my number pop up on his phone, he wouldn't answer. I had already tried to call him forty-two other times but he ignored me. Searching around I wasn't able to locate a phone.

"You two don't have a phone?" I asked, walking back over to him.

Jaquon didn't say anything. I bent over and ran the blade across his chest, causing a slit in his flesh, and he yelped in pain.

"I asked you a question. Where's your phone?"

"We don't have a phone. We use our cells," he struggled to say.

"Then where is your cell?" I asked.

"I left it in my car."

"Why would you do a dumb thing like that?"

Just for the sheer stupidity of leaving his phone in the car, I ran the blade across this chest again, causing another slit in his flesh to open.

"At the rate you are going, Jaquon, you are going to bleed out so you better help me," I said, watching as blood spewed from him. "Are your car doors unlocked?"

He shook his head.

I looked down and saw his keys lying on the floor next to him. I picked them up and saw the contraption that would unlock his door.

"You better not be lying to me, Jaquon, or I will come back up here and slit your damn throat," I said, tapping the blade on his neck for good measure.

I left the apartment and went down the first flight and then the second flight of stairs when I heard a door slam. I paused, looked up, and realized Jaquon tricked me. I ran back up the flights of stairs to find the door to the apartment was now closed. I jiggled the knob and it was locked.

Banging on the door I yelled, "Open the door, Jaquon."

I didn't hear anything, not even the clicking of him attempting to unlock the door.

Banging again I yelled, "Open this door now."

Still there was nothing. I turned and began to pace.

"Stupid, stupid, stupid, stupid," I said to myself as I grabbed my hair, panicking. And that's when I realized I had the keys in my hand.

"Hah. Hah," I said, laughing. "I got you now, Jaquon. Oh, buddy, you are going to be sorry."

I searched through the keys and tried each one until I found the one that turned to unlock the door.

"Yes," I said to myself.

But when I turned the knob to open it, nothing happened. This man had turned the deadbolt, too, double locking it.

"Oh, you are a smart one," I yelled through the door. "But if you got the key to this lock on these keys, then you should have the key to the deadbolt, too, stupid."

I tried each key again, and again I found the key that turned the deadbolt lock.

This time when I turned the knob to enter, the door opened for me. But only slightly. Jaquon had put the chain on the door. I hit the door with my shoulder a couple of times but I could tell Jaquon had his body against it for reinforcement. How in the world did he have any strength at all? Not after I stabbed him several times.

"Open this door, Jaquon," I demanded through the slight opening, but he didn't say or do anything.

I pushed the door some more, thinking I had enough strength to break this chain, but it wouldn't snap. "If you don't open this door, I swear, Jaquon, I'm going to kill you," I yelled.

"Go . . . to . . . he . . . he . . . hell," he managed to say.

Chapter 38

Kea

I couldn't wait to get away from Jaquon. I mean how many more times did I need to be humiliated before I realized that this man was not the one for me? Our relationship was like trying to fit a square into a circle. It wasn't going to happen unless you were willing to alter the shape of the square to fit. And I knew I had altered myself enough for this man to still end up with the same results of having a man who couldn't keep his dick in his pants. I felt like I needed to call Dr. Phil or the Oprah Winfrey Network to be a guest so they could tell me why I kept going back and doing this to myself.

I drove until I found myself in front of Terry's home. We hadn't spoken since she walked out on me. And honestly, she had every right to do so. I was a little fearful showing up because I didn't know how she would receive me. I was coming to her again because of the drama that was happening in my life. I could have gone to Dad's house, where he and Emory were, but I didn't want to put my stress on them when they both had their own issues going on. I swear I felt like my family was falling apart. For a moment, I felt like I was the one who had it together, but who was I kidding? I was fooling myself and I was the only one who couldn't see it until now.

I knocked at Terry's door gently and waited for the door to open. No one came to the door. I knocked again, this time a bit harder. I could hear Terry approaching and she must have looked through the peephole and seen it was me because it took her longer than usual to open her door. I guessed she was contemplating whether she should. Terry decided to open the door and she didn't look happy to see me.

"Hey, Terry," I said, seeing her standing in front of me wearing some black-rimmed glasses, black jogging pants, and a red tee.

"How can I help you?" she asked impersonally. I could see she wasn't going to make this easy for me.

"Can I talk to you?" I asked sincerely.

Terry stepped to the side and allowed me to enter her place. On her coffee table sat a laptop and a bunch of folders, a few open, letting me know she was working as usual.

"Please, have a seat," she said, gesturing me to the chair that didn't have anything in it. Terry's place was neat besides the papers she was working on. One thing about her, she kept an immaculate home.

I sat down in the chair I hadn't seen before. "I see you purchased some new furniture."

"Yep. Got this about six months ago," she said, picking up her laptop as she sat down on the sofa and placed it in her lap. "But you would have seen it sooner if you came by to see me more often."

I nodded, knowing she was right yet again. My stomach began to churn at the awkwardness of our conversation. I couldn't remember a time ever when me and Terry were in a place like this in our friendship.

"Wow. So it's been that long since I've been over here."

"Yep," she said curtly, tapping away.

There were no words spoken for a moment. Just the tapping of her fingers on her laptop. I wondered if this was a mistake, but knew I had to apologize to her for my behavior. Rubbing my knees with my hands over and over again to alleviate the stress that was built up within me, I began to speak.

"Look, Terry, I miss you. I want to apologize for how I acted the last time we saw each other."

Terry kept tapping away. She didn't look up one time while I was talking and kept ignoring me. I knew she had to hear me so I kept going.

"You were right. You have always been there for me. I have been so caught up in my own life that I didn't take the time to see what was really going on in yours."

Terry stopped tapping. She took her glasses off and looked over at me. "You really hurt my feelings, Kea."

"I know and I'm sorry. You are my best friend, the one who tells me like it is. This time I didn't want to hear the truth."

"So you want me to lie to you from now on?" she asked.

"No. I want you to be you. That's why I have you as my friend. Any truth I need to know, I know I can count on you to give it to me straight. I love that about you and I don't want that to change."

Terry crossed her arms and sighed before speaking again. "Is this the only reason why you are here? Because I feel like there is something else going on," she said, sensing I had to be here for another reason.

"Well, I do have some things going on. Today has been a bad day."

"And you need me again," she said coldly, probably not believing my apology due to me possibly having an ulterior motive to be here.

"Terry, I miss talking to you. You are my sounding board."

Terry stared at me before asking, "So what has Jaquon done this time?"

I lowered my head, wishing for once our conversation didn't have to be about him. Why couldn't we talk about the weather or the best mixed drinks to consume? But as usual our conversation always stemmed from Jaquon.

"How did you guess?" I asked shamefully.

"Isn't it always him?" she said with an attitude. "And plus, I know he's back to cheating on you again. I was wondering how long it was going to take for you to find out this time."

Hearing Terry say this baffled me. I frowned, wondering how she knew, because she sounded confident with what she was telling me. "How do you know?" I asked.

"Because, I have proof."

"What do you mean proof?"

For a minute I wondered if her anger turned into revenge, getting back at me by sleeping with Jaquon. I prayed this wasn't the case because I couldn't take another devastating event happening in my life right now. I'd seen enough *Maury* shows to know your best friend sometimes became your worst enemy. As much as I loved Terry, she seemed like the type who would get back at me like this.

I watched Terry pick up the laptop and place it on her coffee table. She searched through her MK purse, which was on the sofa with her, and pulled out her cell phone. Punching in her code, she began searching for something. Then after she found what she was looking for, she scooted closer to me, sitting on the edge of the sofa. She leaned over and handed me her phone.

"That's my proof," she said, pointing at the screen.

I looked at her phone and saw Jaquon getting out of an elevator.

"Where did you take this?"

"I was at a late business meeting in a hotel when I saw him," she said.

"But what does this prove?" I asked, still not wanting to believe that Jaquon was at a hotel cheating on me.

"Swipe to the next picture," Terry told me.

I did what she told me and was stunned when I saw my neighbor exiting the elevator moments later. I looked at Terry, who sat back, crossing her arms again.

"Coincidence right?"

All I could do was shake my head in disgust. He was all out in the open with his infidelity. This information had come to me three times. First, I saw him leave her place with my own eyes. Second, Trinity told me about the two of them together. And now Terry had pictures of them leaving a hotel. If this wasn't evidence enough he was back to sleeping around, I didn't know what else could convince me.

"I didn't see them leave together or get in the same car together, but come on, Kea, it's obvious Jaquon had to be with her. Who else could he have been with?" she asked. "And she's a whore."

The distress I was feeling was more than I could stand. Tears welled up in my eyes and I began to sob.

"Kea, please don't cry," Terry said, sitting back up on the edge of her sofa and placing her hand on my knee.

"You tried to tell me and I wouldn't listen."

"You love him. You had faith that he would do the right thing this time and there was nothing wrong with that. I shouldn't have gotten mad at that. But I did because I hate to see you like this," she revealed. "When you hurt, I hurt. You are my best friend and I love you with all my heart."

"This day just keeps getting worse. I didn't know where to go or who to turn to. I drove until I ended up here."

Terry slid over and patted the empty space next to her. I got up and went over to sit beside her. She took my hands into hers. "You deserved way better than this."

"I know. Call me a sucker for love." I chuckled.

"No. You are loyal and love hard," Terry said.

"Look where that has gotten me. I'm a broken-down mess," I said, wiping my tears.

"What are you going to do?"

"Terry, I have to end it with him. I can't trust him. I never did. And now I want to kick myself because I let the man I truly love go."

"You can get him back," she said.

"No, I can't. I haven't told you the worst part yet."

"Worse than Jaquon cheating on you?" Terry asked.

I nodded. "Derrick is back with Zacariah."

Terry leaned back and blurted, "What?"

"Yes. Girl, we have so much to catch up on. Not only has this day been awful, but this entire week has been this way. Today we buried Derrick's mom."

"Whoa, whoa, whoa, whoa, whoa," Terry kept saying. "Wait a minute. She's dead?"

"Yes."

"What in the hell is going on? I haven't been gone that long."

"Right. My sister is back. My mother got twenty-five to life. And to top everything off, you show me a picture confirming Jaquon's cheating."

"Hold up. You are going too fast. I know I'm smart and beautiful but that's neither here nor there," she said, causing me to giggle. "But you are going to have to go back and tell me what's been going on," Terry said, turning to face me as she put her feet up on the sofa, tucking them beneath her.

"Before I get into everything, can I please use your bathroom?" I asked.

"Sure," she said, pointing. "You do remember where it is, don't you?"

"Yes," I said, standing.

"But go in the one in my bedroom because I'm remodeling the guest bathroom. Please don't judge me by the way it looks," she joked. "I'm going to fix us a glass of wine."

"Okay," I said as I made my way to her bedroom. I had to pass the guest restroom on my way to her bedroom and I saw it had been completely gutted. There was nothing in there but studs. No tub, no toilet, no sink, nothing. I shook my head, taking this as my friend's hand itching to spend some of that big money she was making.

I walked into Terry's bedroom and was amazed at how tranquil the space was. She had remodeled this space also. The floor was covered with this off-white Berber carpet. The walls were painted a soothing light blue. A circular metal chandelier hung over her king-sized bed, which was covered with a white duvet cover. Accent mosaic pillows with blues, browns, and tans adorned it. Two chrome lamps with white shades sat atop two white tables positioned on each side of her bed. Two plush auburn-colored chairs were positioned in front of a fireplace she also had installed. Directly across from her bed was a massive bookshelf, which went all the way up to the ceiling and had this cutout to fit what looked like a fifty-inch flat screen. Books also filled the shelves with pictures and white roses. Admiring her bedroom, I forgot I had to go to the bathroom, which pretty much matched her bedroom.

I did what I had to do and walked back out into her space, again admiring the work she put in to making her home look beautiful. I especially loved the bookshelf. I walked over and looked at the books she had, wondering if I could get one to read. Reading books always relaxed me. As I looked at the books, I saw a picture of me and her smiling from ear to ear when we went on vacation together a couple of years ago. We looked so happy and

I grinned at our joyful times. But my smile was quickly replaced with a scowl. One picture caught my eye in particular. I didn't understand why she had this picture on her shelf.

"What is taking you so long? Did you fall in?" Terry asked as she entered her room. I quickly moved away from the bookshelf and moved over to the lamp, acting as though I as admiring it. I hoped she didn't see me, and based on the way she was acting, she hadn't.

"I love what you did with this space," I said, trying not to sound nervous.

Putting her hands on her hips, she said, "I love it too. It came out even better than I could imagine."

"This space is a lot more calming than you are," I joked.

"True. I needed a space to complement my strong presence but also to mellow me out," she said.

"You did an amazing job with this. I feel better already."

"Yeah, right," she said, frowning.

"It's true." I walked over to Terry and grabbed her hand. "Thank you."

She squeezed my hand saying, "No problem. You know I love you, girl."

"I love you too," I told her back.

"Now, let's go back so you can catch me up on what's been going on," Terry said, pulling my hand to follow her.

I smiled and went with my friend. As open as she wanted our relationship to be, I wondered how real she was being with me. I wanted to question her about the picture but I decided to leave it alone since we had just started talking again. I had enough problems of my own to deal with. I had to confront Jaquon about his cheating and I knew without a shadow of a doubt tonight was not going to be good. Little did I know how right I would be.

Chapter 39

Kea

I was not ready to do this but I knew this confrontation had to happen. By morning I was determined Jaquon and I would no longer be together. I walked up the stairs leisurely, looking at my cell phone, and saw it was after nine. His car was in the parking lot so I knew he was here, unless he was across the way with Sheila again.

When I got to my door, I saw it was cracked. The chain was on the door, which meant I couldn't get in my own damn house. Was he trying to tick me off? What type of game was he playing?

"Jaquon," I yelled.

There was no movement, which pissed me off even more.

"Jaquon," I yelled louder, this time banging on the door as hard as I could to wake him up. My knocks were loud enough to wake up everybody else within our building.

That's when I saw his hand. What was he doing on the floor? I squinted and saw his hand was covered in what looked like blood. My heart dropped. Panic set in as Jaquon fell to his back and that's when I saw his clothing drenched in blood.

"Jaquon," I screamed hysterically. "Baby, can you get the chain?" I asked. He tried to turn to his side as he struggled to get up but he fell back again.

"Jaquon," I called out again, fearfully wondering what happened to him. "Jaquon, get up. Let me in," I yelled. He mumbled something but I couldn't make out what he was saying.

I pulled out my cell and dialed 911.

"911, what is your emergency?"

"Something is wrong with my boyfriend. He's lying on the floor bleeding. I need an ambulance at the East Brandon Apartments. We are in apartment F. The door was cracked open but it's held by the chain so I can't get to him. Please hurry," I yelled into the phone.

"Ma'am, calm down."

"Please get someone here now," I demanded.

"EMTs and the police have been dispatched. But please stay on the line with me until—"

I didn't bother to stay on the line to hear anything else. As soon as she let me know the police and EMTs were on their way, I didn't need anything else from her.

Panicking, I went across the hall and banged on Sheila's door. It took her awhile but she finally came to the door, swinging it open, saying, "What is your problem? Jaquon is not here."

"I need your help breaking down the door."

"Do what?" she asked, looking at me like I was crazy.

"Sheila, it's Jaquon. Something's wrong," I said, going back over to my door with Sheila following me.

She peeked in and saw him lying on the floor, unconscious. "What happened?" she asked with her hand over her mouth.

"I don't know. Did you hear anything? Did you see anything?"

"No!" she answered frantically.

"You didn't see that the door was cracked open?"

"Kea, I didn't pay attention. I didn't see anything," she said with stress in her voice.

The one time I needed her to pay attention, this nosy trick hadn't seen anything. "Help me get this door open."

"Mr. Hanks. Now Jaquon. What is going on around here?" Sheila said, beginning to sob.

"Sheila. Shut up and help me."

"But won't we hurt him if we break the door down? He's right there in front of it. We need something to cut the chain," she suggested.

As dumb as I thought this woman was, she actually was talking with some sense. I guess I shouldn't have judged this trick by her appearance or the lack of clothes she always wore, like right now in a cut-off tee and bootie shorts.

"Do you have anything to cut this chain?" I asked urgently.

She ran into her apartment. I could hear her searching for something. I looked through the crack in my door and saw Jaquon was still unconscious. He was not moving at all and for a moment I wondered if he was dead.

I called out to him, "Jaquon. Baby, stay with me. Don't you leave me."

He moaned, which gave me some hope. He was not dead. I knew we needed to get to him soon though or else he wouldn't make it.

Sheila came running back out into the hallway with some tool. She said, "I found my chain cutters."

I frowned, wondering why Shelia had any tools in her place at all, especially chain cutters. She didn't look like the type of woman who would have tools. The only tool she was used to working with was dicks. But I wasn't about to ask her. She pushed me to the side and put the cutters up to the chain and squeezed. Eventually, the chain was cut and we were able to open the door. To my dismay, blood was everywhere. Jaquon was saturated more than I thought.

"Oh my goodness. Oh my goodness," Sheila said, walking in with me. She dropped the tool to the floor and covered her face again once she saw all the blood.

Kneeling down beside Jaquon, I put my head down to his chest to hear his heartbeat. He was still alive.

"Go get me some towels," I told Sheila. She did as I asked and ran to my bathroom. I lifted his shirt and saw puncture wounds in this chest and stomach area.

"Jaquon, baby. Please don't die," I begged.

Sheila came running back into the living room with a handful of towels. She dropped to her knees on the other side of Jaquon and helped apply pressure to the wounds we could see. Jaquon moaned a bit when we pressed down on his stomach and chest. I looked over to see Sheila with tears streaming down her face. She looked at me but didn't say anything. I wondered if these tears were streaming down her face because she had some feelings for my man. But now was not the time or the place to question her about her relationship with him.

It was not long before the paramedics and police were entering and pushing us out of the way so they could work on him. They sliced his shirt open to see his injuries.

"Ma'am, can you tell me what happened?" an officer asked me.

"I don't know. I found him like this. The door was cracked but I couldn't get in because the chain was on the door. My neighbor had chain cutters and we cut it to get to him," I explained, looking at Sheila, who was sitting on the floor watching.

"He's flat lining," I heard one of the paramedics say.

Another EMT ran over with some paddles I figured were going to be used to shock him. Sheila was to the side on her knees, rocking back and forth, crying hysterically now.

She said, "Jaquon, please don't do this. Don't you leave me."

I stared at her and back at the cop who was observing what was going on. The police officer asked, "And you said she's your neighbor?"

I nodded and he wrote something down in his little pad. This didn't look good at all. I was his fiancée but Sheila was the one crying like he was her man. This just further let me know the two of them had something going on. I knew the officers at the scene were thinking the same thing by the way they were looking at me and Shelia. They probably thought I did this to him. I'd wanted to hurt Jaquon plenty of times and maybe even a couple of occasions I wished he was dead. But I never meant it. I loved this man. As hurt and angry as I was at him, I couldn't show my emotions because Jaquon was fighting for his life. I felt like I had to be strong for him.

"We got a pulse," the paramedic said.

Sheila yelled, "Thank you, God."

Picking Jaquon up off the floor and placing him on the stretcher, the paramedics rushed to get him to the ambulance so they could transport him to the hospital. I hoped he wouldn't flat line again.

"Kea," a voice behind me called out and I turned to see who it was.

"Daddy," Sheila said.

"Sheila," Pastor Wilson blurted, running over to Shelia, who stood to her feet.

Daddy? I thought.

"What? What is going on?" he asked, confused about what was going on.

Sheila fell into Pastor Wilson's arms. He embraced the panic-stricken woman.

I forgot I called him over to help me deal with Jaquon and his cheating ways tonight. I didn't want a repeat of me tossing his things out and it being another altercation, so I thought having the pastor here would keep things orderly. But, as fate would have it, the situation just got a lot more confusing for me.

Chapter 40

Zacariah

I was woken up out of my sleep by the ringing of Derrick's cell phone. I peered over at the clock and saw it was after one in the morning. *Who in the world could be calling his phone this time of the morning?* Then Trinity's crazy behind crossed my mind.

My back was to Derrick and I turned to see him pick up his cell phone.

Groggily he said, "Hello."

I could hear a woman's voice but I couldn't make out who it was and what she was saying. I quickly got my answer as to who it was with Derrick's next question.

"Kea, what's wrong?"

Really? I thought. Would I ever get rid of these women who thought it was okay to call him anytime they felt like it? Anger started to rise within me until I saw Derrick jump up out of the bed with urgency.

"I'll be right there," Derrick said. He hung up the phone and started throwing on his clothes quickly.

This was the first night the two of us had slept in the same bed since I'd been back and now it was interrupted by something Kea called him about. I was infuriated. I asked, "What's going on?"

"That was Kea."

"I figured that by you calling her name," I said with an attitude. Derrick looked at me but continued to dress.

"What is it this time, Derrick?" I asked, unconcerned.

"It's Jaquon. He's at the hospital. He's been stabbed."

"And what, she's calling you to bail her out of jail for trying to kill him?" I asked.

I figured she was the one who stabbed him, which was why she was calling Derrick. After what happened tonight, it seemed like Kea was on the edge of exploding. I couldn't blame her. Jaquon was a compulsive cheater.

"She's not in jail. She's at the hospital with him."

"She didn't do it?" I asked.

"Look, Kea . . ."

Hearing him say her name caused my eyebrows to rise. *No, he didn't just call me another woman's name.* He knew he made the mistake and closed his eyes after seeing the expression on my face.

"I'm sorry, Zacariah. I didn't mean to—"

"Didn't mean to, what, call me Kea? I can't believe you did that," I retorted, feeling insulted.

"Look. I said I was sorry. I'm upset and got confused because I just got off the phone with her. My best friend is in the hospital."

"And?"

"And, I don't want anything to happen to him."

"Well, you could have fooled me by the way you have been shunning him these past few weeks."

"We are working on our friendship. Just because I haven't been dealing with him doesn't mean I don't still love him."

"Is Kea somebody you love too? Are you sure you are not running to the hospital to be by her side?" I asked.

"No, Zacariah. Look, I can't do this with you now. I have to leave."

Derrick snatched his keys off the dresser and didn't wait for me to say anything else. He bolted out of the room. Moments later I heard the beep signaling him opening the door and shutting it behind him. I lay in the bed angrier than I had been in a long time. Here I was being the good girlfriend, being patient and kind and faithful, too. And he still had the audacity to call me Kea.

I punched the bed and screamed to let out my frustration. This trying to be a better person was getting to me. Granted, I was in his bed, in his house and back in his life but I wondered if it was worth it. Especially when it seemed like I was the one doing the majority of the work trying to make this so-called relationship succeed.

Then I thought about Fabian. He had been crossing my mind a lot but I pushed him to the back of my mind, wanting things to work with Derrick. A part of me missed him a lot. He told me to call him anytime I needed him and I felt like I needed to hear his voice now.

I reached over to the side table and picked up my cell, which was plugged in. I unplugged my phone and fell back to my back. Scrolling through my contacts, I came across Fabian's name. I stared at it, debating whether I should do this. *Should I risk all I worked so hard for just to hear his voice?*

I decided yes and clicked his name and then the call button. I saw it was ringing and hesitantly put the cell to my ear. It rang about four times and just when I was about to hang up he answered.

"Hello."

I didn't say anything.

"Hello," he said again.

"Um. Fabian."

"Zacariah?" he asked, not sure if it was me.

"Yes, it's me."

I heard some scuffling around and then him groaning. I wondered if he had another woman beside him. Immediately, I could feel some jealousy enter me. Why was I jealous? He was not my man. Still the thought of another

woman being next to him caused me to feel some type of
way about it.

"Did I interrupt anything?" I took a chance in asking.

"No. I was sleeping. That's all."

"I'm sorry to wake you."

"Naw. It's okay. I told you to call my anytime. Is
everything okay?"

I hesitated before saying, "Yes. No. I don't know."

"Something has to be wrong for you to be calling me at
this time. Is your man home?" he asked.

"He just left."

"That man was crazy enough to leave a beautiful
woman like you home alone?"

His compliment caused my center to stir with ecstasy.
Just the deepness of his voice was a turn-on for me as
I imagined for a moment being in his arms instead of
Derrick's.

"I think calling you was a mistake," I said apprehen-
sively.

"Zacariah, please don't hang up."

"I never should have woken you up. I'm going to hang
up."

"Don't hang up," he said sternly. "If you hang up, I'm
coming over there."

I frowned, saying, "You don't know where I live."

"Yes, I do," he admitted.

"How?" I asked curiously.

"I followed you."

Okay. This was getting a little spooky. Why was he following me? And even more important than that, when?

"Before you start saying I'm stalking you again, I'm
not, even though my statement does make me look like a
creeper."

I giggled and said, "You think?"

"Naw, I saw you a week or so ago coming from the hair salon. I was at the barbershop next door. I got excited when I saw you looking all good but I was undecided about approaching you."

"So you decided to follow me?"

"Yes. And again I know that makes me look crazy but I had to know where you were going. I hopped in my ride, and it just so happened you pulled into this nice two-story house, which I figured was your man's place."

I didn't know what to say to this. Maybe I should have hung up because this was weirding me out. But my interest was so piqued by him, I couldn't hang up.

"I know you told me you are with someone but I miss you, Zacariah."

"You barely know me," I told him.

"I know enough. Ever since you threw your drink in my face, I cared for you."

"Now you talking crazy," I retorted.

"No. The first time I saw you, I felt like you were the woman for me. Call it love at first sight. The love arrow shot me in the heart because I can't get you off my mind. I think about you every single day wondering if you are okay or if you are happy. Are you happy, Zacariah?" Fabian asked.

I paused to think about his questions. I responded by saying, "I don't know."

"If you don't know, then I'm going to take that as a no. Someone happy wouldn't have to think about it. You faltered."

I took in a deep breath.

"Zacariah, come see me."

My heart pounded at the thought of seeing Fabian again. My body tingled at the thought also.

"Please," he begged.

It was late and I didn't know when Derrick was getting back home. What if I went and didn't make it back home before Derrick made it back? Then it would be obvious that I was with someone else. Did I want to risk it?

"Zacariah, are you coming?"

Hesitantly I said, "Yes. I'll come over. Text me your address."

Chapter 41

Derrick

I ran into the hospital's emergency room entrance as fast as I could, hoping I would see Kea there but I didn't see her. I went up to the desk and said, "I'm looking for patient Jaquon Mason. Where is he?"

"And you are?"

"His brother," I lied.

"Sir, your brother is in surgery as we speak. His fiancée is in the waiting room around the corner. It's the second door on your right," the nurse directed me.

I ran until I found the room. When I entered, I saw Kea sitting in a chair with her head down in the palms of her hands.

"Kea," I called out to her.

She looked up and stood. I went over to her and embraced her as she released her emotions on my shoulder. We held each other for a long moment before she pulled away from me. She was wiping her tears.

"What happened?"

"I don't know. When I got home, he was lying on the floor bleeding to death. There was so much blood, Derrick," she said.

I sat her down and sat in the chair next to her, never letting her hand go as I held hers in mine. "Is he going to be okay?" I asked nervously.

"I don't know. You didn't see him. He looked so pale. He flat lined twice," she stressed.

"But he's alive, right?"

"Yes. They had to rush him into surgery. I haven't heard anything yet," she said with more tears streaming down her cheeks. "If only I was there," she said.

"Don't blame yourself. You didn't do this."

"I know but still. I should have been home. I was so mad at him for what happened at your mom's house and I had to get away from him."

"You did what was best for you in that moment. You didn't stab him, did you?"

She looked at me and said, "No."

"Well then. Stop blaming yourself."

She began to break down and struggle to speak. I squeezed her hand waiting for whatever she was going to say.

"I was going to break up with him tonight."

Hearing her say that stunned me. But then again it didn't after what when down at my parents' home. I nodded and continued to listen to her.

"He's still cheating on me, Derrick."

"How do you know? You can't go on the word of Trinity."

"I don't need Trinity's word because Terry had proof. She had a picture of him leaving a hotel. That alone was suspicious since he didn't have a reason to be there. Then moments later someone I knew came stepping out the elevated."

"Who?" I asked.

"Sheila, my neighbor from across the way."

"That's messed up."

"You telling me. Jaquon has cheated on me way too many times to count but he had to sleep with the woman right there where we lived?" she asked me, frowning. "I know they have something going on by the way she broke down when she saw him tonight. She acted like she loved him, Derrick," Kea said with a crackling voice.

"Stop talking about it, Kea. You are making yourself more upset."

"I am upset," she yelled.

"And that's understandable."

"When I saw her crying over him, for a split second, Derrick, I wished he would die," Kea admitted.

Again her words staggered me from speaking. I knew how she felt because I'd been where she was. When Zacariah cheated on me, I wanted to wrap my hands around her throat and squeeze until she couldn't breathe again. The pain hurts so much that you want them to hurt as bad as you do and sometimes you think of desperate ways to make it happen. That's why so many men and women snap when they find out about an affair. A few are in prison today for that very reason; not being able to control their anger.

"I'm a terrible person right?" she asked.

"You are human, Kea."

"That's why I blame myself. I wished death upon him and he flat lined. I could have said a prayer but no, I wished him dead," she kept repeating.

I leaned over and pulled Kea onto my shoulder and let her release the pain built up within her. She was on an emotional rollercoaster that was going a hundred miles a minute and didn't look like it was going to stop anytime soon.

Kea leaned up, wiping her face with the palms of her hands. She said, "I wish I would have chosen you."

The tearful look in her eyes let me know she meant what she was saying. I'd wanted to hear that from her for so long.

"Seeing you with Zacariah was like a dagger to my heart. The only person I can blame is myself. Seeing you with her solidified the fact I still love you, Derrick. I made an irrational choice and chose to let you go and it was the dumbest mistake I've ever made in my life."

Hearing Kea say those words caused me to melt. It was like all the cloudy days I'd been having were quickly brightened with the admittance of her love for me.

"I still love you too, Kea."

She smiled and I leaned over and placed a passionate kiss on her lips. We went deep and hard, trying to make up for all the lost time we missed with one another. As bad as the timing was, I couldn't help myself. I'd dreamed about this moment for so. I didn't want this moment to end, for fear it wouldn't happen again. When we released our lips from one another, Kea reached up and caressed my face.

"I've wanted to do that for so long," she admitted.

"Me too," I retorted.

"Now what?" she asked.

"Honestly, I don't know, Kea. The one thing I'm sure about is I don't want to waste another moment being away from you."

"I agree," she said, smiling, and we leaned in once more to show just how much we loved one another.

Chapter 42

Zacariah

The sun was coming up when I got home and I knew Derrick was going to be sitting on the couch when I walked in. I was afraid to go home because I didn't want a repeat of what happened before when he kicked me out of his house. The only difference this time, I made sure to clean myself up. Still, coming in at this hour would be hard to explain. I didn't have Essence here anymore to be my backup. Man, did I miss her. I thought about her every single day and knew I would never have a friend like her again.

Hitting the button to the garage, it eased up. I saw that Derrick's car was not in his usual space. This let me know he hadn't made it home. I let out a sigh of relief. I was happy I wouldn't have to explain where I'd been but I was upset he wasn't home yet. I wondered if Kea was the reason for him not showing up at home yet.

Regardless, my night with Fabian was amazing.

We were in the throes of passion seconds after I arrived. As soon as he saw me standing on his doorstep, he snatched me up in his arms and placed his thick lips onto mine, kissing me deeply. I didn't resist. I didn't want to. He pulled me into his place and slammed the door behind me with our lips never disengaging from one another. Very few words were said. Fabian picked me up and carried me to his bedroom. I appreciated his take-charge attitude and longed for someone to show me the affection he was giving me. And Fabian's feelings for me were genuine.

The cologne he was wearing was so intoxicating. I buried my face in his neck and began nibbling on it. He moaned as he made his way to his room. His dreads were tied back and he looked sexy as ever. Fabian definitely knew how to take care of himself, from his body, to his teeth, to his hygiene. This man was a well put together piece of dark chocolate.

When we got to Fabian's room, he put me down on his bed and lay beside me. I looked around the space to see this man took the time to light several candles and play some soothing music, which relaxed me even more in his arms. He kissed me deeply again.

Coming up for air he finally spoke, saying, "I'm glad you came. Now it's time for me to show you just how happy I am to have you here.

I smirked and said, "I hope you can keep your word."

"Oh, I can keep my word and I'm going to back it up. Just watch me," he said in his seductively deep voice.

Damn this man was sexy. He kissed me again and let his hand roam my body, exploring areas he'd never ventured to before, all the while staring into my eyes. I interrupted our gaze with another kiss to his lips. My tongue roamed his mouth as his hand pushed its way down my pants and into my underwear. I spread my legs, making it easier for him to penetrate my center. I moaned when his fingers pushed through my opening and dipped into my wetness.

I released our kiss long enough to moan with pleasure as Fabian nibbled on my neck. In and out his fingers went slowly moving at a pace that made me want to push his fingers deeper inside me. My head rose with the circular movement on my clit. I was on the brink of releasing and bucked my hips to meet his fingers. I was cumming. I reached down and pushed his hand farther into me as my body jolted with pleasure. My creamy center oozed. My body quivered. When the sensation of my climax subsided some, my body relaxed. Fabian removed his fingers from inside me and brought his drenched fingers to his lips sucking each one clean. I smirked, waiting for my turn to taste his cream.

I leaned up and tugged at his belt. Fabian fell to his back and let me unfasten his pants. He lifted his hips so I could pull his pants down. His bulge was nice. I couldn't wait to see the real deal. With his pants down around his ankles, I tugged on his boxers to pull them down also. I was eager to meet his dick. I hoped I wouldn't be working with anything small and my wish came true as this monstrous extension damn near smacked me in the face. His dick was nice and thick like I like it. I wrapped my left hand around the base of him and watched as the head swelled with anticipation. I looked up at Fabian, whose head was lifted to watch me place my mouth on him. I smiled and did not want to disappoint as I took his girth into my mouth. Fabian bit his bottom lip as he thrust his hips upward. I pushed my mouth down as far as I could and watched his head drop back to the bed. His hand made its way to my head and he gripped a handful of my hair. This turned me on. I knew it did the same for him because his dick began to swell even more. My head bobbed up and down his shaft, slurping and sucking him to meet to the same brink of ecstasy he brought me to.

Fabian lifted his head saying, "Oh shit."

I loved to hear him. He gripped my hair tighter as his hips thrust upward faster.

"Zacariah," he called out.

I kept bobbing up and down sucking him deep. His shaft grew longer and thicker. He was about to cum.

"Zacariah, wait," he told me but I didn't stop. I wanted to know what this man tasted like.

"Wait," he begged but that only encouraged me to suck him harder and deeper.

"Babe, I'm about to cum," he warned. He jerked my hair back trying to pull me away from him but my jaws clamped down around him. When he realized I wasn't going to stop, he thrust upward gripping the back of my head, moaning. The head of his manhood reached the back of my throat as his hot liquid shot into my mouth. Just like me, his body convulsed with each squirt. When he stopped moving, I bobbed slowly up and down for good measure enjoying the residual effect of his climax. I watched as his stomach heaved up and down. He was spent but I had gotten a second wind.

"Are you ready for round two?" I asked him as I climbed on top of him. He looked up at me flirtatiously like he didn't believe I was ready to continue this. But when my hot center came in contact with his dick, he groaned. I moved my hips back and forth, sliding my drenched center along the length of his semi-hard manhood. I didn't have him in me yet. I was doing this because of the way it felt against my clit. I could cum with the friction of him. But I was also doing this to bring his dick to full capacity to enter me. I loved when a man recovered quickly.

Fabian gripped my hips as he bit his bottom lip again. I got excited by the muscles in his chest flexing. I lifted myself up and reached under me, grabbing a hold of his now-hard dick, and pushed his hardness inside me. Both of us moaned as lowered myself down on the full length of him. Instantly I began to cum. I couldn't hold back. I didn't know if it was because it was this good or because I hadn't had it like I wanted in a while. Or could it be I was feeling this man more than I wanted to admit to

*myself and that alone was sending my body into orbits
I'd never visited before? As I climaxed for a second
time, Fabian leaned up to kiss the crook of my neck as
he gripped my behind and pulled me farther into him.
I wrapped my arms around him and hugged him tight.*

With my head leaned back on the headrest of my car,
I knew my night with Fabian had just made things more
complicated for me. As much as I knew what I'd done was
wrong, I knew there was no way I could let Fabian go. I
may have not wanted to admit it to myself before but I
had no choice but to come to this realization now.

Thinking I should get out this car and into the house
before Derrick pulled up and I would have to explain why
I was in my car, I opened the door to get out. Hitting the
button for the garage to close again, I stood and closed
the door to my ride. As I made my way to the entrance to
our home, something struck me over the head, causing
me to pass out.

Chapter 43

Zacariah

"Wake up, sleepyhead," was what I heard as cold water ran down my face. Struggling to breathe as water entered my mouth and nose, I tried to figure out what was going on. I attempted to open my eyes and started coughing as I began choking on water. I tried to move but realized I couldn't. I couldn't raise my hands up nor could I move my legs. What was going on?

"It's about time you woke up," a voice said.

Still struggling to open my eyes, the visual of the person standing in front of me was blurry. As my view came into focus, the person talking came into view. And that's when I realized it was that crazy-ass Trinity.

"What are you doing here and why do you have me tied up?" I asked, wiggling, trying to get free.

"It took you long enough to wake up. I slapped you, pinched you, even kicked you but you wouldn't wake up. I thought I killed you but I heard your heart beating so I knew you were still alive. My plan wouldn't work if you were dead. Then all of this would have been for nothing. But anyway, I decided to pour cold water over your head and ta-dah, it worked," she said, holding her hands out like she had just done a magic trick.

I squirmed, trying to free myself, but Trinity duct taped my hands behind my back and also taped both my ankles to the legs of the chair.

"Let me go, Trinity," I demanded.

"Now why would I do that when I worked so hard to tape your behind down?" she said, pulling a chair in front of me and sitting down in it. She crossed her legs and glared at me.

I glowered back at her as I still tried to loosen the tape around my wrist.

"I finally have you," she said.

"I never knew you wanted me," I retorted.

"Yes, I did. I wanted you to die," she admitted.

"Why, so you can have Derrick?" I asked.

"Exactly. You are the reason why we are not together," she said, bouncing her leg like we were having leisurely girl talk.

I giggled and said, "Sorry to spoil this for you, but have you noticed he's not here?"

"He will be back eventually," Trinity said. "I'm a patient person. I will wait for him to get home."

"Well, your wait might be long since he's with Kea."

The expression on Trinity's face changed from one of cheerfulness to one of agitation. I loved it. She almost looked panic stricken. She uncrossed her legs and leaned closer to me. She asked, "Why is he with her?"

"Why should I tell you anything, you demented bitch?"

Trinity stood up and poured more cold water over my head. This woman had gotten the bucket we washed our cars with to put the water in. I spit as the liquid ran down my body. The coldness of the water caused me to shiver a bit.

"Tell me," she screamed.

I started laughing. She punched me in the face and that ticked me off. I wiggled wildly, trying to free myself so I could beat the trick's ass. She jumped back like she knew I was going to get free. She swung the bucket she was holding and hit me across the face. I was dazed but didn't go unconscious.

"You can make this easy. Or you can make this hard. It's your choice. But I will tell you, the last person who made it hard for me didn't live," she admitted.

I wondered what she was talking about and looked at the crazed look on her face.

"Now tell me why is Derrick with Kea?" she yelled.

"He's at the hospital with Kea."

She asked, "Why is he at the hospital with her?"

"They are both there with Jaquon," I told her, still trying to wiggle my hands free.

"But I thought he was dead," she said.

"Why would he be . . ." I paused. And that's when I realized she probably had something to do with what happened to Jaquon. She saw the way I was looking at her and walked away from me.

"You did that to him didn't you?" I asked.

"I want you to call Derrick and tell him to come home."

"So you are going to ignore my question."

"I'm the one in control here," she said, walking up close to me and pointing her skinny finger in my face. She nudged my forehead and said, "So you need to do as I say."

I didn't say anything. My anger wouldn't allow me to as I wished to be freed so I could kill this woman.

"Now, I want you to invite Kea to come with him, too," she said.

"Why do I need to do that?" I asked another question despite her telling me she was running this.

"Because you don't want to suffer the same fate as Jaquon, my brother, and Derrick's mom did."

That halted me. Jaquon I was expecting to hear her say, but Ms. Shirley and her brother? That traumatized me knowing how Ms. Shirley was bludgeoned to death. Fear had definitely begun to set in.

"You looked stunned," she said, smiling devilishly.

I didn't see anything funny about killing somebody. I didn't say anything. I steadily tried to wiggle my hands free but it seemed very difficult because the tape didn't seem to be budging.

"I'm even responsible for your little trunk ride," she confessed.

"You did that to me?" I asked.

"Well, I had my brother kidnap you but somehow he managed to screw that up. I guess if you want something done right, you have to do it yourself. Wait," she said, looking at the ceiling and placing her finger on her chin like she was thinking. "I did try to kill you myself but Derrick's mother ended up being the one I took out. She wasn't supposed to be the one to die."

Trinity was talking like she was giving a recipe on how to make a chocolate cake. Her mood swings from calm to damn right frenzied were on some bipolar-type behavior.

"When I took that bat to her skull, I thought it was you lying in that bed getting your brains turned into pulp," she continued to admit. "I mean I really almost got an orgasm on that shit," she said, chuckling. "But when I pulled that sheet back and saw it was Derrick's mom, my heart dropped," she said sadly. "I didn't mean to kill his mother. It's your fault she's dead," she said, turning to me. "It's like you have nine lives or something. Every time I wanted to take you out, the opportunity slipped away from me."

"You are one crazy bitch," I told her.

"Don't call me that," she screamed, grabbing her hair and pulling it like she was going to rip her own hair out of her head. "Don't call me crazy. I can't stand when people call me crazy. I'm not crazy."

All I could do was look at Trinity's out-of-control fit she was having. I shook my head. She saw me do this and instantly tried to calm herself.

"And you wonder why I called you crazy," I said.

Trinity walked over to me and grabbed a fistful of my hair. She jerked my head back so I was looking up at her.

"I told you to stop calling me that," she said through clenched teeth.

"If I wasn't tied up, I would be trying to kill you right now," I told her.

Trinity glared down at me and then let my hair go as she walked away from me. She smirked and pulled the chair back up in front of me, having a seat. Crossing her legs, she said, "You underestimate what I'm capable of. Here you are talking about killing me and I'm the one who's already done it. I can't count how many times I've actually killed someone," she bragged.

"Your time is coming, Trinity. You will get yours," I retorted.

"You think?" she said.

"I know."

Trinity giggled and said, "That may be true but until then, I'm going to continue to do me."

She reached in her pocket and pulled out two cell phones. One of them was mine and the other I suspected was hers. Looking from her phone to mine, she punched in a number.

"Okay. I'm going to need you to tell Derrick to come home," Trinity said.

"And if I don't?"

She reached behind her back and pulled out a knife. She swung her arm around and sliced into my chest.

The pain was terrible but I was not going to scream out for this trick to get off on me feeling this pain. I gritted my teeth as tight as I could to deal with it.

Trinity tilted her head to the side and said, "Trying to be hard until the end."

I didn't bother to respond as the front of my shirt turned crimson from the blood trickling from me.

"Please don't be like Jaquon. You see where that got him."

I looked at the knife, which she turned like she was on *The Price Is Right* showing one knife out of a collection. She wiped my blood from the tip unto my jeans.

"Now. Are we clear?"

I reluctantly nodded.

"Good, because I really don't want to hurt you."

I knew she was lying. Why else would she have me tied to this chair like this? For goodness' sake she had already killed her own brother. Why was I worth keeping alive? Especially since I was the one in the way of her getting Derrick back. Especially since she'd tried to kill me twice already. I knew this bitch wanted me dead. *And with this being the case, should I cooperate at all?*

"I'm going to dial Derrick's number. Remember to tell him to come home and bring Kea," Trinity explained. "Here we go," she said, and put the cell to my ear.

"Hello."

At first I didn't say anything. I knew Trinity heard Derrick say hello because her eyes bulged when I didn't respond to him. She took the knife and stuck the tip of it into my leg, causing a twinge of pain.

"Zacariah, are you there?" Derrick asked.

"Yes, I'm here," I managed to say through the pain.

"Are you okay?" he asked.

"I'm good. Just cut my hand with a knife," I said as Trinity smiled from ear to ear at my comeback. "Are you still at the hospital?" I asked.

"Yes. I'm still here with Kea."

"How's Jaquon doing?" I asked.

"He's out of surgery but not out of the woods yet. The doctors have given him medicine putting him into a coma," Derrick said.

"At least he's made it out of surgery."

"True."

"I know you are tired."

"I am," Derrick said.

"Why don't you come home for a bit? Bring Kea with you, too. I made breakfast," I lied. Trinity was jumping up and down like a little kid happy at my performance. Little did she know her jumping was making the cell phone move and I hadn't heard what Derrick said.

"I'm sorry, Derrick, what did you say?" I asked, glaring at Trinity, who cooled her heels a bit.

"'Are you sure' is what I asked. You want me to bring Kea with me?"

"I'm sure, babe," I said and the fact I called Derrick "babe" angered Trinity, causing her to stick the tip of the knife deeper into my leg. I wanted to yell out but I maintained dealing with the pain.

"You sure?" he asked again like he wasn't believing me and I couldn't blame him. I wouldn't believe me either.

"Both of you, especially Kea, have had a hard night. Come on home so you guys can get something in your bellies and freshen up a bit. Then you can return to the hospital."

"Wow. Thank you, Zacariah," he said. "I appreciate this. I'll talk to Kea and convince her to come too. We should be home within the hour."

"Okay. I'll see you then."

Trinity pulled the phone away from my face and the knife from my leg. She jumped up and down in delight. "Yes, yes, yes, Zacariah, you did your thing."

I didn't say anything as I still worked to loosen the tape from around my wrist.

"My plan is coming together. It's a matter of time before I have my man," she gloated.

Her man, I thought. This chick was delusional if she thought Derrick would have anything to do with her, especially after she'd admitted to me she murdered his mother. She had to know I was going to tell him. As soon as I did, I knew Derrick was going to try his best to kill this trick himself.

"Too bad you and Kea have to die," she said, causing me to pay attention to her rambling. She looked at me and continued. "You really didn't think I was going to let you live, did you?" she said, smirking. "I can't have Derrick going back to either of you. I don't need any competition; not that there is any, but with you two out of the picture, me and Derrick can live happily ever after."

And, just like I figured, she was planning on taking me out. The only reason I went along with her plan was because she wasn't counting on me telling Derrick anything. But that's okay. As soon as they got here, things were going to be on and popping. I just hoped things went according to my plan, or else I might not be here to see tomorrow.

Chapter 44

Derrick

I looked over at Kea, whose head was leaned back on the headrest. Her eyes were closed and I could tell she dozed off while I made my way to my place. I knew she had to be tired after the drama she dealt with yesterday. It had been a very long day for her. Now the sun was beaming like today should be one to smile about. For me, I had a lot to be happy about. I had the woman I loved back in my life. I knew my body was running on pure adrenaline from being by her side. I finally had who I wanted. The only thing about this was how was I going to break this to Zacariah?

When I told Kea Zacariah invited her over for breakfast, she was reluctant. I couldn't blame her. It wasn't like they were friends. Kea was wondering why Zacariah all of a sudden was being nice to her.

"Is she going to poison me?" she asked me jokingly.

"No, Kea."

"You sure? Because something is not right here," she said.

"Look, let's go. Let's get our eat on. I'm starving and I know you have to be," I told her. Kea nodded. "So let's do this so we can get back to the hospital to be by Jaquon's side."

As soon as my car stopped, Kea sat up slowly, looking around to see where we were.

"We're here, sleepyhead," I said, caressing her leg.

She yawned and stretched a bit before turning to me with her beautiful smile. "You sure this is okay?" she asked.

"I'm positive. Come on. Let's go eat," I said, getting out my ride.

Kea did the same.

When I walked into the house, the first thing I noticed was the absence of the scent of any food in the air. Even if Zacariah had ordered out, the smell should have wafted through this space. Walking through the kitchen, I saw nothing. No takeout, no pans on the stove, nothing. I looked back at Kea, who crossed her arms giving me a look like "I told you so."

"Zacariah," I called out, but she didn't answer.

"You see. I told you she was up to something," Kea said, trailing behind me.

I entered my living room and was shocked to see Zacariah tied to a chair with tape covering her mouth. "Zacariah!" I called out, running over to her. I ripped the tape from her mouth.

She didn't waste any time, saying, "Behind you."

When I turned, I saw Trinity standing there with her left arm wrapped around Kea's neck and a blade she was holding cutting into Kea's flesh. "Hi, baby."

"Trinity, what are you doing? What is going on here?" I questioned, looking at the frantic look on Kea's face. Blood trickled from the cut the knife was making into her skin, and I could see Kea was trying not to move so the knife wouldn't go any deeper into her skin.

"I'm glad to see you finally made it home, sweetie," Trinity said coolly.

All I could do was look into Kea's eyes, which were stretched wide. She flinched a little and Trinity dug the blade farther into her neck.

"Trinity, let her go. You don't want to hurt her."

"I really do. I want to hurt both of these women because they are keeping you away from me, Derrick."

"No, they are not," I argued.

"You are living with Zacariah. You didn't even bother to tell me you were back with her, Derrick. You were playing me."

"I'm sorry," I apologized.

"All I asked was for you to be honest with me. That's how we started our relationship together. And that's how we should have ended it," Trinity explained.

"You are right. I should have told you and that's my mistake. But why take out my wrongdoings on these ladies?" I said, looking back at Zacariah and then at Kea. "You know I love you," I lied.

"You're just saying that because you don't want me to slit Kea's throat."

"No. I mean it. I love you, Trinity," I lied again. I would say anything to talk Trinity off the edge.

"Prove it," she dared.

"What?"

"I said prove it."

"How?" I asked.

"Go get a chair out of the dining room and bring it in here."

I did as she asked and went to retrieve the chair. Bringing it back into the living room, I set the chair beside Zacariah.

"Get over there," Trinity demanded, removing the knife from Kea's throat and pushing her in my direction. Before any of us could think to tackle Trinity, she reached back with her left hand and pulled out a gun.

"Now, I want you to tie Kea up. And, Derrick, if you try anything stupid, I will not hesitate to pop a cap in her pretty little head," she threatened.

Kea walked to the chair and sat down. Trinity walked
around so she was positioned at the side of Kea so she
could watch to see if I tied her up correctly. She held both
the knife and the gun up. Kea stared at me, giving me
a questioning look like "how are we going to get out of
this?" Unfortunately, Trinity didn't like the look she was
giving me and reacted violently.

"Don't!" Trinity yelled, hitting Kea in the back of her
head with the gun.

Kea fell forward into my arms, causing both me and
her to fall to the floor. I turned so her body could fall on
top of mine. Kea was not unconscious but she was a bit
dazed.

"Don't look at him like that. Don't be giving him any
signals or I swear I will shoot you," Trinity threatened.
"Get her up, Derrick, and place her back in the seat."

I helped Kea up and placed her in the chair. When Kea
pulled her hand away from her head, her hand was filled
with blood. I wanted to panic but knew I couldn't. I had to
act like the only woman I was concerned with was Trinity.

"Get the duct tape and tie her up," Trinity demanded
and I did as she asked once again. Tying Kea's hands behind her back and her legs to the chair just like Zacariah,
I stood, hoping this was enough to satisfy Trinity into
believing I was on her side.

Trinity went and tugged on the tape wrapped around
Kea's hands and legs. She nodded like she was pleased.
With a smile, Trinity ran up to me and kissed me. As hard
as it was to feel her lips on mine I welcomed them onto
me.

"Babe, you do love me," she said.

"I told you I did."

"But why did you leave me?"

I couldn't think of anything to say and wasn't expecting
this moment to be a twenty-one question essay. Thinking

as quick as my horrified mind would allow me, I thought of something to say. "Sweetie, I was stressed out. I was confused. Then I lost my mother. But that doesn't matter anymore. We are together. I know with you in my life, things will be better," I told her.

"Forever right?" she asked.

"Yes, forever," I said, pinching her chin playfully.

Trinity kissed me again and again I returned her gesture. I considered tackling her for the knife and the gun but I knew now was not the time. All I was concerned with was getting her to go away with me. This way Kea and Zacariah would be safe from any violence Trinity may bring.

When she pulled away I told her, "Let's leave now, get away from them so we can be alone."

"But what if they talk?" she said, looking back at Kea and Zacariah, who watched on.

I took my finger and gently tugged at her chin to face me. I said, "If they know what's best for them, they will not talk."

I hoped both of them heeded my warning to keep their mouths shut. At least until I got Trinity away from here.

That was too much to ask because before I could look back into Trinity's face, Zacariah came hurtling up from her chair, causing both of us to fall to the floor.

Chapter 45

Zacariah

I wasn't going to wait for this crazy bitch to kill me. I had survived so much turmoil in my life, I'd be damned if I was going to allow this blue-eyed monster be what was going to take me out of this world to be with my Maker sooner than God originally planned. All that wiggling to free myself paid off, even though I didn't let Trinity know this. The water helped the adhesive of the tape loosen and my hands were free. I was waiting for the right time to pounce. So I jumped up and tackled both of them to the floor.

Trinity screamed as the gun went flying across the floor. Unfortunately, somewhere during the fall the blade she was holding ended up being plunged into Derrick's side. He lay on the floor screaming in agony as Trinity scurried to her feet. She got up before I did and I grabbed her ankle pulling her back down to the floor.

"Let me go," she yelled, kicking me in the face, stunning me for a moment. This gave Trinity enough time to gather herself again. She scrambled to her feet and went charging for the gun. I managed to get up too and I bum-rushed her again, trying to keep her from getting to the gun first. But she was closer than I thought. Trinity grabbed the gun and pointed at me, causing me to stop fighting with her.

"You stupid bitch," she said, firing a shot at me.

I heard the sound of the gun being fired but I didn't think I was hit. That was, until the pain from the bullet tearing into my flesh brought me back to a reality I didn't wish for myself. I lay on the floor, still staring down the barrel as she spoke. I wished I had handled this differently. Especially when I looked over and saw Derrick lying on the floor a few feet away from me with the knife sticking out of him.

Trinity saw me looking at him and her sorrowful eyes looked down at Derrick.

"You did this to him," she addressed me.

I looked at Kea, who was still a little dazed from the hit across her head.

"Derrick," Trinity called out to him. "Are you okay?"

"I don't know," he responded as he grunted from the pain.

Trinity went over to him and kneeled by his side. She touched the knife and grabbed it, getting ready to pull it out of him.

"No!" I yelled, which halted her. "Don't pull the blade out because it could cause him to bleed out," I warned her.

Finally Trinity listened to what I had to say. She removed her hand from the knife and stroked Derrick as tears began to fill her eyes.

"Babe, I need to get you some help," Trinity said, crying.

"Yes, babe. You need to call an ambulance," Derrick struggled to say.

"But if I call them, they will take me away from you," Trinity said, thinking of herself first.

"No, they won't. I told you them two will not say anything. You have to get me help or else I'm going to die," Derrick said.

"You can't leave me. If I lose you, Derrick . . ." Trinity paused. She couldn't finish her sentence. Trinity wiped her tears away, saying, "You know what? I'm going to take you to the hospital." She stood. "I'm not going to let you die, Derrick. I love you too much."

I was so tired of this trick pretending she loved Derrick so much when she was responsible for all of this in the first place. She was too delusional to see it. I wanted to ruin this happy moment.

"Why don't you stop all your crying and tell Derrick the truth?" I struggled to say.

The look on Trinity's face was one of fear. For the first time tonight, she was scared of me. She knew I could take her man away for good if he knew what she did.

Derrick noticed the expression on Trinity's face as he looked up at her. He glanced at me and asked, "What is she talking about, Trinity?"

"Nothing, honey. She's not talking about anything," Trinity said, kicking me in the ribs and I lay on the floor still spewing blood.

Now it was my turn to giggle. I still managed to say, "Tell him, Trinity. Tell him how you—"

The gun went off and a bullet ripped into my arm. I yelled in pain as I grabbed the area that was aching severely.

"Shut up!" Trinity yelled.

I looked at the smoking gun and giggled at her still. This bitch thought she was crazy. She met her match with me. I came too far to let this trick be the one to make me back down regardless of how many bullets she decided to shoot into me. I hardly ever backed down from anyone, and if it meant me dying, then so be it. I didn't care. I was so done with this. So I just blurted it.

"She killed your mom, Derrick."

Trinity fired her weapon again and this time the bullet pierced my midsection. I winced as fire radiated through me from another bullet piercing my flesh. More blood seeped between my fingers.

"I told you to shut up," I heard Trinity say.

"Is this true?" Derrick asked through his pain.

"No, baby. She's lying," Trinity said. "Let me help you get up so I can take you to the hospital."

"I don't know if I can move," Derrick said.

"I can help you," she said, leaning down to help Derrick stand up. He kept falling back to the floor, roaring in pain. Trinity was still holding on to the weapon but let her guard down by putting it down on the floor. She needed both her hands to help him and put both under his arms, trying her best to lift him to his feet. Finally, Derrick stood with the blade still sticking out of him.

"Put your arm around my shoulder," Trinity said.

Derrick did as she asked and leaned his wounded body into hers. They both moved slowly toward the kitchen, which led to the garage. All I could do was stare at the gun, which was a few feet away from me but it seemed so far. I couldn't find the energy to retrieve the weapon and felt helpless for the first time tonight. I felt myself become weak as I watched the two of them move farther away from me.

Chapter 46

Kea

Trinity must have been trying to get her balance and that was the reason they stopped walking toward the kitchen. It looked as though Derrick was hugging Trinity. She looked up at him with wide eyes as he stared down at her. Tears ran down the side of Trinity's face but the look on Derrick's face was one of retribution.

"I love you, Derrick," Trinity said.

"But I don't love you," Derrick said, letting her go. Trinity's body fell to the floor and that's when I saw that the knife that had been in Derrick's side was now plunged into Trinity's chest.

Derrick grabbed his side and fell to his knees as blood still spewed from him, this time a lot faster than it was when the knife was in him.

"Derrick," I yelled.

He struggled his way over to me and managed to ask me, "Are you okay?"

"Yes. I'm fine. But you are not okay. Derrick, you really need to get to a hospital." I tried to wiggle myself free but I couldn't. Derrick went behind me and managed to loosen the tape around my hands. Once he did that, he fell to his back. I leaned forward and hurriedly undid the tape around my ankles. I needed to get to him fast. Once I freed myself, I jumped up and ran over to him.

"Derrick, baby," I said, pushing down on his wound, which caused him to cry out.

He took his hand and placed it over my hand and said, "I'm good."

I took my other hand and put it over his. I removed my hand from his wound and used his hand to press down to stop the bleeding. I said, "Keep your hand here. I'm going to call the police."

I ran to retrieve the phone, dialed 911, and ran back in the room where all the mayhem went down to see the three bodies lying on the floor. Zacariah looked unconscious. Her eyes were closed and she was not moving. I prayed she wasn't dead. From the first time Derrick gave me that look, I knew he had a plan. But looking around at the carnage that went down I knew it didn't go according to plan.

Unfortunately Zacariah spoiled everything, causing him to get stabbed in the first place. But I couldn't be mad at her because she was trying to take this Trinity out. I thought if I was in her shoes, I would have done the same thing.

It didn't take long for the police and paramedics to arrive. This was the second time in two days that I was kneeling beside someone I loved, hoping they wouldn't die on me. The same police officers who questioned me at Jaquon's stabbing were now questioning me at this scene. From the comment one of the officers made, I knew they suspected I was behind all of this.

"Trouble follows you, doesn't it?" the officer asked.

"The trouble here was Trinity," I said. "And I suspect she had something to do with Jaquon's stabbing also."

I didn't have proof of this but I knew deep down she was behind all the tragedy that had happened in my life recently. If it weren't for a criminal who pled guilty to shooting Mr. Hanks with my mother being behind that, I would have thought Trinity was behind that too. This was one crazy woman.

I watched as the paramedics attempted to work on Trinity first.

"Hold up. Why are you working on her when she caused all of this? You need to start with these two first," I blurted, angry that she would come before Derrick and Zacariah. Trinity was the reason why they were fighting for their lives now and she didn't get the benefit of being treated first. An officer pulled me away from them, trying to calm me down, but I had had enough. I wanted this to be done and over with.

The paramedics put Zacariah on a gurney and took her to an awaiting ambulance while another EMT worked on Derrick in front of me.

Moments later they were putting him on a gurney too and wheeling him off to the hospital. I followed so I could ride with him but an officer stopped me, telling me I couldn't leave. This infuriated me.

"Now can you tell me what happened again?" the officer asked. He was ticking me off now because he kept asking me the same questions like my answers were going to change.

"Look, like I told you before, Trinity is responsible for all of this. I wish you would stop asking me questions like I'm the criminal here," I blurted in anger.

"You don't have to answer any more questions," I heard my best friend's voice say.

Terry walked up and handed the police officer her card, saying, "If you want to question my client anymore, there's my number where you can reach us. What's important is that this woman be seen by a physician. After that, if you still have questions, I will personally bring her in for questioning."

The officer looked like he didn't like the fact that Terry was coming to my rescue. I knew then he was trying to pin this entire incident on me since I was the only one standing, literally. The officer knew this was the end of his questioning and walked away.

"How did you—" I tried to ask Terry.

But, she raised her hand, saying, "That's not important."

I hugged Terry, grateful to see her there.

"Are you okay?" she asked.

"I think so," I said sadly.

"What happened, Kea?"

"Trinity happened."

Epilogue

One Year Later

Epilogue

One Year Later

Chapter 47

Zacariah

I was back on top and with the man of my dreams. And I'm not talking about Derrick. I was engaged to Fabian and my life couldn't have been better. The Lord had another plan for my life when I spent the majority of my time trying to get Derrick back into it. Who knew Fabian was the man I was meant to have by my side? When I was knocking at death's door, Fabian appeared by my bedside like an angel. He told me he heard about the incident on the news and rushed over to the hospital to be with me.

Three gunshot wounds and I still lived. It was nothing but the grace of God why I was still here. And yes, I was talking about God. I had to. He was the reason I still had breath in my body. After my close call with death I realized life was too short. I took things for granted and it was during my time of healing I realized Fabian was who I loved.

It wasn't like this was heartbreaking news to Derrick. He had his close call too and came to see me, apologizing for using me like he did. He told me his intension was to make me feel bad like I made him feel but then things changed where he could see I was becoming a changed woman. That meant a lot to hear Derrick tell me this. I accepted his apology and even introduced him to Fabian.

The day I came home, which happened to be Fabian's home, I was greeted by flowers and balloons galore.

Fabian went all out to make my homecoming a great one. But when that man got down on one knee, I thought I was going to lose it. Was he trying to put me back in the hospital from passing out and possibly getting a concussion from the shock of this?

Fabian took my left hand into his and asked, "Zacariah, will you do me the pleasure of being my wife for eternity?"

Tears instantly welled up in my eyes. And I wasn't a crier. But I was so filled up with joy that this was the only way I knew to show it. I couldn't say anything. All I could do was nod.

Fabian giggled and said, "I'm going to need to hear you say it."

I smiled, still nodding, and said, "Yes, Fabian. I would love to marry you."

Fabian slid the most beautiful two-carat diamond I'd ever seen on my left ring finger. He stood and lifted me into his arms. I was still sore from the wounds but I didn't care about the pain. I was so happy that I found a man who truly loved me for me, flaws and all.

Our wedding was to be in two months and I was a nervous wreck trying to make sure everything would be perfect for our big day. We were living together in his home but decided once we got married, we were going to purchase a new home that captured my flare along with his.

"Babe, are you ready?" Fabian asked, peeping into the bedroom as I put in my earrings.

"I'll be right down," I said.

We were about to go to his parents' house and have a big dinner, which his mother prepared every fourth Saturday to keep the family coming around often. Where I didn't have much family and longed for one even when I acted like I didn't need anyone, God granted me the blessing of giving me one anyway. Marrying Fabian came with a huge family in tow. He had five brothers and one sister. I just knew the females of this family would not welcome me at all. And I guess I felt this way because of my issues I used to have with Derrick's mother before we called a truce.

Both Fabian's mother and sister welcomed me with open arms. His sister clung to me like white on rice, happy that another female was coming into the fold of too much testosterone. I never saw me ever clicking with another female, but his sister and I clicked right away. We had become best friends even, and I hadn't had that since my best friend Essence was murdered.

As hard as I struggled to deal with her death and the fact the police never found her killer, I decided that, in order for me to be able to move on with my life, I had to let the anger go of losing her. I had to see Essence was my sister in heaven smiling down and keeping a watchful eye over me now.

I grabbed my Coach bag and exited our bedroom. I hit the top of the stairs and proceeded to walk down. Fabian was at the bottom looking up at me with so much love in his eyes. I smiled back at him. Damn, I was a lucky woman.

"You look fabulous," he said when I hit the bottom step, taking his hand into mine so he could assist me in taking the last step down.

"You don't look so bad yourself," I said, looking him up and down as he wore some blue jeans, a white polo shirt, and fresh white sneakers. I looked the bomb diggity too, wearing blue jeans, a white tee, a black fitted blazer, and black Christians. Or, as Trina would say, "long heels, red bottoms."

Fabian kissed me deeply. I almost backed away from him because I didn't want my lipstick smeared. But if there was anything I'd learned, life was way too short to

sweat the small stuff. So I kissed my man and decided
once I got in the car I could always put on another layer of
lipstick. Wow, look how far I'd come. And here I thought
all this time Derrick was the man for me. Sometimes
when we hold on to something so hard, little do we
realize the exact thing we are trying to hold on to is not
good or even meant for us. In the case of Fabian, love just
happened. Derrick and I had love between us but nothing
like the love I had with Fabian.

"I love you, Zacariah," Fabian told me.

"I love you too."

I used to say all the time, "whoever said dreams do
come true is a liar." I take that back because now I was
a living witness that they do come true and I couldn't be
happier to finally find the man of my dreams.

Chapter 48

Jaquon

Today I stood in the mirror marveling at the fact that one year ago today I almost died. I looked down at the scars Trinity left for me to live with for the rest of my life. But I quit feeling bad about them once I figured this thing could have been so much worse.

I splashed water up in my face, glad it was Saturday. Derrick and I were supposed to get up and play a game of basketball at the park. Today was supposed to be a nice, comfortable seventy-three degrees. I was happy Derrick and I had resumed our friendship. After I came out of my coma, I was surprised to see him by my side along with Kea. My heart felt good to see them there, my two favorite people. Despite all the negativity that went down, both of them were there for me and I couldn't thank them enough for that.

Arms wrapped around my waist and I closed my eyes because her hands felt so good to my naked chest. She kissed my back and said, "Baby, do you have to go?"

"Yes. You know me and Derrick play ball every Saturday morning."

"But I want you to come back to bed so we can, you know," Sheila said, kissing my back again.

I turned to face her. She rubbed the wounds on my chest, standing there in her silk pink robe. Her nipples penetrated the thin material, which turned me on. I picked her up and her legs automatically draped themselves around my waist.

"You are really trying to make it hard for a brother to leave," I said, leaning back on the sink still holding her up around me.

"I am trying to make it hard," she said, kissing me.

Sheila was the last woman I ever saw myself with. The irony of the entire situation was I ended up with someone who was just like me. So if I ever decided to step out on her, you best believe she would do the same and probably better than I ever could.

While I was in the hospital, she came by to see me too. She made sure to come by when Kea wasn't there so there wouldn't be any problems. And during one of her visits she admitted to me how much she cared for me.

I was speechless. Me, the playa Jaquon, had managed to capture the heart of someone who was just as promiscuous as me. But what really made me consider being with Sheila was her trusting me enough to open herself up to me. In doing so, I even helped her drop her pride and try to work on things with her father. Even though they were back to working on their relationship, we both didn't think it was a good idea for him to know about me. I wasn't looking forward to the day when he found out I was the man his daughter was in a relationship with.

It's still weird seeing Kea, knowing that at one point in my life she was my fiancée. And despite her being by my side, I knew the person she really wanted was my best friend Derrick. Did it hurt? It did for a long while but I didn't let them know that. Seeing Derrick and her together did make my heart twinge at what could have been between me and her. Even Zacariah had love in her life now. All was well, yet not all secrets had been revealed. I still hadn't told Derrick about Zacariah having that abortion, and that there was a 50 percent chance the baby was his. That night Trinity and Kea got into it as his folks' spot, I was planning on telling him. But the commotion ruined any chance of me getting that off my chest. Now I didn't think it mattered since he was no longer with Zacariah. Everybody was happy, so why should I damage things by spilling more heartbreaking secrets? I realized awhile back that would be a secret I would hopefully take to my grave.

Sheila was mine now. As for our future, I didn't know. All I knew was I was going to enjoy the ride while it lasted. Still, who would have thought I would be in a relationship with Sheila? She was the last person I ever saw myself with, yet here I stood holding this woman in my arms. And my dick loved her too, as its rock hardness appreciated her warm center covering it.

"Come on, Jaquon. Come back to bed. I promise I will make it worth your while."

Sheila leaned in and kissed me gently on my lips. I could feel the heat rising from her as out tongues tangled for a moment. She pulled back and rubbed my cheek. She smiled at me and nudged me to let her down. I did as she wanted. Sheila backed away from me, walking very seductively as she took off the silk robe she was wearing. With my dick standing at attention, I knew then that Derrick was going to have to wait while I handled my business.

Chapter 49

Derrick

I called Jaquon to let him know I had to make a pit stop real quick before I got to the basketball court. As soon as he answered, I knew he was planning on being late himself.

"Man, why are you panting like that?" I asked, giggling. I knew what was going on but wanted to pick on him for not calling me to tell me he was going to be late too.

"I'm working out a bit before I get there," he struggled to say. I could hear the sly grin in his voice.

"I'm going to let you get back to . . . working out," I stressed, giggling some more. "I can tell you are going to be awhile so hit me up when you are done with your workout."

"Bet," he said, hanging up as I heard Shelia in the background moaning. I shook my head at them.

I pulled into the driveway of the home I grew up in. I walked up on the porch and saw Pops had the door open and was sitting down in his faithful chair across from one of his friends playing chess.

I walked in, saying, "What up, Pops. Good to see you, Mr. Lester."

"Good to see you too, Derrick," Mr. Lester said, glancing at me but looking back at the chessboard, strategically trying to find his next move to get him closer to winning this game.

Pops stood and hugged me, saying, "Son, to what do I owe the pleasure?"

We embraced and Pops repositioned himself back in his chair. I smiled at him continuing to peek over those same black-rimmed glasses he wore all the time. The only difference today was the room was not filled with cigarette smoke. Pops quit smoking right after Mama passed away. All those years me and Mama tried to get him to quit, it took Mama going to heaven for Pops to give up smoking. I guess in the end she still was the one who made him stop.

"I just stopped by to check on you, see how you doing," I said, looking down at my father making a move on the board.

"Checkmate," he told his friend, laughing.

"You know what, that's my cue to go the restroom," his friend said. Mr. Lester got up and made his way out of the room.

"And don't be blowing my bathroom up either," Daddy blurted.

"And you know that's what I'm about to do," Mr. Lester said back.

"You better spray. And double flush. I don't want to see anything floating in my toilet," Daddy yelled to him.

I giggled at the two of them. Pops leaned back in his chair and placed his hands over his round belly.

I asked, "Are you still coming over tomorrow for dinner?"

"I sure am. I wouldn't miss it for the world. Plus I want to see this mansion you and Kea have purchased."

"It's not a mansion, Pops."

"Didn't you tell me it has six bedrooms, six and one half bathrooms, a completed basement with a home theater, and a three-car garage?"

"Yes," I said, smiling.

"Well, it sounds like a mansion to me. I don't know what you two need with such a big house anyway. Unless you two plan on filling it up with some grandchildren for me," Pops said, looking over his glasses.

"We are working on that, too," I said, chuckling.

"So, Kea doesn't have a bun in the oven yet?"

"No, Pops, not yet."

"Well, what you waiting on?"

"We can't rush God. When He's ready, then we will have a bun in the oven, as you say."

Pops nodded and rocked a bit in his chair. He got quiet staring off in the distance for a minute.

"You okay?" I asked, placing my hand on his shoulder, looking down at him.

"I sure wish Shirley was here to see how happy you are," Daddy struggled to say. He removed his glasses from his face and wiped the tears that were developing away. "I miss her so much."

"I miss her too," I told him, looking over at the living room side table at a picture of my mother smiling back at me.

"Every time I see you, you remind me so much of her."

"Do you want me to stop coming around?" I joked.

"Of course not, son," he said.

"I'm just saying because if you are going to cry every single time I come over, I don't know if I can take it."

Pops chuckled, placing his glasses back on his face.

"I hope you know I'm joking," I told him.

"I know, son."

It did pain me to know that if I would have never got involved with Trinity, my mother could still be alive today. And the sad part about it was when I got sad about my mother, I spent a lot of time remembering Trinity was the one who killed her. That part I hated. Trinity didn't deserve any type of energy given to her. Despite me stabbing her, she lived. Miraculously she lived. I thought she was dead. A part of me wished she was. But, again, I was not God.

After further investigation on Trinity and her brother, they connected them or at least her to several other murder attempts, along with her possibly being the one responsible for her parents' deaths. Trinity was later charged with several different murders spanning four states. To find out she'd done this several times before and had never been caught amazed me. The officers investigating the case figured out Trinity was basically a serial killer, which was very rare in women. But this was easily brought on by the fact she was bipolar and had schizophrenia.

I'm glad me, Kea, and even Zacariah lived through what she tried to do to us. Her lawyer pled not guilty because of mental defect. And, you know what, I couldn't argue with her unstable disposition. Trinity was certifiably crazy. She became emotionally unhinged when she stopped taking her medication, thus becoming a murderer. Trinity will be locked up in a mental ward for the rest of her days, if she's lucky, because as soon as they see her fit to stand trial, I will be there to testify that she be locked up in jail for the rest of her existence. And after they found her brother's body, and Zacariah's testimony that she'd admitted to killing him, my mother, and attempting to murder Jaquon, the legal system wouldn't have any choice but to throw the book at her.

It didn't matter now because she was out my life for good. Luckily, no charges were filed against me because it was self-defense. My goal now was to live my life to the fullest and not dwell on the fact my mother wasn't here.

I was happy me and my dad's relationship was great. Even though the paternity test I and my uncle took proved I was his son, I still couldn't see him as my dad. The only people who knew the truth were me, Uncle Gerald, and Pops. I decided it was best to leave things the way they were. It would only hurt a lot of people and cause friction within our family. Plus, I didn't want Aunt Henrietta to hate my mother, who was not here to defend herself. So Uncle Gerald remained my uncle and our relationship would be just like it was before. There was no way on this earth he would ever take the place of Pops.

"Well, Pops, I have to go. I supposed to meet Jaquon to play a game of basketball."

By now Pops' friend had come back from the bathroom and they were back to playing another game of chess. "All right, son. I'll see you tomorrow."

"Okay. I love you, Dad," I said, opening the screen door to leave.

He turned and looked at me with a smile and said, "I love you too, son."

Chapter 50

Kea

Terry was late as usual as I sat at a dining table at Metro restaurant, sipping on a glass of wine. Two men had already come up to me, hitting on me, which was flattering, but I quickly showed them the ring on my finger letting them know I was taken. The third man I shut down was walking away from my table when Terry approached.

"Girl, I'm sorry I'm late," she said, panting like she ran up in here.

I shook my head and laughed. "Can you ever be on time, Terry?"

"The only things I seem to be on time for are my court cases, and I guess I'm on time for those because those deal with my money."

"Well, you panting like you just ran from the courthouse."

"I did. The courthouse is not that far away. And I was not about to drive this block looking for parking when I had a paid spot there. So I walked. Plus, it's great exercise."

I giggled and looked at the waitress who came over to our table. She must have seen Terry come and figured this was her cue to come over. She happily asked, "Are you guys ready to order?"

I looked at Terry, who still looked flushed from rushing, and told the young lady, "Give us five more minutes please."

The waitress nodded and walked away.

"Thanks for thinking about me. Good looking out," she said, picking up the glass of wine I ordered for her. Terry loved getting her sip on and I knew that would be the first thing that touched her lips when she got here.

"You are welcome."

Terry quickly gulped that down and I eyeballed her to slow her roll.

"What?"

Again I shook my head at my friend and asked, "So how's your firm coming along?"

"I got three more clients today."

"You go, Terry."

"I know. I'm so happy I made the decision to do this. My hard work is paying off."

"Let's toast to your success," I said, lifting my glass.

"But I don't have any left."

I slid the second glass of wine I had sitting next to mine over to Terry.

"Oh. You know me so well," she said.

"I sure do," I quipped. Terry picked up the full glass and I said, "To your success."

"To our friendship," she said, and we clinked glasses before taking a sip of our wine. Well, I took a sip while Terry gulped down that glass also.

"Thirsty, are we?" I asked.

"I need these. I'm trying to get up my nerve to tell you what I have to tell you."

I frowned, wondering what this could be about. Terry did look anxious and there wasn't much that made my friend nervous. I leaned forward, placing my elbows on the table. "Are you okay?"

"Yes. No. Yes."

"Terry, what is it?" I asked worriedly.

Terry stared into my eyes before turning away. She was looking for our waitress and I was suspecting it was for her to bring her another glass of wine.

"Terry!" I called out sternly.

"Okay."

"Just spill it. You know you can tell me anything," I said, trying to comfort my friend.

"Kea, I have something that's been on my chest for a long time I want to get off."

I stared at her while she talked.

"But you have to promise you will never tell anybody."

"Okay."

"I'm serious, Kea. You can't even tell Derrick," she said firmly.

"Okay, I won't," I said, agreeing to her stipulation.

"Kea," she said, but then she paused. It seemed like the words wouldn't come from her mouth.

"Terry, I told you I will not tell a soul. Dag. Do you want me to blood swear it to you?" I suggested.

"Can you?"

"What?"

"I'm just kidding, Kea," Terry said, giggling, but the look on her face said if I agreed with it, I think she would have done it. Now I was feeling like a nervous wreck.

"So what's the big secret you don't want nobody to know?" I asked calmly.

The waitress walked over and asked, "Are you guys ready to order?"

"No. Can you come back, please?" Terry said.

I looked at her, thinking I was hungry. I was early and she was the one late. But I guessed whatever she had to tell me had to come before my hunger pains. "Okay, Terry, spill it."

Terry looked around the space, which was kind of empty where we were sitting. There was no one sitting around us. And I'm glad there wasn't because the next words that came out of my friend's mouth were something no one needed to hear.

"I was the one who killed Essence."

I laughed and sat back in my seat, picking up my menu, knowing she was joking. I said, "Stop playing."

But when I looked at the grim expression on Terry's face, I knew she was telling me the truth. "You?" was all I could say.

She nodded.

My hands went over my mouth as I gaped at my friend. I scanned my mind, wondering what in the world would cause her to take this woman's life. Here I was thinking Trinity could have been responsible. It made sense with all the other lives she'd taken, and tried to take for that matter. Never in my wildest dreams would I have ever suspected my best friend Terry could be guilty for something so horrific. But then it hit me: that day I was in her room and saw that picture on her bookshelf. I didn't know why I put that at the back of my mind but I guessed with everything that had been going on with Jaquon, Derrick, Zacariah, and Trinity, I never once went back to the place of remembering that photo.

The picture was of Essence. I didn't know who this woman was until I found her linked up with Jaquon at Derrick's cookout. And I hadn't seen her before then. But I was good at remembering faces and I knew when I saw that picture, it was her. Why she was on my best friend's shelf was another story.

"But . . . why?" I asked, wanting answers.

"I did it for you," she said.

"Me? Why me?"

"I can't believe you haven't noticed."

"Noticed what?" I asked, bewildered.

"Have you ever really seen me with many men?" she asked.

I thought back on all of our times together, and now that she had mentioned it, I hadn't seen her with many men. She talked about them and how cute they were, and how she slept with them, but I never saw her with one.

Seeing Terry looking intently at me, I shook my head.

"And I guess since you never noticed, you never once thought anything different?" she said.

"No, Terry, I haven't. You like men. Remember you said you were strictly dickly," I reminded her, thinking the air between us was getting really weird.

"Kea, I know you are my best friend but the reason you haven't seen me with many individuals is because I've always loved women."

Terry's words stunned me. My hand flew to my chest before I knew it, and I found myself breathing erratically. I think this shocked me more than her killing Essence.

"I think I may love you."

"You're in love with me?" I asked uneasily.

"Yes," she said sincerely.

"But still, what does that have to do with Essence?"

"That night, after your fight with Zacariah at Derrick's house, you called me. Do you remember?"

I nodded.

"You were so upset and told me everything that happened. Kea, I got mad right along with you. It hurt me to see you in pain, and I knew that if it weren't for this female, your life would be much better. But little did I know that female was Essence."

"But there were a lot of females Jaquon messed with. Why Essence?"

"I killed her because she and I used to have a thing, too."

I gasped at this revelation. I swore if one more piece of truth that'd been a secret was pushed into the realm of what I thought was real, I didn't know if I would be able to take it.

"You and her used to be an item?" I asked hesitantly.

"Yes. She played me, Kea. She was the first woman I'd ever slept with and loved," Terry admitted. "I knew she was bisexual, but that didn't matter to me because at that point in my life I had been with men too. It was not until she left me for someone else. It wasn't until you called me that night that I found out that someone else was Jaquon."

Small world, I thought.

"I was so furious I decided to call Essence. Of course she didn't answer. So I went to where I knew she would be, which was the club. I went in and saw her with some guy and almost approached her until I saw Jaquon staring her down from the bar. I didn't want him to see me so I left."

"But how did you end up . . ." I stopped, not bringing myself to say it again.

"I waited for Essence in the lobby part of the club. I saw Jaquon leave and knew that was my opportunity to confront her. When she came walking out of that club with this dude's arm around her shoulder, I went ballistic."

I watched as Terry's irritation increased.

"How could she go from me to Jaquon and now this stranger she just met? It was in that moment I really felt betrayed. I told Essence what I'd heard, about her being with Jaquon and how he was with you, my best friend. Do you know what she did?"

"What?" I asked.

"She laughed at me. I mean she reared back and had a huge gut-wrenching chuckle at my expense. Here I was upset by her leaving me because I loved her and she was laughing like the state of my heart was something to laugh about."

I could not believe I was hearing my friend tell me about her love life and the fact that she was with the same woman Jaquon cheated on me with. And here I was thinking she may have been jealous because she wanted a taste of Jaquon. I couldn't have been more wrong.

"Essence stepped around me with her little friend and walked away like I wasn't relevant," Terry said with water forming in her eyes. "Nobody makes a fool of me. I had people do that to me all my life growing up and I was not going to let her get away with what she did to me."

"So what did you do?" I asked curiously.

"Somehow deep down I knew things weren't going to go well between us, but I still had that inkling of hope it would. But just in case I needed to be prepared."

"Prepared for what?" I asked, frowning.

"Before going to the club, I picked up some chloroform. If she refused to talk to me, then I was going to make her deal with me, even if it meant me gassing her to get answers."

I listened and saw the waitress begin to walk up. I held my hand up to stop her and she turned and went back in the other direction. Now was not the time. I knew we were taking up space but we were paying patrons and I had already made a mental note to tip this young lady for her patience alone.

"It was three hours later when Essence finally came strolling to her car. I knew she had slept with this man because the sweat of him was still all over her. This infuriated me. I poured the chloroform into the cloth before getting out of my car to confront her. I snuck up behind her at her ride and placed the cloth over her mouth and nose. She tried to fight but it didn't take long for the chloroform to take effect. Little did I know the amount of chloroform I used was too much. I poured way too much of the chloroform into the cloth, almost drenching it. I wasn't thinking it could be fatal."

Terry sounded sincere. I felt my best friend's emotions while she explained the situation.

"She never woke up after I did that. I didn't mean to kill her. I just wanted to bring her home with me so we could talk once she came too. I didn't want her to die."

"But, Terry . . ." I said, not being able to think of anything else to say.

Terry gazed back at me almost blankly. She continued to say, "After realizing she wasn't going to wake up, I dumped her body on a rough side of town, hoping the police would think she was some prostitute."

"But, Terry, you killed someone. And you are an attorney. You could lose everything."

"I haven't lost anything and I'm not going to lose anything because you are not going to say anything. You promised me, remember?" she said, stretching her eyes at me as she leaned forward to stress her point.

"But I didn't know your revelation was going to be this big."

"Does it matter?" she asked.

"Yes, it does."

"So what are you saying, you are going to turn me in?" Terry asked tensely.

I watched as the waitress approached our table, and our conversation ceased. She placed down two more glasses of wine and said, "Here you go. I figured you ladies may need another one."

"You were right," I told her.

"Are you ladies ready to order?" the waitress asked.

"Yes. I will have the fried oysters and your scallops St. Jacques," Terry said, talking like she was unfazed by what she revealed to me.

"And you, ma'am?" the waitress asked me.

I peered at Terry as I picked up my menu and said, "I'll have your roast chicken risotto."

The waitress took both of our menus and said, "I'll have your orders out to you in a bit." The waitress walked away and my eyes locked with Terry's.

"So . . ." Terry said.

"So what?"

"Are you going to keep my secret?"

"I'm still trying to get over the fact you love me."

"Well, I do. But not like I thought I did."

"What does that mean?" I asked, confused.

"Then, I wanted to be with you after my breakup with Essence, but I figured we are better as friends. I couldn't handle losing your friendship. You are my girl, Kea. And that's why I said I love you. I meant more like a sister, you know? Now answer my question, please. Are you going to take this secret to your grave?"

I thought about everything Terry was telling me. Even if I wanted to, could I turn my best friend in? This woman was like my sister and I couldn't see me doing that to her. I knew more than anybody when you tried to do right, things always seemed to go wrong. Looking back on all the years I wasted with Jaquon and dealing with a mother who hated me even when I tried to love both of them, I ended up being the one hurt in the end. I have the scars from my mother having left blemishes externally and the ones from Jaquon eternally left on my heart. I had been mad enough to want both of them dead for what they did to me, so I could see how Terry ended up being in the predicament she ended up in. So was it right for me to judge my friend for being in love and making a mistake, even though this mistake was a big one costing the women who ruined my life their lives?

Hell, look at me. I was with my man's best friend now.

Terry continued to stare at me attentively.

I nodded, picked up my freshly refilled wine glass, and said, "I will take your secret with me to my grave."

Chapter 51

Terry

I am so glad Kea believed that crock of lies I just fed to her. Well, the story was partially true. The fact did remain that I killed Essence and we did have an affair with one another. Where the truth started to get cloudy in my explanation was the fact I knew Essence was seeing Jaquon. I found out about them two before Kea called me that night of the cookout to tell me everything. Essence was my dirty little secret and I was hers. All the time she spent trying to prove she was strictly dickly to Zacariah, other people, and even herself, Essence was lapping me up every chance she got. And I had to admit I was between her thighs numerous times myself.

I can't front. I also wanted everybody to think I liked men too, which I did, but I loved women also. And in the business I was in, loving men and being as sexy as I tried to be all the time helped me to establish my own law firm. For me, my cat had to scratch a few poles a few times to work my way to the top. Don't get it twisted; I had the skills to get me to the top. But this is a man's world and men look after each other. They'd rather see another man elevated than a woman, and that was the problem I ran into a lot of time. So I used what I had to get what I wanted. And I didn't have any regrets about that either.

My only regret was ever getting involved with Essence in the first place. That woman had my heart and I couldn't remember the point in our relationship where she took it. I never thought I would fall for a women like I did her. Ironically I did recall the time she reached into my chest and ripped my heart out. I thought we were in a committed relationship. That was until I followed her one night and saw her having sex with Jaquon on top of his car. And she was outside, no less, for everyone to see. Seeing them together enraged me. The bitch was trying to play me. But I never confronted her on it. I thought about getting her back in other ways, like messing her car up with grease, and putting a dead rat in her newspaper. Yep, that was me. A rat for a country gutter piece of trash, and that's where I left that bitch: in some gutter for the rats to feed off her flesh.

She hurt me so I wanted her hurt. Little did I know Essence was going to use Jaquon to lean on during her time of fear. She could have easily leaned on me to support her. But no, she chose him. I was already mad Jaquon was cheating on my best friend, but he had to make Essence one of his conquests, too.

I eventually confronted Essence about cheating on me. And she had the nerve to tell me she was done with me. She said being with Jaquon further led her to believe she wanted a man in her life and not a woman. Was she serious? We were together for over a year but getting penetrated by him tapped into some core in her body, which made her realize he was who she wanted. Or, rather, dick was what she preferred. Talk about wrong timing to come to that conclusion, after I had spent money on her. After I helped her get her house and her car. After I deposited money in her account almost monthly. After I realized I loved her. Still, I wasn't good enough for her to want to spend her life with me. She had the entire situation twisted up if she thought I was just going to back off and be like, "Okay, I understand." Fuck that. I didn't